After Words

Brenda Margriet

AFTER WORDS

This edition published September 2020
Copyright © 2020 Brenda Margriet Clotildes
Print ISBN 978-1-7773513-0-4
Digital ISBN 978-1-7773513-1-1

Cover Art by Steven Cote

"There is bad news," Leeza said. "If this is a complete list of the men who shipped out on July 21, William and Rodney should be on it. But neither of them is."

"How can neither of these men show up in official records?" Gavin said, staring off into the distance, eyes unfocused behind his lenses. His eyelashes were long, almost brushing the frames when he blinked.

Suddenly he turned to her, his abstracted expression vanishing. "What if Rodney is a middle name? They only have middle initials listed."

His abruptness startled her, and she took a moment to collect herself. "That's an excellent idea. But it doesn't explain William. There are plenty of Smiths, and even a William, but his middle initial is B."

"What if that's a mistake? Either in the transcription online, or in the original records? A capital H could be easily confused with a capital B depending on the handwriting or type." Gavin's eyes glowed with enthusiasm.

Her exhilaration rose to meet his. "That makes so much sense. Could it be that simple? And if it is, does that mean we've found him? That we'll be able to learn from the original records who William is?"

"It has to get us closer. But we might be jumping to conclusions." Gavin placed the laptop on the coffee table and turned to Leeza, his expression sobering. "We shouldn't get our hopes up."

She laughed, giddy with anticipation. "I know you're right. I can feel it. Maybe some of his family is still alive, and we'll be able to give them his diary. He'll finally be home where he belongs."

She grinned at Gavin. He stared at her, not returning her smile, just studying her as if—well, as if he'd never seen her before.

"What?" she said.

He didn't reply.

Instead, he kissed her.

Dedication

To my brothers and sisters –
those by blood, love and marriage –
for reading my books and telling me you like them.

CHAPTER ONE

July 21st, 1941
The journey starts here. I don't know if I'll be able to record everything about it but I'll try. My mother made me promise that I write in this journal as often as possible. She believes that writing your thoughts in journals keeps you sane. So I promised her, to comfort her. I've left home. We left today at noon from Halifax. It was difficult seeing the coast slowly shrink as we left. I hope this trip won't be too long, I don't want to get seasick.

The book didn't look dangerous. It looked like a grubby, slightly damp-damaged journal, with less than half of the unlined pages covered in loopy, childlike handwriting.

Leeza Boychuk should have known better. She knew words were weapons, knew that, whether written or spoken, they could destroy happiness, batter pride, and bring the haughtiest low. But it was only much later that she came to realize the power of the book she held in her hand.

It was barely bigger than her palm. The spine was black leather, as were the curling corners. The rest of the cover was a thick, rough, red cardboard. How had it ended up jammed between a trade paperback of Robert Ludlum and a hardcover of Clive Cussler? She put it in the big tote she used as a purse to examine later and continued to fill the box at her feet with the books remaining on the shelf.

"Did Grampa-Great really read all of these?" Drew asked. Her son stood with a stack of novels clutched in his large hands, gazing with disbelief at the hundreds of books still lining the walls. He had offered to help clear out the backroom, but she didn't think he'd anticipated quite the amount of work it would be.

Mind you, neither had she.

"I imagine so. He loved to read." She folded the flaps of the now filled box and tucked them neatly under each other.

"What are you going to do with them? You don't sell used books at Millar's." Drew handed her what he held so she could start a new box and reached to the top shelf for more. At just over six feet, he was almost twelve inches taller than her, his height inherited from his father.

She was *not* going to think of her ex-husband. Not when she was already emotionally drained from dismantling her grandfather's life.

"No, we don't. I'm donating them to the thrift store the Hospice Society runs." In fact, most of the contents of the house were heading that direction. Her grandfather had lived alone, amazingly independent for a man who died only weeks shy of his hundredth birthday. He'd spent his last days at the local Hospice House, and supporting that organization was the best way Leeza could think of to thank them for their warm and loving care.

It took the rest of the afternoon, but they finally managed to pack all the books away. Boxes were stacked two and three high and covered much of the floor space.

"Almost ready for the new renters," Leeza said, stretching her back. "The thrift store truck is coming tomorrow." Drew grunted acknowledgment as he guzzled water. Otto Friberg might have read all the books at one time, but it had been a long while ago if the dust coating them was anything to go by. Leeza could feel the grit on her teeth and took a long swallow from her own bottle. "They're taking everything that's left. Are you sure there's nothing else you might want?"

Drew nodded. "I have the photo of him during World War Two, with him on the tank, and the one of the two of us at my high school graduation. That's enough. If I was staying around, I might have taken some of the furniture, but since I'm not..."

Leeza's heart pinched, but she kept her expression open. "Yes. It will be easier to buy what you need once you get there."

"I'm hoping to find a furnished place to rent. Or maybe share an apartment. Or flat, I suppose I should say." He grinned, brown eyes gleaming.

"Well, when in England..." Leeza smiled, determined not to shadow Drew's grand adventure with a melancholic mother. When he'd first told her he had quit the bank and was heading to Europe for an indeterminate amount of time, she'd assumed he meant weeks, possibly a few months. She'd known he was restless and dissatisfied, even though a job in finance should have suited the Bachelor of Commerce degree he'd completed a couple of years before. She figured he was going to take some time for himself before settling on a new career path. But then he told her he'd accepted a placement at the High Commission of Canada in the United Kingdom—specifically, London. He had been blazing with excitement then and hadn't lost that excited glow in the weeks that had followed. She would do nothing to dim that joy.

They stepped out the front door into the chilly briskness of a darkening last day of November. Drew headed off in his soon-to-be-sold sporty sedan to have dinner and spend the evening with friends. He only had a few more days in town, and she wanted to share every second she could with him. But he had his own life and she had...well, her work, at least.

Leeza tossed her bag into her SUV and headed to her bookstore.

It wasn't really *hers*, although, after ten years as manager and as many years working her way up to that position, it felt like it was. It was just one branch of a national chain, and she was growing increasingly frustrated with what she saw as ill-judged decisions and restrictive red tape. As manager, she didn't often work an evening shift, but a flu bug was going through the staff and with Christmas less than a month away and the holiday buying frenzy ramping up, she was needed.

She parked at the back of the shopping complex and entered through a rear door. The mall was rather frantically decorated with red and gold and green and glitter, and tinkling, jingling instrumental versions of carols echoed off the tile floors. Just *thinking* about spending Christmas without Drew burned the back of her throat. Passing a coffee shop, she distracted herself with a deep inhale scented with peppermint and hot chocolate. Maybe she'd come back after checking in at the store. It would give her a chance to ask her partner on shift tonight if he would like something, too.

Gavin Fletcher was helping a customer at the till when she hurried into Millar's. He nodded at her, the light glinting off his glasses, and she acknowledged him with a brief smile as she passed on her way to put her tote and jacket in her office at the back. She ran her hands through her hair and twisted her spine, trying to see if any dust from Grampa-Great's books had transferred itself to her. She had planned to go home to freshen up, but she'd underestimated how long it would take to pack them all—she was usually *un*packing books, not putting them away— and had run out of time.

Deciding she looked presentable enough, she headed out on the floor. Several customers were browsing the shelves, but no one waited at the counter. She saw Gavin was making use of the lull to straighten a display of three-for-the-price-of-two hardcovers at the front of the store.

When she'd hired Gavin five years ago, she hadn't expected him to stick. He had been in his early forties at the time—he was a year younger than her, as she knew from his employee records—and not the typical applicant for a part-time job, given his previous career as a financial planner. He'd quietly explained he was looking for a change since the death of his wife, and she'd bet herself it would take no more than six months before he ran screaming for the door.

Thankfully, she'd been wrong. While he'd resisted her attempts to give him full-time hours, he was her most dependable employee. There was nothing wrong with the Millennials who made up the rest of her team, but it was certainly pleasant to have someone her own age around.

She joined him at the table, keeping an eye on the flow of customers while she helped reorganize the jumbled books.

"How's it been today?" she asked.

"Steady." Never talkative, he was a restful person to work with, going about his duties with efficiency and a casual friendliness.

"That's good," she said. Sales had been depressed all year, and this was the last chance they had to make up for earlier losses. Black Friday had just passed, and while in Canada it wasn't the retail juggernaut it was in the United States it had been a decent success.

Gavin stretched an arm up to the books at the top of the display, his long, lean fingers lining up the edges with precise movements. He wore a white button-down dress shirt and sedate tie under his uniform vest. She'd never seen him less than professionally turned out, although his ties were not quite the right width for the current style, and she assumed they were holdovers from his days in finance. Of course, she'd rarely seen him away from the store. He attended few of the social events she organized for her staff. Maybe he favoured baggy jeans and over-sized hoodies when he was at home.

Riiiiiigggght. The thought made her smile.

Gavin, his eyes on the display, said, "Did you get everything packed away?"

Her smile faded. "Yes."

"It's hard," he said quietly. "I know."

"Thanks." She appreciated his understanding, especially since losing a grandfather who had lived a full and adventurous life couldn't be compared to losing a soulmate. Gavin never mentioned his wife directly, which Leeza interpreted to mean he had loved her too deeply to share her memory with a relative stranger. "The truck comes tomorrow to take it all away, and the new renters move in on the fifteenth. It's the end of an era."

A customer approached the till and Leeza went to ring the sale through. The rest of the evening was busy enough to preclude any more private conversation, which was a good sign given it was the first night the mall was open extended hours. But the cash register would have to ring as often as the mall elves jangled the bells at Santa's Workshop if they were to get close to meeting the targets set by head office.

CHAPTER TWO

July 23rd, 1941
I've been playing cards with Rodney ever since
we left. The boat is gigantic. There must be
thousands of men on board. There's a
swimming pool (the water is freezing!),
movies, bingo and really neat things. The ship
is called the Orion. There's a battleship that's
escorting us across the Atlantic in case
Germans attack us. I can't wait to get there, it's
only been two days since we've left and it seems
I've been on the ship a week!

Just after nine o'clock Gavin ushered out the evening's last customer and unfolded the clanging metal gate to close the entrance. They worked in silence as they did the duties necessary to wrap up the day, the routine well established and familiar, and then walked together through the deserted mall and out to the parking lot at the rear of the building. He stayed with her until she reached her SUV, his presence quiet and comforting in the dark night.

"Thanks," she said, encompassing his work at the store and his chivalry in walking her to her vehicle in the single syllable. He waited patiently as she searched for her keys in the tote slung over her shoulder. "Sorry," she muttered, "I know they're in here somewhere." She pulled out a small makeup bag, a plastic container of carrot sticks and the little red book she'd found at Grampa-Great's and balanced them in one hand as she scrabbled with the other. Inevitably, the stack tilted, and the book fell to the snowy pavement. Gavin bent to retrieve it as she triumphantly freed the keys from the depths of her bag.

"Is this your grandfather's?" Gavin asked, studying the book. "Where did he serve?"

"Where what?"

"Where did he serve as a soldier?" He shrugged apologetically. "I didn't mean to snoop, but it was open to the inside cover when I picked it up."

"Let me see." He handed the book back, and in the glow from the overhead light she read *William Henry Smith, A Company,* the words written in faded pencil in the same sprawling, looping hand she'd seen when she first discovered the book.

"That's not my grandfather," she said, frowning. "His name was Otto Friberg. I found this today among his books. It didn't seem like something the thrift store would want, so I kept it." She turned the page and read the date of the first entry—*July 21st, 1941.* "He did serve in World War Two but didn't talk about it much. He always deflected when I asked about it. And now it's too late." The loss of her grandfather pierced her again.

"I'm a bit of a history buff," Gavin said diffidently, as if admitting to a shameful disease. "If you want, I could take a look at it for you."

"Thanks," she said. "I haven't had a chance to read it myself, but I'll let you know."

He nodded and stepped back so she could open her door. He waited until she'd turned on the ignition and the locks automatically clicked before sketching a salute and heading to his own vehicle a few slots away.

A history nerd, Leeza thought with an amused shake of her head. *Who would have thought?* She'd known the man for five years and this was the first hint into his personal life he'd offered.

His headlights shone in her rear-view mirror as they left the parking lot, and she felt an odd sting of desertion when they turned onto a side street and disappeared, leaving her to make her way home alone.

All thoughts of the journal were lost in the furor and confusion of Drew's last days in town. Between working extra hours as the flu bug continued to make its way through her staff and spending as much time as she could with her son, all thoughts of the little red book vanished.

On Friday evening she drove Drew to the Prince George Airport. The one large suitcase he was checking was swallowed by the luggage conveyor, and they stood just out of the way of the line up for security.

"I guess this is it," he said, smiling down at her. It struck her anew that he was a grown man, an adult with his own life. It was funny how often she seemed to forget that.

"Yes," she said, and stepped in to hug him. "Take care. I love you."

"I know." He squeezed her tight, but his voice was distracted, already moving through the steps of the journey that would take him half a world away.

She couldn't let go, not quite yet. Her voice muffled against his shoulder, she said, "I'm proud of you." And she was. She'd raised him to be an independent, open-minded man—but now she was cursing herself for it. She pulled away reluctantly.

"Did Dad tell you if he was coming?" Drew scanned the crowd over her head, hitching his backpack up one shoulder.

"He didn't say anything to me." Not that he was talking to her these days. *And good riddance.*

"Well, we said goodbye last night. I guess he figured that was enough." Maybe she was being oversensitive, colouring the words with her own pain at Drew's departure, but she thought she heard a touch of uncertainty in his casual tone. What kind of father *wouldn't* come to see his son off, knowing it would be months before they'd meet again?

My lying, cheating ex-husband of a father, that's who, she thought confusedly.

She hugged Drew once more, her arms stretching to wrap around him—the same arms that had cuddled a colicky baby and taught a young boy how to play catch and helped a sulky teen learn how to do laundry.

"I love you," she said again.

"Love you, too, Mom."

He joined the security line. The airport was busy but not large, so she was able to watch him walk through the scanner. He turned back, gave her a jaunty thumbs up and a wide smile, and disappeared.

She had no reason to stay any longer. There would be no chance to see him again before he boarded. But she sat under the tall arching beams of the Arrivals Area, staring through the wall of windows that overlooked the car park and the main runway, simply breathing, reconciling herself to this new reality. She sat for more than an hour, watching the dusk fade to dark, until the lights of the airplane carrying her life streaked down the runway and vanished into the night.

No son.

No grandfather.

No husband.

She still had her parents, but they were in Arizona, snow-birding in their motorhome like many Canadians. Otto, her father's father, had started deteriorating in the late summer, so they'd stayed throughout the autumn, delaying their annual drive south, waiting for the inevitable. When it had finally come to pass, and the exhausting strain of watching a beloved parent's final days was over, they'd announced their intention to remain in town until their only grandchild left for London, with the unspoken addendum being that, with Grampa-Great gone, there would be work to do to close up his house and pack away his life.

Leeza and Drew had convinced them otherwise. Winter in Northern British Columbia pretty much guaranteed icy, snowy roads, and they'd already postponed long enough. It hadn't taken much cajoling to get them to depart shortly after the funeral, and they were now basking in the bright, dry desert sunshine and not expected to return until spring.

An announcement over the airport's public address system jolted Leeza from her thoughts, and she rose, slightly stiff after her vigil, and headed to her car.

As part of her divorce from Scott, the home where Drew had grown up had been sold and the money divided between them. Leeza had used her portion to buy a modern, up-and-down condo in a developing neighbourhood, choosing to start fresh in more ways than one. Drew had never lived in the condo, never even stayed a night, so she couldn't understand why the house felt so empty when she returned from the airport.

Whatever the reason, she couldn't seem to settle. She tidied the already tidy kitchen and then turned the television on, only to flick through the channels and turn it back off. Her e-reader lay on the end table next to her, filled with old favourites and a to-be-read list that would keep her going until the next century, but it held no attractions—a first in Leeza's world.

The thought of books reminded her of the little red journal she'd discovered on Grampa-Great's shelf. She retrieved it from the hall table near the front door where it had lain since Monday night. Sitting in her corner of the sofa and curling her legs under, she turned to the first page.

Despite the faded pencil lead, the handwriting was easy enough to read, although the rounded, sprawling cursive looked childish and unpracticed. A quick flip of the pages showed most of the entries were very short, some only a sentence or two. Habit kept her from reading the final words—she'd never understood people who flipped to the end of a book before reading the rest. The first two entries were breezy and carefree—a young soldier going off on a grand adventure, the attitude held by many young men before the truths of war caught up with them— but the third made her catch her breath.

July 26th, 1941
Last night, some kid, I'd say about nineteen, was crying in his bunk. Everyone was asleep and didn't seem to hear him. I couldn't help but hear him. I was wide awake, those beds are really uncomfortable. He must have missed home and his mother. He's not the only one. We all miss home but we don't cry about it. We'll see home again, someday.

She didn't *want* Drew to be homesick, but a tiny part of her heart hoped he missed her, at least a little. And then she felt guilty about that wish. The young man in the troopship was going to *war*, going to risk his life for his country. Of course he was homesick. Drew, on the other hand, was blazing a new life for himself, and she shouldn't hope for anything that might derail that plan.

The last line in the entry tolled in her mind like a solemn bell. Had William seen home again? Reading the last page might give her a clue. But if it somehow revealed he *hadn't* come home, she didn't want to find out tonight. The sympathy she felt for William's mother, sending her son off into the unknown, was shattering enough, without the certain knowledge that she had waited in vain for her son to return.

She continued reading, already drawn into this young man's world. The entries were often weeks, sometimes months apart. He sounded so young, so innocent, and for the most part he wrote about the monotony of army life and the English girls he and his best friend Rodney inevitably met. In only a few minutes she'd read through more than two years of his life. Toward the end of 1943, the tone of the journal changed as William sensed they might finally be deployed. A feeling of restlessness and anxiety permeated his terse entries.

Closing the little book, she caressed the rough cover with the tip of one finger. William had written he'd known Rodney all his twenty-one years, which meant he was probably born in 1920, the same year as Grampa-Great. Even if he had survived the war, he was more than likely dead by now. Yet he'd come to life again in his words, and despite the backdrop of war upon which he'd written, she felt soothed. It was like looking up at the stars and realizing how infinitesimal humanity was. There was freedom in knowing she was only a part of a larger whole.

When she fell asleep that night, she dreamed of William walking up the gangplank and into the troopship. He turned back to wave at her, and the face he wore was Drew's.

CHAPTER THREE

July 29th, 1941
Finally! After eight days we've arrived safely in
the Bristol Channel! Absolutely no threats from
the Germans on our way over! We'll be docking
soon enough at a place called Avonmouth. My
first time on European soil!

None of her staff called in sick on Sunday—
hallelujah!—so Leeza seized the chance to meet up
with a friend for coffee at Café Voltaire. Charlene
Petryshyn was one of the few people she'd kept in
touch with after her split from Scott. She was also
single and divorced—although not as recently—and
Leeza was more comfortable with her than her other,
still-married friends.

"Have you heard from Drew?" Charlene asked
as they took their places at a tiny, round table near
the window. Befitting her career as a successful salon
and spa owner, Charlene was perfectly turned out
even on a blustery Sunday afternoon. Her hair was
artfully streaked and styled, her makeup subtle and
flattering. She wore a fashionably styled black wool
coat, saved from severity by the brightly patterned

silk scarf at her neck.

She made Leeza feel underdressed in her regular day off uniform of jeans, sweater, and untouched face.

Cupping her hands around her mug, she said, "Yes, he texted when he arrived. He starts work tomorrow and we're going to try and arrange a video call in the next day or so. We just have to figure out the time zone thing."

Charlene sipped her cappuccino without marring her lipstick. "How you holding up?"

Leeza dipped her chin. "I knew it would be tough, but I didn't think it would hit me this hard. I'm having trouble sleeping." And when she did manage to drop off, her rest continued to be disrupted by dreams that merged William with Drew. She'd read the entire diary yesterday, compelled to discover what she could about the young soldier's fate. This morning she'd woken up gasping from a nightmare, the details of which she couldn't remember. The dregs of terror were still with her.

"You've had quite the year. I'd be surprised if this *wasn't* difficult." Charlene patted her hand. "Have you gone on a date yet?"

Leeza shook her head. "Not going to happen," she said. "I am nowhere near ready for another relationship."

"Who said anything about a relationship?" Charlene grinned naughtily and Leeza couldn't help but smile. "You're not waiting for Scott to come back, are you?"

"No! Of course not." Even in the early days of Scott's betrayal, she'd never wanted him back. She might have wanted the life she'd thought she'd had back, but not Scott. Not once she found out the full extent of his perfidy.

"Because he's with someone else."

Leeza raised an eyebrow. "Well, duh."

"I don't mean the cow he left you for. That's been finished for a while now."

"He's with *another* woman?" Leeza gaped. "Already? And how do you know?"

Charlene's brash expression slipped, her eyes flickering nervously.

"Charlene! How do you know?"

"He calls me. Every once in a while."

Leeza drew a quick, indrawn breath at the spark of pain. "You're *my* friend."

Charlene's eyes flashed. "You're *both* my friends. I know he was a jerk and a dickwad, but people make mistakes."

"He made mistakes all right," Leeza said. "Their names were Marian, Chloe, and Yvonne." And those were just the ones he admitted to.

"I'm not sticking up for him, but I won't shut him out," Charlene said. "Sometimes he needs someone to talk to."

"Why you?" Even Leeza could hear the plaintive tone in her voice.

"I shouldn't have said anything." Charlene patted her hand again. "Never mind him. It's you I'm worried about, believe it or not. You need to get out of that house, especially now that Drew's gone. Take a class, join a club, start a project—whatever it is, just get out there." She narrowed her eyes. "When's the last time you did something just for fun?"

"I *used* to think it was fun having coffee with you," Leeza muttered.

"I don't count. And neither does work."

Leeza sighed. "Work hasn't been much fun lately, either. I'm getting bad vibes from corporate. They closed ten stores across Canada this summer. I think we might be next."

"All the more reason to stop moping at home. You need to network."

"Networking is as bad as dating. Do you know how long it's been since I had a date? Or went on a job interview?" Leeza scowled. "I'm too old for this."

"You're never too old for a new adventure." Charlene rolled her fingertips on the tabletop, her gel polished nails clicking. "Tell you what. I'll give you a free day at the salon. Just tell me when. Massage, hair, facial, the whole shebang. Start this next phase in your life on the right foot."

It sounded fantastic. "I can't let you do that."

"Yes, you can. I'm the boss, remember." She rose from her chair. "I've got to get going. Unlike you, I have things to do. Call me. I'll set it all up." With a swoosh, she was gone.

Leeza finished her drink slowly, letting the quiet bustle and clatter of the café wash over her. Charlene's rather astringent pep talk had stirred an idea. She'd loved doing research when she took her English degree many, *many* years ago. Since she hadn't been able to get William's journal out of her subconscious, maybe she needed to face it head on. And in doing so, maybe she could find his family and return the book to them. His words deserved to be read and treasured by those of his own blood.

Two hours later, she sat back in her chair and ran her hands through her hair in frustration.

The name William Henry Smith was in no way unique, and she'd thought she might have trouble figuring out *which* William Henry Smith was the author of the journal.

What she hadn't counted on was not finding him at all.

Doing a Google search for *William Henry Smith* had been the logical place to start. Ironically, given Leeza's own profession, the most famous person of that name was the British bookseller W. H. Smith, who was also a prominent political figure in the mid-eighteenth century.

After the many entries related to that Smith, she did discover a William Henry Smith in an online Canadian War Memorial—but he lost his life in World War One. He'd only been eighteen.

She tried changing her search by adding *World War Two*. Nothing.

Remembering what was written on the inside cover of the journal, she typed *William Henry Smith* and *A Company*. Nothing.

With trepidation she tried just *William Smith* and came up with results for the American actor and a geologist, among hundreds more.

She searched for Canadian war records and came up with links to so many different databases that it would take her hours to go through them all.

If she could narrow down which regiment—was that even the right word?—he belonged to, surely that would give her a clue to his identity.

Too bad she had no idea how to do that. What she needed was someone more familiar with World War Two history. Someone who would know where to look.

She closed the lid of her laptop and placed it on the coffee table in front of her. Her back ached from sitting so long, so she rose to stretch it out, and then went to the kitchen to get fresh water. Pouring the cucumber and mint infused liquid into her glass, she eyed her cell phone, lying innocently on the counter.

She'd never called Gavin for any reason other than work, and even then, only rarely. To call him now, for this purpose, would change things between them. It was stepping over a line into the personal that she wasn't sure she wanted to initiate.

Of course, he'd offered to help. He'd taken the first step, hadn't he?

"For Pete's sake," she said aloud to the empty

kitchen, "just call him. What's the big deal?"

It rang three times and she was about to hang up when he answered. In the background she could hear high-pitched voices and tinkling music.

"Hello, Leeza," he said.

"Hi, Gavin. Sorry to bother you on a Sunday. Do you have a minute?"

"Of course. Just let me get somewhere a little quieter." She heard smothered sounds, and when he spoke next the voices and music were gone. "There. That's better."

"I didn't mean to interrupt anything."

"That's all right. What can I help you with?"

Oddly reluctant to get to the point, she dithered. "It sounds like you're at a party."

"I am. My granddaughter's second birthday."

"Oh!" She hadn't even known he had grandchildren. He seemed far too young, although it was certainly biologically possible. She wasn't ready to be a grandmother yet. Which was lucky, given that Drew hadn't been in a serious relationship for, well, ever.

"Is there something you need?" Gavin's quiet voice interrupted her meandering thoughts.

"Yes. No. Well, maybe." God, she sounded like an idiot. Getting a grip, she went on with slightly more coherence. "Remember that book you saw, the one I dropped in the parking lot? How much do you know about World War Two?"

"I remember. What's your question?"

"How can I find out what regiment or whatever it's called a soldier belonged to?"

"There are databases online."

"I've been searching most of the afternoon, and I can't find him. I'm obviously not looking in the right places. I was wondering if you might want to give it a go."

"I could try." His voice was calm as usual,

26

although an undercurrent of energy rippled through the speaker. "I'd need to read it, of course. How long is it?"

"Not very. It took me less than an hour."

"Did you want to give it to me on Tuesday? That's when I work next."

She felt a pang at the thought of letting the journal out of her care but knew she could trust Gavin. "That works."

"Okay." He paused and she waited, accustomed to his deliberate style of conversation. "Do you know what regiment your grandfather was in?"

"No, I don't think I ever heard him mention it. Why?"

"It seems a logical place to start. Unless he was in the habit of collecting diaries, maybe the journal belonged to someone he knew."

"I never thought of that. It makes sense." If that was the case, though, it was even odder that the book had been tucked onto a shelf with dozens of novels. Thinking of the box where Drew had found the photo of his Grampa-Great on a tank, she said, "There are some old photos and letters I haven't gone through yet. I can see if there is anything helpful. And I can call my dad. Maybe he knows."

"Sounds good," Gavin said. He paused again. "I should get back to the party."

Unreasonably disappointed he couldn't talk longer, she hurried to agree. "Yes. Of course. Sorry to drag you away."

"Not to worry. See you Tuesday." Another of his customary pauses. "I'm glad you called."

He sounded sincere, and her chest warmed. Ending the connection, she stared at the screen for a moment, and shook her head. He was an acquaintance doing her a favour, nothing more.

Then why did she feel so giddy he had agreed to help?

CHAPTER FOUR

August 5th, 1941
Slowly getting used to England. It's a little
different from home but not too much. I've had
the chance to see new places over the last few
weeks. England is alright. I've met some new
people. Oddly enough, I've gotten to know
things about Rodney that I never knew before!
Imagine, after being friends for 21 years, since
I was born, I still don't know everything about
Rodney! Rodney can drink five beers and still
act sober. We sneaked in after curfew last night
and a major came to talk to us. I could hardly
stand while Rodney chatted away as if he had
never drunk five beers. If he hadn't been there,
I would have had my leave revoked for God
knows how long. What could I do without old
Rodney?

Leeza handed Gavin the journal on Tuesday in a
stew of emotions. She'd grown protective of William
Henry Smith, and hoped he would feel the same. It
was crazy, given she only knew the young man as
words on a page, but his innocence and youth and
good humour and ultimate humanness shone in

those sporadic entries, and she felt connected to him in a way she couldn't explain.

Gavin had said he'd call when he had something to share, and she'd done her best to wait patiently. But the journal consumed much of her thoughts. Even when she and Drew had video-chatted on Wednesday, her thoughts had drifted to a different young man in a different London—and another mother praying for her son's safety and well-being. Returning the journal to William's family was in danger of becoming an obsession.

In a mix of relief and trepidation she saw Gavin's name appear on the screen of her phone early Friday evening.

Wiping her hands quickly on a wet rag, she answered. "Do you mind if I put you on speaker?" she asked. "I'm doing some baking."

"I can call back if you're busy," he said in his precise way.

"No!" She didn't want to wait longer. "I just have to drop the last cookies on the sheet. I can do that and talk. Tell me—what have you found?"

"I can tell you what I *haven't* found. I haven't found your William Henry Smith."

She let out a disappointed breath. "I was so hoping you'd have better luck." Methodically, she spooned out small blobs of dough, her mind elsewhere.

"I'm sorry."

"So that's it?" She licked her finger clean and opened the oven. Sliding in the tray, she said, "Is there nothing else we can do?"

"If you don't mind, I'd like to keep the journal a little longer. I have some ideas on what we might do next. Have you had a chance to ask your father if he knew anything?"

"I did. If he ever heard his dad mention his regiment, he's forgotten. But chances are Grampa-

Great never did. He didn't talk about the war."

"What about the letters and photos you said you had?"

She set the timer on the oven and began piling dirty dishes into the sink. "I looked through them, but none of the letters had anything to do with the war. There are a couple photos of young men in uniform, but I couldn't see anything that might give us a clue."

"Can you see insignia on the uniforms?"

She frowned. "I don't know. And even if I could, I wouldn't know their significance."

"Do you mind if I take a look? Maybe there's something I might recognize."

"Of course." She surveyed the baking cooling on the counter. "Do you like chocolate chip cookies?"

"Yes." A soft upward lift turned the word into a question.

"Are you busy right now?"

Inviting an employee over to help her find a man who in all likelihood had been dead for decades probably wasn't quite what Charlene had in mind when she'd suggested Leeza needed to get out more. But it was a start. It *was* time to begin building a new life and stop grieving the old one.

As she'd told Charlene, she wasn't in the right place to think about a serious romantic relationship. But a new friend? She could always use one of those. She respected Gavin and enjoyed his company. She didn't think the boss/employee dynamic was a barrier, given their backgrounds. And if, after they'd finished looking into William's journal, they had no further reason to meet outside of work, it would be a natural regression to their previous relationship.

Gavin was a controlled experiment with no potential for a negative outcome.

She quickly washed, dried, and put away her baking equipment. On her way to get her grandfather's box from the spare room, she checked in the bathroom mirror to make sure she didn't have flour on her face—and if she quickly swiped on fresh lipstick and brushed her hair so her medium-length bob was neat and tidy it was only to make sure she was presentable for company.

The doorbell rang as she descended the stairs from the second floor carrying the box of memorabilia. Balancing it on one hip, she took a breath and opened the door.

Gavin stood on the step, spot lit by the porch light, the early evening midnight-black behind him. "Come in," she said, an unnecessary nervousness making her pulse trip lightly in her throat. "Has it started to snow?"

Which was a ridiculous statement, since she could see very well for herself that it hadn't.

He stepped past her, wintry air swirling in with him. "Not yet, but it feels like it will soon," he said, politely ignoring her inanity.

"They're calling for five to ten centimetres overnight." Breathing deeply, she concentrated on acting the mature, sensible woman she was. "Here, let me take your coat." She placed the box on the hall table.

Gavin handed her his black wool coat after tucking a navy-blue scarf into the sleeve. She hung it in the closet, and when she turned back, he had picked up the box.

"I can get that," she said.

"No problem." His gaze rested gently on her face. His light brown hair was cut short, and for the first time she noticed it was thinning at the temples, although there was no hint of grey in the tawny strands. He wore a heavy knit sweater in dark blue, the blue plaid pattern of his shirt revealed at the collar and cuffs. His jeans were crisp and new looking—another first for her, as he never wore denim to work.

He shifted his grip on the box and she realized he was waiting for directions. "The kitchen's that way," she said hurriedly, pointing past the stairs. "We can use the table there."

Without a word, he started down the hall. She trailed after, feeling foolish and uncomfortable. He placed the box on the dark oak table, next to the plate of cookies she'd laid out earlier and turned to look at her again.

"Would you like coffee?" she asked.

"What about a glass of milk?"

She smiled. "Of course. Have a seat." She waved a hand vaguely at the box. "Everything's in there if you want to take a look."

She poured two glasses of milk and carried them to the table. He'd lifted out a handful of papers and taken a seat in one of the wheel back chairs.

He thanked her with a nod and methodically sorted the letters and photos into two piles.

"Your grandfather's name was Otto?" he said without looking up.

"Yes. Otto Friberg."

"Scandinavian?"

She nodded. "Swedish. His family emigrated to the United States in the late eighteenth century, then somehow ended up settling in Nova Scotia. We don't know much more than that, though."

He lifted his glasses onto his forehead and raised a photo close to his face. "He was born when?"

"1920."

He lowered the photo and peered at Leeza, blinking short-sightedly. "And he just passed away recently?"

"He would have been one hundred on Christmas Day."

"That's incredible," he said in respectful awe.

"And he lived independently until near the end. He was an amazing man. Have a cookie." She pushed the plate toward him.

He took one, his attention on the next photo, and absentmindedly dunked it in his milk before taking a bite. He chewed and swallowed and looked at her again. "These are delicious." He finished the first and reached for a second while scrutinizing the third photo.

She had a wistful flashback to after school snacks with Drew. She'd worked part-time for most of his elementary years and was usually home by the time he'd been dropped off by the bus. Chocolate chip cookies and milk had been part of the tradition. Missing him had inspired her to make the cookies tonight, and while the ache of his absence wasn't gone, it was softened by Gavin sitting across from her.

"Do you have a magnifying glass?" he asked. The photos were spread out in front of him. There were four, all showing groups of men wearing uniforms. Someone—presumably her grandfather—had written first names on the backs. Unhelpfully, none of the names were William, and nothing else indicated where or when they had been taken.

"I don't think so."

"That's fine. I can use my phone." He pulled out a newer model smartphone and opened the camera app. Leeza stood and leaned over his shoulder as he zoomed in on the top corner of a photo showing three men—including her heartbreakingly young grandfather—sitting in front of a tent, a row of similar tents marching off into the distance.

"What do you see?" she said, heart thumping.

"Where's your computer?"

"Just a minute." She hurried to the living room and plucked her laptop from the coffee table.

Returning to the kitchen, she opened the lid and entered her password even before putting it down. "Here."

He deftly manoeuvred the mouse to her web browser and tapped briskly on the keyboard, his long fingers spelling out *Fifth Canadian Division Nova Scotia Camp Flags*. When the page loaded, he clicked over to the Image results tab and the screen filled with brightly coloured rectangles.

Leeza caught her breath. "What is it?" she said. "What are you looking for?"

Touching the phone's screen, he spread his fingers to get a closer look at a flag blowing from a narrow pole planted next to the tents. It wasn't possible to see the entire emblem, but details were still visible. Leeza's gaze jumped between the phone and laptop.

"That one," Gavin said with satisfaction. He pointed at an image with blue, gold, and red vertical panels. In the centre panel, the letters NSH stood out boldly above a blue X with a gold shield bearing a red lion. "The North Nova Scotia Highlanders."

CHAPTER FIVE

October 10th, 1941
I know. I have to write more. Training should
start soon. Some of the guys have been leaving
a lot lately. They've met some girls that they
liked. I don't think it's such a good idea. The
girls are getting attached to them but half of
these guys are using them like paper towels.
This one guy said he's been out with at least 25
girls in about 2 months, that's almost
impossible.

"I can't believe you saw that so quickly," Leeza
said a few minutes later.

Cookies and milk hadn't seemed quite enough
for celebrating Gavin's discovery, so she'd poured
wine and they'd moved to the living room. She sat in
her accustomed corner of the couch and he chose an
upholstered chair next to the modern gas fireplace.
He appeared composed and calm as usual, but a
gleam in his eye and a quirk of his mouth hinted at a
deeply hidden excitement.

"Once I saw the flag, it only made sense to start
with units based in Nova Scotia, as that was where
your grandfather was from. We're lucky there was a

wind that day."

The thought startled Leeza. "Of course. If it had hung straight down, we wouldn't have been able to compare it." Though it was not entirely visible, the design of the North Nova Scotia Highlanders camp flag was unmistakable in the black and white photo.

"I don't know if it gets us much further," Gavin said. "William should have shown up with the searches we've already done, even without knowing the unit he was in." His fingers tapped lightly on his knee. "And we're only guessing he was in the North Novies with your grandfather."

"Is there a way to compare the events in the journal with the movements of the—what did you call them? The North Novies?"

Gavin bobbed his head. "That was the nickname they gave themselves. They were an instrumental part of the D-Day invasion of Normandy." He shook his head. "But you know that. You've read the diary."

The final, heartrending entries were what had lit Leeza's determination to find William's family and restore the journal to them. "It makes it more real, somehow," she said softly, staring sightlessly at the ruby-red wine. "It's one thing to read the hard facts of troop movements and famous battles in a textbook or online, but this—this was like being there along with him." She glanced at Gavin to find him gazing steadily at her. "He was younger than my son is now, when he left home. I can't imagine how his mother said goodbye."

"It's bad enough when they move across town," he said with a wry grin.

"How many children do you have?"

"Two. A son and a daughter. And now a daughter-in-law and a son-in-law."

"And a granddaughter."

His imperturbable expression lightened like sun on a snowy peak. "Who is the most beautiful, smart, graceful, wonderful child ever."

Leeza laughed, as he'd meant her to. "Of course she is."

He gestured with his glass in the direction of a set of floating shelves on the wall next to the fireplace, on which numerous pictures featuring Drew were displayed. "Your son, I'm guessing?"

"Yes." She rose and approached the shelves, letting her finger drift over a photo of Drew wearing a grubby soccer jersey and beaming from a mud splattered face. "He left a week ago for London. He has a job at the High Commission of Canada there."

"You must be proud. And lonely."

She glanced at him, surprised he'd made such a personal remark.

He said, "You've been separated from your husband for more than a year, haven't you?"

Her surprise escalated to shock. "Yes. But how—"

"I pay attention," he said in that calm, quiet voice. "He wasn't at the staff Christmas party last year, and a couple months later I heard you mention to Carrie your divorce had been finalized." Carrie was Leeza's only full-time staff member.

"Oh." Her marriage troubles weren't a secret, but she didn't talk about them much, either.

"I just want to let you know..." He trailed off, cleared his throat, and started again. "What I mean is...I know what it's like to be lonely."

"You can't compare my situation to yours," Leeza said. "You lost your wife to a horrible, dreadful disease. I kicked my husband to the curb when I found out about his affairs." Try as she might, she couldn't keep the bitterness from her voice.

Gavin's eyes widened behind the heavy frame of his glasses. "Affairs? Plural?"

She took a healthy gulp of wine. "Yes. In one way, that made it easier. If it had been a single affair,

I might have tried to forgive him, tried to patch things up. Multiple affairs made it easier to cut my losses. No need to attempt to fix anything when he had been such an asshole." She clapped her hand over her mouth. "Sorry."

"No need." Amusement crinkled the corners of his mouth. "The same word had crossed my mind."

"On the other hand," she said, unable to stop herself, "multiple affairs did reinforce what an idiot I was for not suspecting. I never did, you know. I thought we'd reached a plateau in our lives, and I was happy, content. Maybe the spark was gone, but that's natural, isn't it? He was never rude or mean or insulting. We'd always been an independent couple, never living in each other's pockets. So, when he said he was busy—busy!"—she snorted—"I assumed it was with work, not other women."

"You trusted him."

"Of course I trusted him!" The words burst from her at an embarrassingly loud volume. She gripped her now empty glass, keeping her eyes averted from Gavin, but knowing he watched her. "Sorry. Didn't mean to unload like that. That wasn't very professional."

He leaned forward to place his glass on the coffee table and she snuck a quick glance. His expression was smooth and undisturbed as usual. "Since we're sitting in your living room and not at work, I think you can be forgiven." He rose. "I should be going."

A spurt of relief unlocked the knot in her chest. It was trickier than she thought, this new dynamic with Gavin, spending time together away from the bookstore. It would take a while to find the balance.

She walked him to the door. "Thanks again for helping find William."

"We haven't found him yet," Gavin said, shrugging into his coat. "We're only assuming he was in the North Nova Scotia Highlanders. I'll do some more digging this weekend."

"Me, too." The sense of discovery was back, firing her excitement. "I'll let you know if I find anything."

He placed a hand on the doorknob. "Goodnight, Leeza." He opened his mouth as if to say more, and then simply nodded and slipped outside.

"Goodnight, Gavin," she said to the closed door.

With less than two weeks before Christmas, Leeza was putting in plenty of hours at the store. She hadn't hired as many extra staff as she might have in previous years and was picking up those shifts herself. Her reasoning had been two-fold. It was a good way to reduce costs to help with revenue shortfalls, and an even better way to keep herself from missing Drew too much.

On the Sunday after learning of William's possible—probable?—connection to the North Nova Scotia Highlanders, she went into the store with an unaccustomed aura of nervousness hovering around her. Gavin was scheduled to work the entire day, and for most of it there would just be the two of them on the floor. At first, she'd been thankful he had left so quickly after her mortifying confession of Scott's infidelities, but the more she thought of it the greater significance his departure seemed to take. She'd obviously made him so uncomfortable he'd had to escape. She could only hope he'd ignore what had happened and let them slip into their usual, efficient routine.

Gavin was unlocking the accordion gate at the front of the store when she arrived shortly before opening. Melting snow glinted in his sandy-brown hair, and he wore a dark-grey down-filled jacket that hung to his hips. A black leather case sat on the floor at his feet.

She smiled brightly, determined to act as if nothing had changed. "Good morning," she said, chipper enough to set her own teeth on edge.

He greeted her with a nod, bent to retrieve the case, and allowed her through first, securing the gate behind them. Leeza headed for the back and he followed silently. He went left to the employee locker room and she went right to her office. She hung up her coat, tucked her purse into a desk drawer, and then turned to the door, emitting a short shriek when she spied him standing in the opening.

"Sorry," he said. "I wanted to say something before the day gets busy."

"Sure." She linked her fingers, and then unlinked them. *Calm,* she thought. *Act normal.*

"You're not an idiot."

She blinked. "Okay?"

He huffed out a breath. "I'm talking about your husband. You're not an idiot for trusting him. We trust the people we love. That's why they can hurt us so badly. I don't think any less of you for having a jerk of a husband. You're an intelligent, caring, beautiful woman, and he doesn't deserve you."

She blinked again, this time to hold back the tears burning under her eyelids. "Thank you. I thought I might have creeped you out, telling you so much. I don't usually talk about him, not anymore. I don't know why I did with you."

He smiled, and something warm uncurled in her belly. *Oh, no,* she thought, *that's not good.* The silence between them felt right, felt comforting.

"I'll get the till going," he said and disappeared.

She stood there, gathering herself, the glow in her stomach reassuring and disturbing at the same time. Before she had a chance to move, he reappeared in the door. "Oh, and I have news. About William."

"You do?" Relieved to put any awkwardness behind them, she said eagerly, "What is it?"

"Too complicated to get into now," he said. "It's more negatives, but interesting ones. We'll talk later." And he disappeared again.

CHAPTER SIX

December 16th, 1941
Lots of things have happened at home! First of
all, Maureen has lost her 2 front teeth and the
tooth fairy brought her 50 cents. Mom says she
was jumping with joy for days after. Mom is
doing great, so she says. I know its been
difficult for her since my father died 5 years
ago. He worked with trains and one day, by
accident, he got hit by a train. My mother went
into a very big depression. I guess she's better
now compared to 5 years ago. Mom says my
younger brother David, who is 17, really wants
to join the army also. I don't want him to. He's
still in school and he's actually smart. I don't
want him to waste his time. I have to write back
to them.

To Leeza's dismay, sales that day were very quiet,
especially considering it was the second last Sunday
before Christmas. Customers came and went, but
most spent their visit browsing, not buying. Each
time one left without making a purchase, she lost a
little more hope that the store would survive much
longer. As manager, she had limited powers to adjust

either stock or pricing. While she did all she could to make sure staff were knowledgeable and displays inviting and worked hard at the hundred other things that made a bookstore attractive, it wasn't making a big enough difference.

The other drawback to the slow day was it made it hard to keep her mind off Gavin's cryptic announcement. During the longish lulls between customers, her mind ran like a hamster on a wheel. What had he found out? If he hadn't identified William, what else could it be?

What with one thing and another, she was thankful when closing time came. In her office, she reviewed the day's sales. Gavin moved about the store, and she heard the soothing sound of covers shushing together as he re-shelved misplaced books, the soft thump as he laid others on the stacked displays to replace the few—very few—that had been purchased. Dismally, she doublechecked the totals. *Not good,* she thought. *Not good at all.*

"All set?"

She looked away from the depressing figures and nodded at Gavin standing in the doorway, wearing his coat and carrying the case he'd had with him earlier. "Be right there."

After securing her computer, setting the night alarm, and turning off the lights, she made her way through the dim space to the front. Gavin again ushered her through the gate first, and then locked up. All the other stores were in the process of closing as well, and the clattering clash of security fences and clicking of heels echoed off the tile floor and high ceiling. The main lights in the mall had been lowered and festive decorations hung eerily in the shadows.

"You're being very patient."

She looked up at Gavin. Odd how she'd never really noticed how tall he was. Almost as tall as Drew. He regarded her with a quiet, amused expression that nettled her.

"I'm trying to be," she said tartly. "But don't bet on it lasting much longer. Now, what did you find out?"

He lifted the flap on an outside pocket of the black leather case and removed the diary, safely stowed in a plastic zipped bag. "Here. I thought you'd want it back." She took it, glad to have it. She'd missed being able to read William's words whenever she wanted.

Gavin said, "I brought my laptop. It's dinner time. How about we go somewhere to eat, and I can show you what I found?"

A few minutes later they were at a four-top table in the Italian restaurant located in a standalone building in the mall's parking lot. The server had greeted Gavin by name and seated them in a corner far from the door.

"The usual?" she asked Gavin.

"Yes, but please bring a menu for Leeza." The server hurried off.

Leeza raised her eyebrows. "Regular hangout?"

He ducked his chin, his expression sheepish, and she caught a glimpse of the boy he used to be hiding under his usually stoic exterior. "You could say that."

She was prevented from quizzing him further by a loud voice booming over her shoulder. "Gavin! So good to see you!"

A man bustled over, the aromas of yeast and tomato sauce wafting in his wake. Gavin rose and was immediately enveloped in a boisterous hug. The man was short and round and wore a white chef's jacket with a red apron tied at his waist. He released Gavin with a couple of vigorous slaps on his back and turned to Leeza. "I'm Leonardo," he said, offering her a menu with a flourish. "This is my *ristorante*. Welcome! If you have any questions about the menu, please ask. But first, a drink?" He waited expectantly, dark eyes bright and snapping. Despite her first impression of a cartoon-like representation of an Italian chef, something cheeky and knowing in that gaze warned her he was more than he portrayed.

"I'll have a glass of red," she said. "Whatever you recommend."

"*Bueno!*" He waved encouragingly at the menu. "Please, take a look. I'll be back for your order right away."

"He seems quite the character," she said as Gavin took his seat again.

"Yes." She waited for him to elaborate, to give her the background on his obvious connection with the restaurant, but instead he made room on the table for his laptop and opened the lid. "You decide what you want while I get this ready."

The list of pizzas was unusual and extensive. While salads and lighter fare were available, this was not a place for the gluten intolerant. Which she wasn't, thank goodness. "What's your usual?"

"Blue cheese," he answered, staring at the computer screen as his fingertip moved quickly over the mouse pad.

"Really?" she said, startled. "On pizza?"

His mouth quirked at the corner. "I had it in Venice once, years ago. Leonardo is the only chef in town that serves it."

Unwilling to be as adventurous, she decided on the more mundane but prettily named margherita. Leonardo brought her wine and a Coke for Gavin, took her order with every expression of delight and bustled off again.

"Coke and blue cheese?" she asked.

Again, that shamefaced look—a look she was beginning to find very appealing. "I'll drink the Coke before the pizza comes, then just have water with the meal. Even I can't mix the two." He turned the laptop so they could both see the screen. "Now, about William. First, the good news."

She scooted her chair forward and twisted her neck to see the screen better. The headline read *Nova Scotia Highlanders* and a graphic showed a blue and gold circle with a red lion in the middle, all on a white X. It was a slightly different version of the image on the flag in Grampa-Great's photo. "Tell me."

"I think we can confirm that William was a member of the North Novies." Suppressed excitement glistened in his eyes. "Look." He scrolled down the page quickly, and then pointed. She read:

> *The regiment subsequently mobilized The North Nova Scotia Highlanders, CASF for active service on 24 May 1940. It embarked for Great Britain on 18 July 1941 on board the S.S. Orion. On D-Day, 6 June 1944, it landed in Normandy, France, as part of the 9th Infantry Brigade, 3rd Canadian Infantry Division, and it continued to fight in North-West Europe until the end of the war.*

He said, "William's very first diary entry on July 21, 1941 states that he 'left today at noon from Halifax.' I think it most likely that this date"—he tapped the screen—"is when the units left their bases. It would have taken a bit of time for them to travel to Halifax, get all personnel and equipment on board, and set off."

"That makes sense."

"Then, in his second entry, William names the ship he is on." He paused, eyebrows raised expectantly.

It took Leeza a moment. Then enlightenment dawned. "The *Orion*," she said.

"Exactly." Gavin's satisfaction was evident.

"William was a Novie," Leeza said, resting her chin in her hand and scanning the screen. "It should be easier to find him now, right?"

"You'd think so." Gavin's tone was wry. "Since he didn't come up when we searched just his name, the first thing I tried was combinations of North Nova Scotia Highlanders and Smith. I didn't expect that to work, but it was a necessary step. Nothing popped." He grinned, apparently undeterred by that failure.

"What do we do next, then?"

"I think we should compile a list of places that might have access to information about soldiers who served in that regiment and start contacting them directly. As much as the internet is a wonderful resource, not everything is online."

"What kind of places?"

"Well, the Royal Canadian Legion would be one. The current reserve unit is based in Truro, so we could start there. Maybe the Canadian War Museum and Veterans Affairs Canada. The other piece of good news is that there is a museum dedicated to the North Novies in Amherst. It took some digging to find the website, but I managed."

"It was hard to find a website on the internet?" Leeza puffed out a laugh at the thought.

The skin crinkled around his eyes. "Hard to imagine, I know. But I first saw it on a site listing places to visit in Truro and that link just about broke my computer—I think it had been hacked somehow. I had to get at it another way."

Gavin was interrupted by the arrival of their individual pizzas. Leonardo served them with flair, inquired if they needed anything else, and at their assurances they were fine, faded away.

Leeza's first bite had her closing her eyes in wonder. "This is pizza?" she said around a mouthful of savoury tomato sauce, perfectly gooey cheese, and the faintly black licorice zest of basil. "I've never tasted anything like this. The crust—" She cut herself off to take another bite. "Oh, my. *Sooo* good."

She opened her eyes to see Gavin staring at her with an intense expression. The sounds of the restaurant dwindled, and she became acutely aware of the heat of the pizza slice in her hand, the flavours in her mouth, the dab of tomato sauce on her lip. She licked it off, and Gavin's gaze sharpened even more. Her heart gave a hard, quick thump.

Then he blinked and turned that concentrated focus to his pizza, cutting the thin crust neatly with a knife and fork and raising it to his mouth. The volume of the world returned to normal and she swallowed.

As if nothing had changed—although something had, she just wasn't ready to decide *what*—Gavin said, "Have you heard from your son recently?"

The rest of the meal was spent in ordinary, safe small talk, but Leeza continued to feel on edge, so she didn't linger when her pizza was finished. Gavin made no fuss when she requested separate cheques. He walked her to her vehicle as was his custom, and his goodnight was calm and friendly, his eyes giving no hint of the furled fierceness she'd seen before.

At home, curled on the couch with a cup of tea, Leeza could almost believe she'd imagined...whatever it was she'd seen. For five years Gavin had been, well, *Gavin*. Her most reliable, dependable, mature employee. He'd been a part of the fabric of her life, had woven himself in without disruption or disturbance. She'd rarely thought of him outside of work.

Now it seemed he was rarely out of her thoughts.

CHAPTER SEVEN

January 10th, 1942
Rodney met a girl near London. He's pretty
much always there now. I'm stuck here alone.

Charlene surveyed the bare living room and glared at Leeza. "What are you, in mourning? Where are the Christmas decorations?"

"I've been busy," Leeza said defensively.

"Not too busy to put up a couple of wreaths and a swag or two, surely. And don't tell me it's because you're *too busy*." She put finger quotes around the last words. "I was joking when I asked if you were in mourning, but I suppose you *are* mourning Drew, in a way." Her gaze was shrewd yet sympathetic.

Charlene might not be the most tactful of friends, but that didn't mean she wasn't insightful. Leeza couldn't admit she'd hit the nail on the head. "Fine," she said. "Stay right there."

As she excavated under the stairs to find the boxes that held her Christmas decorations, Leeza reflected this wasn't the way she'd expected to spend her Thursday evening.

After her disconcerting meal with Gavin on

Sunday, she'd been hesitant to talk to him about anything not work-related. But the journal had such a hold on her that she'd been unable to let the investigation drop, so she'd made a couple of phone calls, including one to the regimental museum he had mentioned. What she'd learned had been so confusing she *had* to discuss it with him, despite any self-consciousness. But when she'd called that evening, he'd been unable to talk.

"I'm sorry," he had said. "I'm just heading out for dinner."

"That's all right," she'd replied. She should have hung up right away, but instead asked, "Another family get-together?"

"Not exactly." He paused and she heard him draw in a breath. "It's a blind date, actually."

"Oh." A pang of something perilously close to jealousy tightened her throat.

"My son set it up. She's the mother of a friend of his who lost her husband a year or so ago."

"Well, have a great time," she said heartily. "Good luck."

"I can call you later, if you like. I don't imagine we'll be out too late."

"Now that's not very optimistic. Don't hurry on my account. I just had a couple things to tell you, but nothing dramatic."

"I really do want to hear your news. How about tomorrow?"

"I'll be at the store most of the day. Really, it can wait. Have a good dinner." She hung up. The silence had hummed around her, and she'd immediately dialed Charlene's number and invited her over to break the gloom.

She carried two bins to the living room, and then coerced Charlene into helping her drag in the box containing the tree from the garage. Determined to get into the spirit, she put a Christmas carol playlist on her phone and poured them each a glass of wine.

As they struggled to lift the top third of the pre-lit tree into place, Charlene grunted, "I'm all for women's equality, but heavy-lifting is a man's job." She hissed. "Damn it, I broke a nail."

From her stance on the three-step stool Leeza felt the post click into place. "There."

"Speaking of men," Charlene said with studied nonchalance, "I talked with Scott yesterday."

Leeza climbed down and picked up a box of shiny silver icicles, stifling a surge of irritation. Her ex-husband had taken enough from her in the last year. Was he taking her last friend, too? Ignoring Charlene's words, she handed her the icicles, chose a box filled with gold stars, and climbed back up the ladder. Hopefully, she would take Leeza's lack of response as the unspoken hint it was.

She didn't. "He wanted me to ask you a favour."

Leeza stared, hand frozen in the act of hanging a star on an upper bough. "What on *earth* could he need from me?"

Charlene fiddled with the string of the ornament in her hand, not meeting Leeza's eye. "He wants to talk about selling the cabin."

Originally owned by Otto Friberg and his wife, Leeza had spent much of her childhood vacations at the cabin on a lake less than an hour from Prince George. After the death of his wife, Otto had decided to pass it on, and Leeza and Scott had purchased it. Over the years Scott had spent less and less time there, but she and Drew hadn't let that stop them from enjoying it in all seasons.

"That's not the deal," Leeza said automatically. "We're saving it for Drew." An agreement drawn up in the divorce settlement had stated the cabin would remain in both Leeza and Scott's names, and that both had to agree to sell before it could be put on the market. Leeza fully intended to hold onto the cabin until Drew made a firm decision whether he wanted it or not. He loved the place and she wasn't about to sell it out from under him.

"Drew's in London. Who knows if he's coming back?" Charlene's tone was soft but remorseless. She hung an ornament and chose another from the box.

"He hasn't been gone two weeks yet," Leeza stated. "Give him a chance." Her knees shook at the thought he might *not* return to Canada and she stepped off the small ladder carefully and sat on the arm of the sofa. "Besides, there's no hurry to sell."

Charlene studied the tree, seeking a place to put the last icicle. "Scott thinks he has a buyer."

Rage swelled in Leeza's chest. "He has no right to be talking to anyone about the cabin," she said wrathfully, "and he's a coward to send you to do his dirty business. If he wants to discuss selling, he can call me himself. Since you seem happy being the go-between, though, you can tell him no how, no way. I don't care if he has a bus full of buyers. I won't agree to it. Not until Drew makes a definite decision. And he better not even *think* of trying to convince Drew to sell, or I'll—I'll..." She trailed off, unable to come up with a suitable torture.

Charlene regarded her, impeccably designed eyebrows raised. "All right then," she said. "I'm guessing that's a no?"

Leeza goggled. Charlene's eyes were bright with amusement. After a moment of stunned silence, they burst into laughter.

"I'll pass on your message." The fun faded from Charlene's face. "But I warn you now, I don't think he's going to accept it."

"Too bad." With defiance, Leeza climbed the ladder once more and began randomly placing stars on the tree. "This is non-negotiable. He's just going to have to lump it."

Charlene left around nine-thirty, after helping Leeza finish the tree. She had said nothing more about Scott or the cabin, but the evening had been tarnished, despite Leeza's efforts to push the conversation from her mind.

After stuffing the now empty boxes and bins back into storage, she prepared for bed. Plugging her phone into the charger on her nightstand, she settled back against a pile of fluffy pillows, tugged the comforter up to her chest and turned on her e-reader. Other people might spend their evenings watching television. To Leeza, reading in bed for an hour or more before letting sleep catch her was a daily joy.

Only a few pages into the latest Jennifer Crusie, her phone buzzed an interruption. Gavin's name appeared on the screen.

She bit her lip, heart rate accelerating. She shouldn't be feeling such delight at seeing his name. They were nothing more than colleagues working a project together.

It buzzed again.

The fact that he was calling her the same evening he'd been on a date should not fill her with this warm sense of satisfaction.

It buzzed a third time.

She snatched it from the table, the cord stretching as far as it would go. She unplugged it hastily. "Hello?" she said, her voice husky and rough.

"You were asleep," Gavin said immediately. "I'm sorry, I shouldn't have called. I knew it was too late."

"No, it's fine," she said. "I'm in bed, but I wasn't asleep yet."

The silence in the speaker seemed restless, tense. He made a small, choking cough. "Still, I should have waited for tomorrow," he said, "but I couldn't. It was terribly rude of me, but I thought only of you all through my date. Your news, I mean. What you found out." He stuttered to a stop.

Her heart sped up even more. He'd thought of her while he was with another woman. "Of course, my news," she said. It was her turn to hesitate. She placed her e-reader beside her on the bed and drew her knees up, tracing the floral print on the comforter with one finger.

"If you'd rather we talk another time—"

She cut him off. "No, now is good." His voice, soft and low, was comfort and pleasure and excitement. Her body softened against the pillows. "I'm glad you called."

Another silence filled the space between them, one of anticipation, of shared discovery. "So, what did you find out?" he asked.

She put the phone on speaker and leaned it against her knees. "You remember you sent me the link to the North Nova Scotia Highlanders museum?" A noise of assent came through the phone. "I've been going through the website, and I discovered they have a Book of Remembrance where the death of every soldier is listed. It's not online, but I had a few minutes today, so I called."

"And is William included?"

"No. And neither is Rodney."

"Neither of them?" Gavin said in surprise. "We can't tell from the diary exactly what happened to William, but Rodney—well, we know he never came home. He should be listed."

"It's so frustrating that William didn't include last names. I mean, it makes sense, because the diary was only for him, and *he* knew who he was talking about. But it would have been so helpful. When there was no William Henry Smith listed, I had the man I reached—a lovely gentleman, very patient, name of John—look in the book for Rodney. The entries are chronological, so he started from the earliest date, based on the entry in the diary, until well after the war was over. And I didn't ask him to look just for the name Rodney. I asked him to check any that might remotely be somehow shortened or converted to it. Nothing."

"Did he have any suggestions for where we should look next?"

His matter of fact acceptance of yet another roadblock eased Leeza's discouragement. "One of the museum's artifacts is a scrapbook that was donated years ago. It's been digitized and all the newspaper clippings and photographs are available online. It's searchable, but if we want to confirm nothing was missed when they built the database, we'll have to study every single page."

"Send me the link when you have a chance. We can divide that between us."

The nagging worry he would tire of the search dissolved completely. "John also mentioned there are a number of Smith families in the area, but he's pretty sure he would know if any of them had a connection to the North Novies. He's going to ask around anyway."

"Did you make any other calls?"

"I was going to try Legions in the north end of the province, but I ran out of time."

"I'm not working tomorrow. I'll see what I can find out."

Another pause. Leeza closed her eyes and enjoyed the silence. She was alone, but not lonely. This project with Gavin might have started as a way to avoid missing Drew, to forget the failure of her marriage, and to get Charlene off her back, but it was more than all that now.

It was a link to Gavin, and one she didn't want to break.

"I should let you go," he said softly.

"I suppose." She reached for the phone still

propped on her knees. "How was your date?"

The words popped out before she could stop them. Their echo in her brain sounded needy and sullen. Please god Gavin took it as a friendly inquiry, not a jealous interrogation.

"She's a very nice woman. But I don't think we'll be seeing each other again."

Leeza let her breath out. "I'm sorry," she said, sincere and relieved at the same time.

"It's okay," he said. "I'm very picky and I know it. I'm not looking for an exact replacement for Nancy. But I know how good marriage can be, and I won't settle."

He'd never spoken of his wife by name before. Leeza said wistfully, "When it's good, it's very, very good, isn't it?" *And when it's bad it's indescribably awful*, she thought.

"Yes. Well, goodnight. I'll call you if I find out anything tomorrow."

Call ended popped up on her phone screen. She stared at it in astonishment. Why had he hung up so abruptly? What had happened? It was as close to rude as she'd ever known him to be and was so un-Gavin-like as to be incomprehensible.

She connected her phone to the charger again and picked up her e-reader slowly. Hopefully, Jennifer Crusie's sharp, witty, rapid-fire dialogue would distract her from this new mystery in her life.

CHAPTER EIGHT

January 25th, 1942
Rodney's not with his girl anymore. She left
him for an American. I hear he's much taller
than 'Rodney the shorty'. Me and the guys can't
stop laughing at him.

Gavin's aloofness continued during the next few
days, and Leeza fretted over the change in his
attitude, despite frequent vows to ignore it. Their last
conversation replayed itself in her head on an
endless loop, and she couldn't figure out what had
made him flip the switch so quickly. The last thing
she'd said had been agreeing with him that marriage
could be lovely, when it worked. Surely that hadn't
been it.

He sent a terse text on Friday saying he'd been
unable to get in touch with anyone at the two Legion
offices. It appeared they were closed for the holiday
season. No one would be available until after
December 26, and possibly not until the new year.
On Saturday she had seen him for a moment as she
was leaving Millar's and he was arriving, but he'd
done no more than nod politely as they passed.

Her relationship with the other man in her life wasn't much better. She'd attempted to connect with Drew several times during the last week, but he'd answered her texts and emails only briefly, and hadn't had time to video chat at all. As Christmas drew nearer, her loneliness grew. She couldn't—wouldn't—blame him for diving right into his new life, but that didn't stop her from feeling unaccountably neglected.

Monday morning, she woke up, restless and unsettled even before she opened her eyes. A heaviness in her temples and a tightness at the base of her skull warned a headache was brewing. But with only four more days before Christmas she couldn't afford to stay home sick. She chased a couple of pills down with an extra strong dose of coffee and headed into work.

For an hour or so she managed to ignore the throbbing behind her eyes, the dryness of her mouth. Before long, though, she snapped at Carrie when the young woman thudded a pile of books onto the counter with a noise that made Leeza's teeth rattle. When she blinked, flares of light filled her vision, and her lids rasped annoyingly against her eyeballs. The jingling Christmas music, at first just a background bother, became so irritating she wanted to rip her own ears off, and she escaped to her office, shutting the door to provide some relief. She turned the overhead light off, leaving only the glow of her computer screen in the windowless room, and sank into her chair. Tossing back more pills, she closed her eyes and waited for the medication to take effect.

She didn't think she'd dozed off—she only wished she had, as then the pain might go away—but it seemed only seconds later that the door opened.

"Yes?" she said, trying not to whimper as the clatter of shoppers and music assaulted her ears. She opened her eyes a slit and swivelled toward the door, keeping her head firmly against the back of the chair, fighting a rising nausea.

A figure, silhouetted against the glaring light outside, stepped in, and the noise level dropped to manageable as the door shut. She closed her eyes again.

"Carrie says you're not feeling well," Gavin said.

"You're not scheduled to work today," she said, concentrating desperately on not vomiting.

"I forgot something in my locker yesterday. I stopped in to get it." A warm hand rested on her forehead. "You don't have a fever."

"It's just a headache," she muttered from behind clenched teeth.

"Migraine?"

She would have shaken her head to deny it but was afraid it might explode like an overfilled balloon. "I took some meds. They'll kick in soon."

"You're flinching at sounds and the light is hurting your eyes. You need to go home." His thumb smoothed the skin between her brows, up her forehead to her hairline, then back down. The repeated motion alleviated some of the pain and her neck relaxed a fraction.

"I can't," she said. "I've got to be here."

"The store will do just fine without you for one day."

All of a sudden, it was too much. Drew's desertion and Grampa-Great's death, her divorce and the store's imminent demise. "You don't understand," she said, tears burning the back of her throat, overwhelming emotions defeating even the nausea. Grasping to explain, she blurted out the simplest, least intimate of reasons. "If the store doesn't do well this month, I think they'll shut us down. I have to do everything I can to stop that."

The finger on her forehead paused in its soothing motion, and then resumed. "As bad as that?"

"Yes." She moved her shoulders restlessly. "I probably shouldn't have told you."

"It's okay. I won't spread it around."

She dared to open her eyelids. Gavin was crouched at her side, his face an eerie blue in the light from the monitor, his glasses reflecting the animated fractal screen saver. She couldn't see his eyes. He lowered his hand from her forehead and the loss of its warmth made her shiver.

"I'm feeling better." At least she didn't feel like she was going to lose her breakfast anymore. She pushed herself up in the seat and he shifted slightly, putting a hand on her knee.

"I'll make you a deal," he said. "If you can walk from here to the front till without issue, I'll let you stay. Otherwise, I'm taking you home."

She scowled, and simply lowering her brows caused the headache to kick back up a notch. "I told you, I can't go home."

"Headaches with visual and auditory distress usually involve nausea. Do you really want to toss your cookies all over a customer?"

"I said I'm feeling better." She planted her hands on the desk and stood up. Gavin rose with her. "There's no need to hover," she said. "I'm ready to go back out." She took a step toward the door.

And staggered, her legs weak and trembling.

Immediately, Gavin had one arm around her waist, the other hand supporting her elbow. "Well, that answers that. I'm taking you home."

She wanted to argue more, but he was right. Damn it, she *hated* giving in to physical weakness. It made her feel ridiculous and incompetent. "Fine," she muttered. "I'll have a nap and be back in a couple hours."

"You can believe whatever you like," he said, "as long as you come with me now."

By the time Gavin parked her SUV in her garage, the nausea had returned and all she wanted to do was lie in a dark, quiet room for the rest of her life. She had to keep her eyes closed and cling to the wall as he removed her boots and coat, breathing deeply and steadily to keep control. Then he helped her up the stairs and she melted onto the bed.

"You'll need to call a cab to get back to the mall," she whispered, her teeth aching in rhythm with her temples. "I'll pay you back."

"No worries," he said. The comforter shifted as he tugged it out from under her so he could wrap it around her shoulders. "Sleep now. We'll talk later."

The door snicked shut behind him and she sighed in relief. Now she could let the tears of pain and frustration loose. Curled on her side, the drops ran over the bridge of her nose and down her cheek onto her clasped hands. She relaxed into the comfort of the mattress, and imperceptibly slipped into sleep.

Consciousness came and went in waves, and she was aware of time passing. Once she thought she heard the door open and close, but that must have been her imagination since Gavin would have been long gone.

The red digits on her bedside clock read 2:20. With drowsy surprise she realized the display didn't sear like lightning through her brain. Rolling onto her back, she waited for the roil of nausea, but it didn't happen. Her head felt hollow and light, but pain free.

Moving carefully, she swung her feet over the edge of the bed. When all remained well, she stood and made her way to the en suite. Washing her face and brushing her teeth brought her back to near normal.

Halfway down the stairs, however, her legs trembled, and she admitted to herself returning to Millar's today was not in the cards. As she reached the landing and turned toward the kitchen, a voice from the living room said, "Feeling better?"

She shrieked and lurched against the wall.

"Whoa, there, sorry!" Gavin rushed to her and clutched her elbows, holding her upright. "I didn't mean to startle you."

"You're still here," she said, her racing heart slowing. "Why are you still here?"

"I didn't like to leave you alone." He stood close, the grip of his hands firm, the heat of his body wrapping around her.

"You checked on me." She could see gold flecks in the hazel eyes framed by his glasses.

"Just from the doorway, to make sure you were okay." His thumbs rubbed small circles on her biceps.

Tears filled her eyes again. God, she was being such a wimp today. But it was *lovely* to have someone take care of her. It had been so long.

"Thank you." She laid her palms flat on his chest and raised herself up on tiptoe. When her lips touched his cheek, his hold on her arms tightened and relaxed. She settled back on her heels.

He looked at her with an odd expression on his face—surprise and embarrassment and something boyish she couldn't quite decipher. The silence that filled the space between them was warm and familiar. She smiled.

His hands dropped from her elbows and he took a step back. Clearing his throat, he said, "Are you up to hearing what I learned while you were sleeping?"

A different kind of excitement raised her heartbeat this time. "Of course. Let me make tea first."

CHAPTER NINE

February 15th, 1942
We had our first march in a long time a few
days ago. It was nice seeing the whole unit
marching to Chichester Cathedral. There's also
been a change in commanders. I think all the
companies will have new commanders. I better
not get a jerk.

Gavin escorted her to the kitchen and insisted she take a seat at the table while he filled the kettle. Still enjoying the sensation of being cared for, she didn't argue. Watching him do the menial task was soothing. He moved with competent grace, not in a hurry but with no wasted motions.

"Be right back," he said, and disappeared down the hall, returning almost immediately with his laptop which he placed in front of her.

She frowned. "How did that get here?"

"I was going to do some work at the coffee shop next to Millar's, so I had it with me when I stopped at the store."

"You said you were there to get something from your locker."

"I'd forgotten my gloves on Saturday. It was kind of a kill two birds with one stone trip." The kettle whistled and he hurried to the stove. She directed him where to find the teapot and teabags and mugs and a couple minutes later she held a steaming cup of fragrant tea in her hands.

Gavin sat next to her and clicked open a document.

"Is that the diary?" she asked, peering at the screen. "Did you transcribe it?"

He nodded. "It makes it a lot easier to search. There are a few words I couldn't quite decipher"—he pointed to a row of question marks in the middle of one entry—"but I don't think I'm missing anything vital. I know William's mention of the *Orion* pretty much guaranteed he was a Novie, but the fact Rodney isn't listed in their Book of Remembrance worried me. I figured it couldn't hurt to find further corroboration, so I scanned through the entries looking for anything that might confirm or deny it."

He scrolled down and pointed again. Leeza read:

Feb 27th, 1942
General Montgomery came today. Seemed like a nice guy. We're getting all these new commanders now. My new commander is Major Rhodenizer. All the guys in the company hope he's better than the other guy we had before.

Leeza said, "I imagine it's Major Rhodenizer that's important. Montgomery doesn't exactly narrow things down."

"Bright girl." Bringing up his web browser, he clicked a tab at the top. "It was almost too easy. A quick Google of Major Rhodenizer immediately links him to the North Novies." As the screen filled with a list of search results, Gavin shifted in his seat to face her directly, his eyes glowing. "Major Leon Rhodenizer led the North Nova Scotia Highlanders on D-Day. He was pronounced missing on June 7, then discovered to be a prisoner of war a few months later. At the end of the war he was liberated by the Americans and returned home."

"William and Rodney must have been North Novies then."

"Yes. No doubt about it."

She took a closer look at the page Gavin had called up. "Do you mind?" she said, gesturing at the laptop.

He shook his head and slid it closer to her. "What do you see?"

"This one." She clicked on a link with the headline *Major Rhodenizer Called to Ottawa*. It led to a scan of a newspaper clipping. Ignoring that for now, she deleted the end of the web address in the browser bar, leaving only what she guessed to be the main site. Hitting return, she nodded in gratification. "I thought so. This is the scrapbook I was telling you about. The one John, the gentleman at the museum, directed me to."

Gavin's brows rose. "I hadn't noticed that. Well spotted. That's disappointing, though. If the scans of Rhodenizer show up in a simple Google search, then it stands to reason William and Rodney are not in it."

"That's what John said when I had him on the phone. But the search function only works on the text that's been added as a caption to the digitized images. If a soldier was mentioned in a newspaper article, but his name wasn't included in that additional text, searching won't find it. That's why he suggested we go through it page by page."

"I have looked at a few pages, but not systematically. It does feel like a last resort, though." He picked up the teapot and offered it to Leeza. She shook her head and he topped up his own mug.

"What do you think we should do next, then?"

He sipped his tea thoughtfully. "I think it's time to build a database of our own. We need to go through the diary and write down every town, every name—anything that might give us a starting point. And if online searches aren't getting us what we need, we have to find people and organizations that will. I know I mentioned that before, but we haven't concentrated any effort on that yet."

"Given the response from the Legions you called, I'm guessing we won't have much luck until the new year."

He closed the lid of his laptop and stood up. "No, probably not. And I'm afraid I won't have too much time to devote to it over the next week or so anyway."

"Lots of family events over Christmas?" She kept her tone light and cheerful, though the thought of the solitary Christmas she'd be having was like a black wound in her heart.

"I have to finish shopping"—at her raised eyebrow he shook his head, shamefaced—"I know, I know. I shouldn't leave it to the last minute. Then, my son has invited me to stay at his house on Christmas Eve so I can be there first thing in the morning when my granddaughter wakes up. After lunch they're heading to the other grandparents. My daughter is spending Christmas Day with her husband's family, too, but we'll all get together at her house on Boxing Day for our dinner. My boss gave me the day off." He winked.

She shook her head in mock dismay. "She must have been crazy. Holidays sound like quite the balancing act for your kids."

"It's hard to share them, sometimes, but I'm sure that's what the other parents are saying, too."

"Well, it sounds like a lovely few days."

He must have noticed something in her

66

expression. His gaze sharpened. "What are your plans?"

She waved one hand airily. "Oh, I have lots to keep me occupied."

"I assume Drew isn't coming home?"

"No, but we knew that when he left. It would be ridiculous to expect it."

He didn't take his eyes off her. "What about your parents?"

"They're spending Christmas in the desert, like they normally do." They had encouraged her to go see them, knowing she'd be alone, but with the store in such a vulnerable state she was reluctant to take the time off.

"If you want—"

"Honest, I'll be fine. I intend to spend the entire day in my pajamas, reading comfort fiction and eating only food that's bad for me. You don't need to worry. And someone has to work Boxing Day, so if not you, it might as well be me."

His solemn stare made her want to fidget but she held herself still. After a pause, he said, "If you want some company, just let me know."

She smiled brightly. "You bet." Eager to escape the conversation, she said, "Can I call you a cab? And no arguing, I'm paying for it. Also, in case I didn't say it before, thanks for bringing me home."

He looked like he wanted to press further, but he said, "I'll call. And you are more than welcome. I'm glad I was there to help, and glad you're feeling better. I've never seen anyone so pale."

If anyone asked, Leeza wouldn't have been able to tell them what she and Gavin talked about as they waited for the cab to arrive. She wanted to blame her despondency on her earlier headache, but she knew that wasn't true. Gavin's questions about Christmas had brought home once more how alone she was.

While she definitely didn't want pity, she

wouldn't have minded a friend.

Leeza allowed herself the luxury of changing into loungewear as soon as Gavin left and spent the rest of the afternoon on the couch. There was an odd, echoey feeling in her head and if she moved too quickly, she wobbled, so she felt only faintly guilty about not returning to Millar's. Just because she wasn't in the store didn't mean she couldn't do some work, though.

She logged into her email and took care of a few issues that could be handled remotely. As she was scrolling through her inbox, a message from Roberta St. Pierre, Vice-President of the Western Canadian Region, popped up, bold and black and unread.

It wasn't an email, but a notification of a teleconference scheduled for 9am Tuesday, December 29. The subject line was non-committal, giving no details on what the meeting might be about. Her gut curdled and her earlier nausea returned. *Stress will do that to you*, she thought.

Her finger trembled on the touch pad as she hovered the cursor over the *Accept* button. If her instincts were right, this was not going to be a pleasant meeting. Due to a computerized inventory and sales system, Corporate knew what revenue was, right to the minute, in every store. She couldn't hide from reality.

With a sensation akin to taking that last step off the high diving board, she accepted the appointment.

As if triggered by that action, her cell phone vibrated. She scooped it off the table at her elbow, seeing Scott's name with dismay. She really had no energy to deal with her ex right now, but he rarely called so it must be important. At least to him. She swiped to connect.

"Hi, Leeza."

"Hello, Scott," she said, thankful that hearing his voice no longer caused the searing pain it had in the early days of their separation.

"How have you been?"

"I'm fine."

"Good. That's good." He hesitated, and she found herself comparing the tense anxiety of this silence with the welcome anticipation she felt when Gavin paused in his conversations. She had grown used to his deliberateness, enjoyed the slower pace of time with him. But with Scott, she was just waiting for the other shoe to drop.

When he didn't speak, she gave him an exasperated prod. "Why did you call, Scott?"

"Nothing important. I mean, nothing serious. Have you heard from Drew since he got to London?"

Which told her he hadn't spoken with Drew himself. *Your only child,* she thought angrily, *and you can't be bothered to keep in touch.* "Yes, we've spoken. Numerous times."

"He's doing okay?"

"Yes, he's fine." She was fine, Drew was fine, everything was fine. She gritted her teeth.

Another pause.

Staring blindly at her slippered feet, she said, "Look, I'm at work." What he didn't know wouldn't hurt him. Isn't that what he'd thought all those times he'd cheated on her? "If there's nothing else—"

"Charlene told you I'm not with Yvonne anymore."

It wasn't a question. She replied coldly. "Yes. And that you've moved on to someone else already. I can't believe you're using Charlene to pass on your messages. She's my friend, too. Don't you realize what an awkward position you're putting her in, making her a go-between?" Suddenly aware of how loudly she was speaking, she drew a long breath and continued in a lower volume, "If you've got something to tell me, just tell me, okay."

"Geez, okay, I will." She was obviously not the only one irritated by this conversation. But he deserved every criticism. "Did she mention the cabin?"

She should have known this was where the conversation was going, but she was a little slow on the uptake this afternoon. "Yes. And the answer is no. We're not selling until Drew makes up his mind."

"That could be years!"

"Then so be it. You signed the contract, and the deal is we *both* have to agree to list the property. And you won't get that agreement from me, not until Drew decides what he wants."

"I've got someone interested, but they aren't willing to wait."

"Too bad for you. You shouldn't even be discussing the possibility. You'll just have to tell them the cabin is not available."

"It's a really good offer, Leez."

She recognized that wheedling note. Throughout their marriage, he'd used it—successfully, at least in the early years—to cajole her out of a bad mood or into bed. Sometimes both at the same time. But it had lost its power the moment she'd found out about Yvonne. And the others.

"I'm hanging up."

"Wait! What if I talk to Drew, find out what—"

"No! You are not talking to Drew about this, not now."

"Are you worried he'll agree?"

"He just left home to start a new life in a new country. I won't have you pressuring him to make a decision that he might regret later."

"He's a grown man, Leez. You need to stop protecting him."

It was an old argument. Maybe she had been a

bit of a helicopter mom, but when Drew had been born after two miscarriages, and the doctors had told her she would probably never have another child, she'd made a vow to raise a son that was happy, healthy and strong. The urge to defend him would never go away, no matter how old he was.

"Call him, Scott. You should. After all, he's your son and he lives halfway around the world. But do *not* talk to him about the cabin." She disconnected without waiting for a reply.

CHAPTER TEN

March 5th, 1942
It's total chaos. They've set an age limit and lots
of our guys have had to leave because they
were too young or something along those lines.
I'm not exactly sure. Some of the guys are
heartbroken. Me and Rodney were lucky
though. They didn't split us up. I don't know
what would have happened to me if they would
have. That would have been terrible.

Sales picked up in the last few shopping days of
the season, but not enough to salvage a miserable
year. When the doors closed at six o'clock on
Christmas Eve, Leeza knew that, even with the
Boxing Week influx still to come, she hadn't
managed to save the store. Hiding her worry, she
wished Carrie a Merry Christmas with a cheerful
smile as the young woman hurried off to join her
family. Then she wound her solitary way through the
dark, snowy streets to her dark, quiet home.

Tossing her purse and keys on the hall table, she
turned on the Christmas tree lights and felt her
spirits brighten a tiny degree. In a spirit of defiance
she turned on her favourite holiday album and sang

along with Boney M as she changed into pajamas, heated up a slice of the quiche she'd made the night before, poured a glass of wine, and settled into her corner on the couch with her e-reader.

At two minutes to midnight she was jolted from a light doze when her laptop rang out, signalling a video call. She sat up slowly, her back and neck stiff, rubbed her eyes with the heels of her hands, and with joyous excitement connected with Drew.

"Merry Christmas, Mom!" he said.

"Merry Christmas, Drew." She stared at the screen, resisting the impulse to trace her fingers over his beloved image. "It seems ages since we've had a chance to talk."

"I'm sorry about that. I'm working way more hours here than I did at the bank, but it's all fascinating. It's seeing Canada from a whole different angle, and I'm loving it."

"Don't be sorry. I'm glad you're enjoying it."

He leaned into the screen. "Did you get my present?"

She held the gaily wrapped box, about the size of a hard cover book but much lighter, so he could see it in the camera. "I did. You have no idea how much self-control it has taken not to rip it open days ago."

"I knew you wouldn't, no matter how much you wanted to. You never let me open any presents until morning, not even when I begged. You're lucky this year. You get to open yours only minutes after midnight. I've been waiting for hours already." He reached off to the side and lifted the gift she'd sent him onto his lap. "Yours got here just in time. It's pretty heavy, but I'm not going to ask how much it cost to ship. I'm glad we both have something to open. It's not the same when it's just a gift card or money transfer."

When Drew next checked his bank account, he'd

find she had done the latter, but she wasn't going to bring that up now. He didn't need her money—she *knew* that—but it made her feel better to give it.

"You go first," she said, adding teasingly, "since you've been waiting *sooo* long already."

With childish abandon he ripped a great swath of paper off the top of the box, opened the flaps, and pulled out the bubble wrap she'd used to protect its contents. His arm paused, hanging in the air, as he looked intently into the container.

"Wow." He lifted out the shadow box frame carefully and moved the packaging off his lap. She watched his face and sighed in relief at the reverence she saw there. "Is this Grampa-Great's?"

"Yes." She'd found the cap and badge in the back of a drawer in his dresser and had put them aside for just this purpose even before Drew left Prince George. It belatedly occurred to her that Gavin might have found them useful during his initial researches, but it didn't matter now. "I made sure there was a space for you to add the photo of Grampa-Great on the tank. I thought they should be together."

"It's awesome. Thank you." He touched the glass gently, and then tore his gaze away and met hers through the screen. "I really mean it. I miss him, and this is extra special." He swallowed, and then shook off his sentimentality with a grin. "Okay, your turn."

Keeping with tradition, Leeza slowly peeled off the tape sealing the gift and gently unfolded the paper back as Drew harangued her to hurry up. It was an old game between them. Finally, she revealed a heavy white cardboard box embossed with the words *Alexander McQueen*. She looked up. "You didn't."

He grinned. "Open it."

Once Drew had announced he was leaving for London, Leeza had spent a lot of time researching the city, hoping to stem her worry by getting to know it—at least virtually. One click had led to another and she found herself browsing the website of the famous British designer. Later she'd told Drew about the beautiful but totally out of her price-range clothing she'd drooled over. "Except for the scarves," she'd told him. "They looked lovely at first, delicate and ladylike. But then"—she'd shuddered—"I noticed the skulls. There were skulls on all of them."

The box she now stared at was just the right size and weight for a scarf. A potentially hideous scarf she'd have to pretend to like.

"Go on, Mom," Drew encouraged, his eyes dancing.

She opened it gingerly.

He cackled, not even waiting for her reaction. "I got the box from my boss. *She* can afford Alexander McQueen. The scarf is from a vintage shop near my flat."

The silk slipped luxuriously through Leeza's fingers. She spread it out, admiring the old-fashioned roses, peonies and hydrangeas printed in a riot of colours on it. "It's beautiful," she said in heartfelt relief. "Absolutely gorgeous."

"According to the clerk, the pattern is called *An English Country Garden*. I thought that was appropriate."

"I love it." She draped it around her neck, where it clashed ridiculously with the purple and orange teacups on her flannel pajamas, and stroked the material admiringly.

"I miss you, Mom."

She looked up. "I miss you, too, sweetie." Her eyes searched his serious face and she struggled to keep back tears. Her thoughts jumped to William and Rodney's mothers. They would have missed their sons at Christmas, too, with the added anguish that they were soldiers, and could be sent into battle at any moment. She had no idea how they had borne it.

"And I miss Grampa-Great. Christmas isn't the same without celebrating his birthday, too." He looked down at something off screen she couldn't see. "I wish he could have made one hundred."

"He was really looking forward to it," she said. "He always complained his birthday got lost in the holiday celebrations, so he made me promise for his hundredth it would be a birthday party, not Christmas dinner. I'm still surprised he didn't hold on long enough to lord it over us."

"Me, too." For a moment, his expression reminded her startlingly of the day she'd left him at summer camp for the first time—lost and lonely.

"Is everything okay?" She had to ask, although what could she do to help?

He smiled, though it didn't quite reach his eyes. "Yes, it is. Just feeling a bit homesick. It comes and goes, but most of the time I'm fine. Things are a lot different here. I do love my job, though—it's so much better than banking—and I'm meeting all sorts of new people. It's just—not home."

She wanted to tell him it was all right to change his mind, to come back to Prince George. But that wasn't what he needed to hear. "You know what I've always said—you've got to give big changes a few months. It's so easy to make an emotional decision before you've given it a chance."

"Don't get me wrong, I'm not regretting coming here." His voice lightened, and with it Leeza's worry. "It is honestly amazing, and it gets better everyday. Just last week, I helped a British company…"

He went on to tell her of his successes, and by the time they signed off about an hour later she was no longer worried about him missing home too much. Instead, she was trying not to flip too far the other way and start angsting over whether he'd come home ever.

Despite not going to bed until after one a.m. and reading for a good hour after getting under the covers, Leeza was awake well before nine o'clock. The day stretched out ahead of her, and she wryly recalled her brave words to Gavin. There was no way she'd be able to spend all day in her pajamas doing nothing but reading and eating—she'd go stir crazy.

Hours later she surveyed her kitchen counters with satisfaction—and no little trepidation. Strewn across them were dozens of cookies, muffins, and sweet breads. "You have enough to start your own bakery," she muttered to the empty room, the air redolent with spices and warmth.

Her phone started ringing, and Gavin's name appeared on screen. She wiped her hands quickly on a towel and swiped to answer, tapping the speaker icon. "Merry Christmas!"

"Merry Christmas to you, too. Are you enjoying your time alone?"

"I baked," she said as she searched for the lid to match a plastic storage container. "I might need to buy another freezer. Or open up a shop."

"Does it include chocolate chip cookies?" he asked. She couldn't miss the hopefulness in his tone.

She laughed. "Yes. And ginger snaps, cranberry muffins, banana bread, and apple betty."

"Wow." He paused, as if stunned by the bounty. "It sounds like you'll need help eating it all."

"Are you volunteering your services?" Spending the afternoon with Gavin suddenly seemed like the best idea she'd had in a long time.

"If I was, and if you invited me, we could eat your delicious baking and spend some time online looking for William and Rodney."

She looked down at her flour-covered sweats and baggy T-shirt. "Give me an hour," she said.

After a quick shower, it took Leeza longer than it should have to decide what to wear. It was a casual afternoon at home with a friend—nothing more than a *friend*—but it *was* Christmas. In the end she decided on sleekly fitting black jeans, a silky red blouse, and Drew's gift knotted at her neck, hoping the combination was both relaxed and festive.

As she took his coat, Leeza noted that Gavin had also made an effort for the day. He wore a tie decorated with jolly Santas ho-ho-ho-ing on a green background, charcoal trousers, and his white button-down was crisp and neat. Not that he wasn't always nicely dressed. It was one of the things she found most attractive about him, that he—

She choked her thoughts off. Yes, Gavin was attractive. But he wasn't—*attractive*. Not in *that* way.

"Merry Christmas," she said, her cheeks heating.

He raised an eyebrow, and her blush deepened. "And to you," he said calmly.

She gestured toward the kitchen, but instead of following her direction he took her hand. The shock of his touch whipped up her arm into her chest, heated lightning along her nerves. Her eyes widened when he gave her a little tug. "How about a proper Christmas greeting?" he said.

She thought he was going to kiss her, and she stiffened, uncomfortable and unsure. Instead, he pulled her into his chest and squeezed her lightly. "In my family," he said, "everyone gets a hug on Christmas Day."

Before she had a chance to react, he released her. His eyes searched her face, and whatever he saw there seemed to please him as he grinned before striding off to the kitchen. She followed, her body tingling from his embrace, her head spinning. It had felt so *good* to be held. The remnants of his warmth clung to her breasts and thighs, the places on her back where his hands had touched.

He came to an abrupt halt in the entrance to the kitchen, and she almost collided with him. He shot her an amused look over his shoulder. "When you bake, you *bake*," he said.

The counter was stacked with containers in all shapes and sizes, and a few plastic zipped bags as well. "I like it," she said, a touch defensively. She might have gone a bit overboard today, but what did it matter? "It helps me relax."

"And smells great." Gavin moved forward and picked up the plate on which she'd arranged assorted treats. "Here at the table? Or in the living room?"

"The living room might be more comfortable." And she wanted to get away from the scene of her compulsion. "I'll make some tea."

A few minutes later they were settled beside each other on the couch, the plate of goodies—minus a couple of cookies, thanks to Gavin—on the table in front of them, tea mugs at hand. Leeza had her laptop on her knees and looked expectantly at Gavin. "All right. Where do we look next?"

"Have you heard anything back from your gentleman at the Nova Scotia Highlanders Regimental Museum?"

She shook her head. "No. John said he'd keep looking, but he didn't sound very hopeful." She navigated to the bookmark folder she'd made for her research and clicked a link. "I went back to the site, though, and looked a little closer. Now that we know a bit more, I thought I might see something new. I found this."

CHAPTER ELEVEN

March 13th, 1942
Friday the 13th. They always scare me, I'm a
very superstitious person. A lot of things
happened on that day. I broke my foot when I
was 12. I broke my hand when I was 14 and I
almost got run over by a horse when I was 17.
Funny enough, its raining outside now.

On the page detailing the regiment's history,
where it mentioned the North Novies leaving Halifax
for Great Britain, Leeza pointed out the date was
July 21, 1941. Switching to another page listing The
Originals—the North Nova Scotia Highlanders who
left Halifax for England on the *S.S. Orion*—she
pointed out the date was July 18.

"I think we can stop wondering about the
discrepancy in William's diary. Whatever the reason
for both dates to be recorded, if the regimental
museum includes them, we're probably safe to
ignore the issue."

Gavin's shoulder brushed hers as he studied the
screen. "I'd still like to know why, but that's just my
own curiosity. I doubt it would help us find William."

He was so close she was enveloped in his scent—clean and woodsy with a hint of chocolate from the cookies he'd eaten. She found herself leaning in and stiffened, drawing back slowly, hoping he hadn't noticed.

"Look what else I found." She scrolled down the long list of names and stopped in the F's. Using the cursor, she highlighted one name. *Pte. Friberg, Otto A.*

Gavin glanced at her appraisingly. "Your grandfather."

She nodded, not quite certain she could speak without her voice betraying the uncomfortable thrill that had shot through her at the sight of his name on that list. The researcher's sense of distance she'd cultivated while looking for William and Rodney had been shattered when she'd seen it. He had been on that boat, along with hundreds of other young men, many of whom would never return to Canada. It brought home the evilness of war in a way nothing else had for her.

"There is bad news, though," she said, dragging her thoughts back to the matter at hand. "If this is a complete list of the men who shipped out on July 21, William and Rodney should be on it. But neither of them is."

Gavin gave her one more long look, as if he could see her distress, but let it slide. "Neither of them?" he said, eyebrows raised.

She'd felt the same disbelief. "It's like trying to catch a dragonfly. Every clue seems to flitter away before we can get a grip on it."

He lifted the laptop off her knees and propped it on his own. With a few quick keyboard clicks, he searched the list of names to no avail. "If I hadn't seen it for myself, I'd be starting to wonder if the diary was real. How can neither of these men show up in official records?"

He spoke as if he'd forgotten she was there and didn't seem to notice when she didn't reply. She stole a glance at his profile. He was staring off into the distance, eyes unfocused behind his lenses. His eyelashes were long, almost brushing the frames when he blinked.

Suddenly he turned to her, his abstracted expression vanishing. "What if Rodney is a *middle* name? They only have middle initials listed."

His abruptness startled her, and she took a moment to collect herself. "That's an excellent idea." She made a note on her phone. "I'll email John and ask him if they can check that. But it doesn't explain William. There are plenty of Smiths, and even a William, but his middle initial is B."

"What if that's a mistake? Either in the transcription online, or in the original records? A capital H could be easily confused with a capital B depending on the handwriting or type." Gavin's eyes glowed with enthusiasm.

Her exhilaration rose to meet his. "That makes so much sense. Could it be that simple? And if it is, does that mean we've found him? That we'll be able to learn from the original records who William is?"

"It has to get us closer. But we might be jumping to conclusions." Gavin placed the laptop on the coffee table and turned to Leeza, his expression sobering. "We shouldn't get our hopes up."

"If Christmas Day isn't the day for having hopes fulfilled, what day is?" She laughed, giddy with anticipation. "I know you're right. I can feel it. Maybe some of his family is still alive, and we'll be able to give them his diary. He'll finally be home where he belongs."

She grinned at Gavin. He stared at her, not returning her smile, just studying her as if—well, as if he'd never seen her before.

"What?" she said.

He didn't reply.

Instead, he kissed her.

The shock of his mouth on hers froze her in place, eyes open, hands limp in her lap—but only for a moment. Her lips parted, softened, and her eyelids closed so she could concentrate fully on his touch. Her palm cupped his jaw, feeling the smoothness of his shaven skin, the hardness of the bone underneath.

His tongue dipped into her mouth, teasing, questioning. She met it with hers, his unfamiliar taste enticing and intoxicating. His hand rested on her hip and she willed him to slide it up, to brush her breast, to intensify the delicious ache building inside her. But it remained motionless, firm and warm, as his mouth continued its exploration. She squirmed closer, eager to press against him. Then his hand moved—to her upper arm, holding her back.

"Leeza," he said, lifting his head, breaking the kiss. "Wait."

"Wait?" she repeated, dazed. "For what?"

"We should talk."

Talking be damned, she thought. *Kiss me again.* Then the serious set of his mouth, the sober expression in his eyes, registered. She scooted back, putting distance between them.

"I'm sorry," she said stiffly, heat scorching her cheeks.

"Don't apologize," he said, his tone sharp. Her eyes widened. "I kissed you, so if anything, it should be me apologizing to you. But I'm not going to."

Now she was thoroughly confused. If he wasn't sorry he'd kissed her, why had he stopped?

"I suppose some people might think it inappropriate, any sort of romantic relationship between us," he said, "since you're my boss. But that's not a problem for me. Is it a problem for you?"

She shook her head. Thoughts were pinging

around in her brain so fast she was incapable of transmitting them verbally.

"Good. I've never subscribed to the idea that colleagues shouldn't date. We're mature adults. Our professional relationship isn't going to change because we have a personal one."

She nodded.

"I know you haven't been divorced long. Do you think you need more time before exploring what this is between us?"

She shook her head.

"Good," he repeated.

His burst of candor appeared to have run its course. He sat there, looking at her, and the silence between them lengthened.

She opened her mouth, and then closed it. Finally, she gathered her courage and asked the question burning her tongue. "*Is* there's something between us?"

He tilted his head inquiringly. "Don't you think so?"

"I don't know." Which was a small lie. To herself she could admit experiencing spikes of attraction over the last few weeks, but she hadn't even considered he might be feeling the same.

He didn't appear disappointed with her answer, which irked her. "Well," he said cheerfully, standing up, "when you figure it out, let me know."

"That's it?" She rose, too, and planted her hands on her hips. "You kiss me, say we have to talk, interrogate me, and now you're leaving?"

He brandished his tea mug, holding it like a shield between them. "Just to the kitchen. To get more tea. Want some?"

She felt like she was precariously balanced on a teeter-totter, wobbly and unstable. "Sure?" she answered with an upward lilt.

He reached for her mug and disappeared into

the hall. She collapsed on the sofa. What had happened to nice, safe, comfortable Gavin? In his place was a commanding, confident man who made her want things she hadn't wanted—hadn't *allowed* herself to want—in a long time.

They spent the next few hours trawling from website to website, searching through the list of World War Two databases that Gavin had compiled. He made no gestures that even remotely suggested he might repeat his kiss, yet she couldn't relax. She was conscious of his every move in a way she'd never been before.

Shortly after six o'clock, Gavin leaned back on the couch. "I think we've done enough for today," he said, taking off his glasses and rubbing his eyes. Without the heavy frames his face looked younger, vulnerable. He placed them back on his nose. "I should probably head home."

"Did you want to stay for dinner?" she asked, not sure what answer she hoped he'd give. Despite the emotional upheaval of the afternoon, she didn't want him to leave. Or stay.

She wasn't sure of anything anymore.

"No, thank you," he said, rising and going to the front entrance. "I promised some friends I'd pop by tonight."

"Oh." She trailed after him. His comment left her deflated, reinforcing as it did her own aloneness. "Well, have fun."

He stood at the front door and wrapped his scarf around his neck before shrugging into his coat. "The store is only open until six tomorrow, right?"

"Yes."

"Why don't you come for dinner after?"

"Aren't you going to your daughter's?"

"Yes."

A hard lump formed in her chest. "You want me to meet your family?"

His eyes narrowed. "You've gone awfully pale. Are you okay?"

"You want me to meet your family." She stated it as fact but couldn't quite believe it.

"Yes, I do. But not if it's going to make you uncomfortable." He brushed the tips of his fingers along her jaw. "I know how to be patient. I've waited a long time already."

She heard his last sentence but filed it away to study later. It was taking most of her brain power to deal with the implications of his invitation. Coming so soon after his kiss, it could only mean one thing. And despite that she truly *was* over Scott, she may have overlooked the myriad other complications of starting a new relationship.

"You can't just invite me at the last minute," she said. "It will inconvenience your daughter's plans."

"One more won't make any difference. There's always enough food for an army."

"I should bring something. Baking? I could bring some baking."

Gavin stepped closer and she lifted her chin to look at him. "Does this mean you're coming?" he said.

She lifted her chin higher. "I guess it does."

Leeza stood at the front door of Gavin's daughter's home. *I don't even know her name,* she thought in mild panic.

A festive wreath hung in the centre of the frosted glass panel. To her right an inflatable snowman bobbed in the slight breeze, and the dark was broken by warm light falling through the large window on her left. A huge Christmas tree displayed there blocked most of her view of the interior.

She took a deep breath, shifted the gift bag she carried to the other hand, and raised her fist to knock. Before she could do so the door was opened by Gavin, leaving her standing gawkily with one hand in the air. She dropped it to her side.

"Hi," she said, nerves making her breathless. *This is ridiculous. I'm a grown woman.* She straightened her shoulders and smiled. "Happy Boxing Day."

He smiled in return. "Come on in." He stepped back and she entered a hall cluttered with boots of all shapes and sizes, with coats hanging over the newel post of the staircase leading to the second floor. The mess was cozy and relaxing, and her spine slumped in relief. Casual was good. The more casual, the better, as far as she was concerned. It would make her feel less of an interloper.

"Let me take your coat," Gavin said. She slipped it off her shoulders and handed it to him then swept her hands over her hips nervously. She'd raced home after work and changed her slacks and blouse for a long, flowing red skirt and thin black sweater with cold shoulders before making the short drive to Gavin's daughter's.

"I don't even know her name," she said abruptly.

"My daughter? It's Sarah." Gavin took her elbow and directed her past the staircase to the rear of the home, a babble of voices growing louder with each step. "Relax," he said. "She doesn't bite. She grew out of that when she was a toddler."

Leeza laughed, as he'd meant her to, and did her best to follow his instruction. It had been more than thirty years since she'd met a boyfriend's family. Not that Gavin was her boyfriend—what a silly term for a man in his forties—but she and Scott had been high school sweethearts and really meeting his parents didn't even count because she'd known his family a long time before they had started dating and so—

She cut off her mental drivelling. Gavin ushered her into a large great room that included a kitchen, dining room and sitting area. The swell of conversation died in an instant, and Leeza felt pinned by numerous gazes.

"Everyone, this is Leeza. Leeza, my family, and a few extras." Gavin directed her to the couple in the kitchen. The woman was about Leeza's height, with hair the same sandy brown as Gavin's pulled up into one of those elegantly messy buns Leeza admired but couldn't imitate even when her hair was long enough. Beside her was a slim, tall man about Drew's age with militarily cropped blond hair and wearing an apron sporting a caricature of a reindeer, including plush antlers and a blinking red nose. "My daughter, Sarah, and her husband, Xander."

"So nice to meet you." Leeza held out her hand.

Sarah laid down the wooden spoon she'd been using to stir something on the stove and shook it. "Thank you for coming." Her tone was polite but neutral, and Leeza's nerves kicked up again.

"Papa! Papa!" A black-haired rocket shot around the couch and collided with Gavin's legs. "Up! Up!"

Gavin laughed and picked up the tiny girl. To Leeza's eyes, she didn't look big enough to be walking, let alone running. "Leeza, this is Emmelyn." Gavin lowered his head so his cheek touched his granddaughter's. "Emmelyn, say hi to Leeza."

The child inserted two fingers into her mouth and stared at Leeza with wide, dark eyes. She wore a bright pink dress and her chubby legs were bare.

Another couple approached. Despite the fact he was a few inches shorter, Gavin's son looked so much like his father that Leeza had no doubt who he was. "I'm Nolan and this is my wife, Amrita," he said. He looked at the woman next to him with loving pride. Amrita, taller than her husband with the same long dark hair as her daughter, offered a shy smile, her eyes warm with welcome.

"Hello," she said. "Gavin has told us a lot about you."

Heat flushed Leeza's cheeks. "Oh, dear," she said. "That must have been boring."

Nolan gestured her to take a seat on the couch. "Actually, we've been fascinated about this journal you found. Dad's being quite mysterious about it." He winked. "I'm really hoping you'll tell us more."

CHAPTER TWELVE

June 23rd, 1942
Me and Rodney just got back from London, we
had a great time. We went dancing and met
lots of girls. There was this really nice girl that
I met. Her name was Daphne. We chatted
together for a while and I bought her a few
drinks. She's a little shorter than I am and her
hair is beautiful. She wants me to come and see
her again.

Moments later Leeza found herself seated next to
Gavin, with a wine glass in her hand, telling the story
of William Henry Smith. Other than Gavin's family,
the small crowd included two more couples, friends
of Sarah and Xander's, and a month-old baby. Leeza
wasn't quite certain who the baby belonged to, as the
swaddled bundle was passed from hand to hand and
appeared quite content no matter who was holding
her.

Certain no one wanted a blow-by-blow account
of the research she and Gavin were doing, she
glossed over the hours of online drudgery and
focused on the pull the mystery had on her. "I don't
know where I'd be without your dad," she said in

conclusion. "He's the one who's made the biggest discoveries."

Gavin had slid off the couch during her re-telling and was sitting on the floor at her feet playing with Emmelyn and a set of plastic farm animals. Her heart squeezed when he made the tiny girl giggle by galloping a horse up her chubby knee. Maybe she was more ready for grandchildren than she had thought...

He looked up. "Negatives are almost as important as positives," he said. "Everything is a brick in the path leading to William and Rodney."

"Well, I'm just glad you offered to help, and that I was smart enough to let you. I'm keeping my fingers crossed that you won't get bored and quit on me."

"I wouldn't have missed this for anything." Leeza hoped she was the only one that heard a deeper meaning in Gavin's quiet words. Heat rose from her chest to her cheeks as he held her eyes. "I haven't enjoyed myself so much in a long time."

Leeza *knew* he was talking about kissing her, and not just investigating the journal. She ran her tongue along her lower lip and Gavin's gaze dropped to her mouth.

"Dinner's ready!" Leeza started as Sarah's voice called loudly from behind. She turned her head in time to catch the narrow-eyed look the young woman shot her father. Gavin, engaged in getting Emmelyn to the table, didn't appear to notice.

Leeza wondered how many women Gavin had introduced to his children since the death of their mother. It had been at least five years, after all. He'd worked at Millar's that long, and it had happened shortly before then. Surely he'd brought home a new friend at least once or twice.

Hadn't he?

The dinner table was filled with cheerful

confusion as plates were filled, toasts made, and the meal enjoyed. Leeza let most of it wash over her, joining the conversation when invited, but otherwise simply revelling in the feeling of being part of a large family group again. She'd known she was lonely but hadn't really realized just *how* lonely until now. It had been lovely of Gavin to invite her, yet she wondered if it would only reinforce her isolation, not relieve it.

After the main meal had been consumed, consensus was to wait before tackling dessert. Leeza insisted on helping clean up and assumed dishwashing duties. Gavin offered to dry, but Sarah shooed him away, plucking the towel from his hand. "We're good, Dad. You go sit. I'm sure Emmelyn will keep you occupied." She took his place next to Leeza.

Leeza watched him go wistfully. Sarah had said or done nothing unpleasant, but an aura of suspicion clung to her, and Leeza missed the buffer Gavin provided. Hoping to find a friendly footing, she said, "Thanks so much for letting me come. I didn't want to impose but your father insisted it would be fine. He can be quite determined, I'm finding."

"I *was* a little surprised when he called yesterday." Sarah shook water droplets off a wine glass before wiping it with the towel. "He's never done that before."

"I'm sure he's much too polite to invite a guest at the last minute regularly." Xander, who was putting away leftovers, placed a stack of empty serving bowls beside her and gave her an absent smile. He was a quiet, unobtrusive man who nevertheless exuded an air of calm confidence—much like Gavin, Leeza realized. Given what Leeza had seen of Sarah's personality, he had better be self-assured so as not to be overruled.

Sarah waited until he moved away before replying. "I'm not talking about the late invite. I'm talking about bringing someone to dinner."

Leeza hesitated, absorbing Sarah's words, and then continued wiping the bowl she held. She wanted to ask the other woman to clarify but was almost afraid to hear the answer. Her reluctance didn't matter, though—Sarah went on.

"By someone, I mean a woman. This is the first time he's invited a woman to a family dinner since my mom died."

If Leeza had been tongue-tied before, she was now incapable of speech. Her relationship with Gavin took on a new, slightly alarming aspect. She placed the bowl into the rinse sink and started on another dish, concentrating on her work. Sarah didn't seem concerned about her lack of response. Under the cover of conversation from the lounge area, she said, "He was devastated when she died. We all were, but Dad was—well, to be blunt, it was awful. For a while it was as if I had lost both my parents. I don't know if he's ever really recovered. He just found a new normal. And that new normal has not included women. Until you."

Leeza finally found her voice. "I'm flattered," she said lightly. "Gavin is a lovely man, and he's become a good friend."

"You're his boss." There was no missing the censure in Sarah's tone.

While Leeza was certain that wasn't the main issue Sarah had with her, it was at least a concern she could deal with—using the same arguments she'd used on herself, and that Gavin had reinforced just yesterday.

"Yes, I am." She turned to face the young woman. "He is a valued employee, one I highly trust. I would never allow our personal relationship to interfere with our professional one. And if you think your father would allow it to happen, either, you don't know him very well."

Sarah, looking startled at Leeza's vehemence, nodded slowly. "I just don't want him to get hurt."

"I can understand that." She went back to scrubbing the dish in the sudsy water.

Sarah continued drying in silence. The atmosphere between them wasn't exactly easy, but Leeza felt the younger woman had lost some of her nervous tension.

For the rest of the evening, Leeza couldn't stop thinking about what she *hadn't* said to Sarah. That the more time she spent with Gavin, the more Leeza worried *she* would be the one to get hurt in the end.

Leeza had no chance to talk privately with Gavin over the next few days. Not that she had anything private to talk to him about—but she had gotten used to spending time alone with him and missed him when he wasn't around.

In the carousel that was her mind, she worried about that—about wanting to be with him—which made her go out of her way to avoid him during the two shifts they worked together in the days following dinner at Sarah's. Outside of work, she hadn't heard from John at the Nova Scotia Highlanders Regimental Museum about Gavin's ideas—Rodney as a middle name and the H being mistaken for a B—so she had no reason to get in touch because of that, either.

She shouldn't regret that fact as much as she did.

Now it was Tuesday morning, and she would soon have something to take her mind off Gavin. Millar's was set to open in thirty minutes, and she was the only person in the store, although two employees were due to arrive shortly. The door to her office was closed, with a note taped to the outside saying she was in a meeting and that no one should disturb her.

She had dialled into the conference call and was listening anxiously to the tinny hold music, picking at a rough fingernail as she waited for the Vice-President, Western Canadian Region, to come on the line.

Leeza had met Roberta St. Pierre several times over the years and respected her for her direct manner and business experience. She had begun her career as a part-time clerk at a Millar's store in Winnipeg, but while she'd started in the same position Leeza had, she'd climbed much higher on the organizational ladder, achieving one of the loftiest rungs at the corporate head office. In Leeza's opinion, she was an efficient and supportive leader. Too bad she was handcuffed from implementing many of her ideas by those above.

A series of beeps was followed by the crackling sound of speakers coming online.

"Good morning," a gruff female voice said. "This is Roberta. Can everyone hear me?"

Leeza listened as store managers from Manitoba to British Columbia answered Roberta's roll call, chiming in when it was her turn. By her count there were five managers on the line, all of them from markets approximately the same size as Prince George—and none from the bigger centres like Edmonton or Vancouver.

This is not good, Leeza thought.

"I won't make you wait any longer," Roberta said once she'd confirmed everyone's presence. "You are all aware of the struggles bookstores are having across North America. I want to thank each of you for your dedication to Millar's, and all you've done to surmount the challenges our industry is facing."

This is definitely not good.

"I called this meeting to inform you that your locations of Millar's are to be closed. I assure you the decision was made after careful deliberation, and with much regret. But changes must be made for the betterment of the many over the few. It is our intent to focus resources on markets with higher stability and revenue potential."

Cutting out the dead wood, Leeza thought. *And who can blame them?*

"Specific details of the steps to be taken will be provided via email. This will include your personal compensation packages. Requests for transfers will also be considered." Roberta paused, letting the shocking but not surprising news sink in. "I am sure you have questions. If I can answer them now, I will, but you should understand some things cannot be discussed in this setting."

After a short silence, a voice that Leeza recognized as the manager of the Red Deer location spoke up. "Is this information to be shared with our staff at this time?"

"A national media release about these closures will be going out in twenty-four hours. I highly suggest you meet with employees before this decision is made public."

Leeza had already been thinking of how to announce this to her staff. She'd have to tell Carrie first. As the only full-time employee, this would affect her the most. But she didn't look forward to telling any of her team. She'd built a good group, hiring mostly students with a love of reading, writing, and words. They were her tribe, and she'd miss them. They'd be worried about finding new jobs, of course. She began to draft letters of recommendation for each in her head.

At least with Gavin she didn't have to worry about his financial situation. He'd never worked at Millar's for the money.

Leeza's computer dinged, signalling the arrival of the email Roberta had mentioned. After confirming that everyone had received it, she closed the call with a few final words.

"I know this is unwelcome news to everyone. Please feel free to reach out to me if you want to discuss it further. And if there's anything I can do to make this process less difficult, just ask."

Leeza disconnected and slumped back in her chair, rubbing her temples. She'd known this day was coming, but somehow that didn't make it easier to digest. Millar's had been a part of her life for so long. What would she be without it?

But that was a question for another day. Right now, she had to figure out how to pass on the bad news to her staff.

CHAPTER THIRTEEN

July 3rd, 1942
Got a letter from mom today. Everything's fine.
Maureen and David are fine also. I'm trying to
get a pass to have the whole weekend off so I
can spend it with Daphne in London.

Leeza called Carrie into her office as soon as she arrived. There was no way to soften the blow, but the other woman took the news as calmly as could be hoped. Her eyes shiny with unshed tears, she said, "I can't say I haven't been expecting something like this. The dangers of being a small fish in a big pond, I guess." She offered a watery smile. "You've been a great boss, Leeza. I know you did what you could."

"I'm sorry it wasn't enough." Leeza felt her own throat close. Damn it, this was hard. "I want you to start looking for work right away. We'll be staying open until the end of January, then any unsold stock will be shipped to one of the other locations. But if you find another position in the meantime, I want you to take it."

"Let me get used to the idea of leaving before you kick me out the door," Carried replied with a return of her usual spirit.

"You just bought a house," Leeza said. "Don't be too loyal. You need to look out for yourself."

Carrie patted Leeza's hand. "Don't worry. Sheila and I will be okay." If Carrie's wife had a stable career, Leeza wouldn't be as worried. But Sheila was an artist, and while an excellent one, Leeza suspected Carrie was their main source of income.

Knowing it would be impossible to arrange a meeting with all staff members at one time, Leeza met with those shifted to work as they came in, asking each of them to keep the news confidential until the next day. Those not scheduled to work she called directly, leaving Gavin until last.

He answered her call after the second ring.

"Leeza," he said, and just the sound of her name in his warm, comforting voice alleviated some of the tension tightening the muscles in her neck.

"Hello, Gavin."

"Have you heard from the museum?"

She'd been so caught up in dealing with the day's calamity that it took her a minute to register his words. "No, no, I haven't. Well, not as of last night. I haven't checked my private email today."

"Is there something wrong? You sound a little...off."

Gavin's concern cracked the facade of strength she'd been projecting to her staff. Determined to keep it together just a little longer, she drew in a shaky breath. "I have some bad news. The public notice will go out tomorrow, but head office announced this morning that they are closing five stores in Western Canada. And we're one of them."

"Oh, Leeza, I'm so sorry. I know you love Millar's."

She swallowed around the lump in her throat. "It's not about me right now. I've spent all day telling my staff that they won't have a job come February."

"You sound beat."

She was. "I'm fine. It's not like I didn't suspect this might be on the horizon. I just feel like a—" She cut herself off. Admitting she was a failure wouldn't help the situation. "For now, all shifts are as scheduled. I expect some staff will be leaving as soon as they find other work, and I can't blame them for that. I imagine I'll be pulling quite a few hours to make sure the closing goes smoothly."

"Just let me know when you need me. I won't look for anything else until Millar's is closed."

"Thanks. I appreciate that." She pressed her thumbs into her eyes and swivelled her chair gently, seeking solace in the gentle movement. "I should let you go. Sorry to be the bearer of bad news."

"Don't worry about me. Do you have plans for tonight?"

She snorted inelegantly. "If I had, I would have cancelled them by now. I won't be fit company for anyone." All she wanted to do was go home and wallow in solitude for a few hours.

"I'll be at your house around six-thirty. Don't make dinner."

"No, really, Gavin. I'll be fine. I need some time alone."

"I've delivered my fair share of bad news over the years," he said. "I'll be there at six-thirty."

And he hung up.

She stared at the handset as if it could explain what had just happened. Gavin was the last person she'd expect to force himself somewhere he wasn't wanted.

Except that she *did* want him. She positively yearned for someone to share this crappy, crappy day with, someone to lighten the burden, to listen to her regrets and complaints.

Thank god he was coming over.

Leeza sat at the breakfast bar in her kitchen, sipping from her second glass of wine and watching Gavin make dinner. If he needed something, he asked, but he didn't allow her to get off her stool to help. Other than a few basic spices, he'd brought everything with him. "Comfort food," he'd said when he arrived, holding up two bulging cloth bags. "Spaghetti and meat sauce, with Caesar salad and garlic bread."

He crushed cloves of garlic by smacking the heel of his hand on the flat side of a wide-bladed knife, and then minced it with quick, certain movements.

"Are you sure I can't help?" she asked, safe in the knowledge he'd refuse her offer. She really didn't want to get up, as the stresses of the day were just starting to fade from her neck and shoulders. Also, watching him was having an odd affect on her nervous system. Maybe it was the wine, but his deft fingers, the sureness of his motions, the confidence in his demeanour, were creating tingles in her belly she was having trouble ignoring.

"Yes, I'm sure." He added a little of the garlic to a couple tablespoons of butter in a small dish, mixing it vigorously before returning to the cutting board and picking up an onion. "You spent the day giving bad news to people you like. You need a break."

That reminded her of what he'd said on the phone that afternoon. "Earlier, you mentioned you knew what it was like to deliver bad news. You were a financial planner, right?"

He cut the ends off the onion, peeled it, and began to dice it. The sharp aroma tickled her nose. "Yes. While I did have to give people unwelcome news about their finances once in a while, it was managing people that was hardest. I was head of one of the larger firms in town. I never had to lay anyone off, but I did have to fire a few people over the years.

It isn't easy." He tossed the remaining garlic and the onion into the skillet, in which he'd already browned the ground beef.

"It shouldn't be," Leeza said, resting her chin in her hand, elbow on the counter. "If you're any sort of decent human being, giving bad news *should* be difficult."

"That's true. What I found was—"

Her phone, lying on the counter beside her wine glass, vibrated across the shiny granite countertop. Scott's name appeared on the screen. She picked it up but didn't answer.

"Aren't you going to take that?" Gavin used a small knife to cut out the stem of a red pepper, and then switched back to the larger chef's knife to chop it.

She sighed. "It's my ex. I don't think I have the energy to deal with him tonight."

The phone stopped vibrating. If he left a voice mail, she'd call him back later. Maybe tomorrow. Or the next day. But before those thoughts had fully formed, the phone started up again.

A faint frisson of alarm tickled her fingertips. "Maybe I'd better take it," she said, sliding off the stool and moving into the lounge area as she connected the call. "Hello, Scott," she said.

"So, I talked to Drew," he said without preamble. "He says he'll give me a decision about the cabin in a couple of days."

"You did what?" She stopped walking, frozen in disbelief.

"It's a good offer, Leez. We don't want to miss out."

The heat of her ire vanquished her fatigue like mist in sunshine. "I can't believe you went behind my back and talked to Drew when I *expressly* told you not to."

Scott's tone hardened. "You can't stop me from

talking to my son. As you've told me more than once, he's a grown man. He can make his own decisions."

"This isn't a decision he should have to make right now. You're preying on the fact that he's far from home, the fact that he'll want to do what pleases you, to coerce him into giving you what you want."

"For god's sake, you sound like I'm trying to steal his inheritance." Disgust vibrated in Scott's voice. "When's the last time any of us were at the cabin, other than to make sure it wasn't falling to pieces? It's better for everyone if we sell now."

When Leeza had a chance, she was going to think more about *why* Scott seemed so determined to sell. But after the day she'd had, it was a relief to raise her voice and shout out her frustration. "I refuse to discuss this any further."

"Leeza—"

"Goodbye, Scott." She disconnected with a fierce stab at the screen, controlling the impulse to heave the fragile device across the room. She did give in to rage enough to emit a short shriek, and then dropped onto the couch, cast her phone to the cushion beside her, and leaned back, closing her eyes.

As her fury slowly subsided, she became aware of the scent of simmering sauce, the sound of bubbling water. Soft footfalls grew louder, pausing immediately behind her. She stiffened when two warm hands settled onto her shoulders, and then relaxed again.

"Want to tell me about it?" Gavin said, his voice drifting down on her as his hands began to squeeze and rub gently.

She sighed. "I'm sorry. You seem to have done nothing lately but take care of me. You must be tired of it by now."

"You're going through a rough patch. We all need help sometimes."

She wondered briefly if he was thinking of the months after his wife had died, those months that Sarah had described, when he'd been lost and distraught. Keeping her eyes closed, she told him about the cabin, about Scott's request and Drew's place in it all.

"This is the third time he's brought up selling the cabin, if I count when Charlene mentioned it for him." She shifted reluctantly out from under Gavin's hands. His touch felt so good—too good—and she shouldn't learn to depend on it. Whatever was between them was still too fragile to trust. Lifting her feet onto the couch, she twisted sideways so she could see his face and said, "I'm beginning to wonder if he has a pressing reason for selling that I'm not aware of."

"Like a purchase he wants to make?" Gavin rested his hands on the back of the couch and leaned forward, his face thoughtful.

"I suppose he might want to buy something for his new girlfriend," Leeza said with distaste. "But it would have to be pretty spectacular to need to sell the cabin for it."

"What about a debt?"

"Anything's possible, but not likely. If there's one thing Scott is good at, it's money. Besides, when we discussed the cabin during the divorce proceedings, he had no problem with delaying the sale, and I can't see him getting into money troubles so quickly."

Gavin straightened and headed to the stove. "He's a real estate agent, right? Maybe he wants to invest in property?"

Leeza frowned. "You know what, I really don't care why he wants to sell. And no matter what Drew says, it's *my* agreement Scott needs." She stood up, slapping her hands against her thighs, brushing Scott and his problems off like dust. "I don't want to talk about it anymore."

"Okay." He stirred the sauce, and then scattered a couple handfuls of pasta into the large pot of boiling water. "Dinner will be ready in about ten minutes."

CHAPTER FOURTEEN

September 5th, 1942
I got a letter back from mom today. I wrote to
her about Daphne and she doesn't seem very
pleased. She doesn't want me to see her
anymore because she wants me to marry a
Canadian girl. I didn't know she felt that way.
She's a thousand miles away so she won't know
if I'm seeing Daphne or not. Thank the Lord for
England.

Leeza reclaimed her perch on the stool and went back to watching Gavin cooking in her kitchen.

Sometimes his presence was so restful she almost forgot about the passion of his kiss. Of course, it had been four days since he'd sparked feelings she'd thought well in her past, and he hadn't made a second attempt. Maybe he'd decided the friend zone was a better place to be. She tossed off the last of her wine.

"What are you thinking about?"

She blinked. She'd been so caught up in reflection she hadn't noticed him standing on the other side of the counter, studying her. "Nothing."

"You get a vee right here"—he leaned forward

and tapped her between the brows—"when you're upset."

She wasn't upset that Gavin hadn't kissed her again. Of course not! "It's been a day," she said, dodging a direct reply. "I need a distraction."

"Did you ever check your email, see if there was something from the museum?"

"No, I didn't. Good idea." She retrieved her phone from the couch and Gavin tended to the pasta as she scrolled to her emails. "Nothing," she said, disappointed for more than one reason. A response would have given them something to talk about other than the dismal day.

"Don't give up hope yet," Gavin said. "There's a very good chance the museum is closed for the holidays. If we haven't heard by the new year you can follow up with a phone call to your gentleman friend."

"I feel like we've stalled out." Seeing Gavin was near to serving, Leeza went to the cupboard and took out plates. She laid them on the table then went back for silverware. "If Rodney is a middle name, how does that get us closer to finding William? And if the curator agrees the B on the list of Originals probably should have been an H, all that does is confirm what we already knew—that William crossed on the *Orion*."

Gavin took the salad he'd made earlier from the fridge and handed it to her, and then pulled the garlic bread from the oven and began to slice the fresh, crumbly loaf. "If we find Rodney, we might be able to find some of his family still living. And they might know who William was. Or is, although that's a long shot."

"I did have one thought, about something else we could try." Leeza took the sliced bread and placed it on the table next to the salad. As Gavin drained the pasta and tossed it with the sauce, she said, "I wondered if there might be a group or community or page on Facebook that helps people find lost soldiers. There must be lots of people looking for more information on men and women who served in World War Two. If nothing else, Canadian soldiers left thousands of war babies in Europe. People in those groups might be able to point us in the right direction."

"It can't hurt." Gavin smoothly transferred the pasta from the pot to a low, wide bowl and carried it to the table, gesturing to Leeza to take a seat. She did, amused at how comfortable he was, acting as host in her home.

He waited until she loaded her plate before helping himself. One mouthful of spaghetti covered in sauce later, she put her fork down and stared. "This is delicious. Fletcher certainly doesn't sound like it, but are you part Italian? First the pizza place and now this?" She lifted her fork and took another heavenly bite.

He smiled. "Not on my side. Nancy's mother was Italian. My wife wasn't much of a cook, but I enjoy it. I spent a lot of time in the kitchen with my mother-in-law."

The last time he'd mentioned Nancy, he had shut down the conversation shortly after. Leeza waited, but he continued eating, seemingly unperturbed.

With her eyes on her food, she said, "You must miss her very much."

When he didn't answer right away, she risked a quick glance, and was caught in his direct, bold focus. Her heart bumped hard against her sternum and her mouth dried.

"I will never forget her," he said quietly. "But as time goes on, I don't think of her every day, and when I do, it is with gratitude and thankfulness for what we had together. Not pain. Not grief."

Leeza swallowed, blinking away the moisture that gathered in her eyes.

Gavin went on. "I know it will never be the same as what I had with Nancy, but I think I'm ready to take the chance again. To find someone to love."

The intensity in his eyes was too much. Leeza shoved back her chair and sprang to her feet. "Didn't you bring Parmesan? I thought I saw it in the stash of groceries you brought over. Let me get it."

"Leeza." The softly spoken word halted her in mid-flight. She stopped but didn't turn around to face him. "I know you're not in the same space as I am. But that's okay."

She laid her palms on the smooth, cool stone of the counter, let the chill calm her racing pulse. "We've known each other for five years. So why does this seem like it's happening so fast?"

The scrape of chair legs on laminate flooring gave her enough warning that, when she sensed his presence behind her, she didn't jump.

"I'm not saying I'm in love with you," he said.

That should have eased her anxiety, but perversely she felt a stab of hurt. *Why not?* she wanted to ask. Was she that unlovable? Scott certainly thought so.

He went on. "But you have to realize I'm attracted to you. And I'm hoping you're willing to explore what we have between us." He put gentle pressure on her shoulders and turned her to face him. She focused on the second button of his shirt, but he lifted her chin, forcing her to meet his eyes. "If nothing else, we're becoming good friends. Researching William's journal with you has given me a purpose, and I want to walk that road with you as far as we can. For the rest..." He shrugged, a smile tugging at one corner of his mouth. "I didn't mean to mention any of this tonight. I'm sorry. The last thing I wanted to do was add to your stress."

She stood quiet under his hands and searched her feelings. *Had* he added to her stress? Sure, she'd freaked out a little bit, but now? Was it anxiety or excitement she felt buzzing in her gut?

"You've been honest with me," she said slowly, "so I'll be honest with you. When I'm with you, I feel...something." His grip on her shoulders tightened briefly. "I'm just not sure if I'm as ready as you want me to be."

"That's okay. I mean it. I'm perfectly fine with that. We'll take this at your pace." His hazel eyes searched hers, tiny creases of anxiety pinching the outer corners. "Can we finish our dinner now?"

"All right." A curl of unease wouldn't let her completely relax. She'd said she would be honest, and while her words held the truth, she felt she owed him something more. As he lowered his hands and moved to the table, she touched his arm, stopping him. He turned back, eyebrows raised quizzically.

Before she lost her nerve, she raised up on tiptoe and pressed her mouth to his.

She'd intended it to be a kiss of future promise, of willingness to be open. But the moment his lips softened under hers, it became something more. She leaned forward, her thighs and belly and breasts meeting the heat of his body. His mouth opened to let her tongue in and for long seconds she drank in his taste, and then she dropped back to her heels, breaking the kiss, and met his dark, wide-pupiled gaze.

He nodded, as if signing a pact between them, and then took her hand and led her to the table.

Leeza slept better that night than she thought she would, what with all the conflicts and confusions of the day.

Gavin's goodnight kiss had been short but

intense, a challenge tossed down like a gauntlet. He might be willing to wait for her, but he wasn't going to let her forget him, either. She was having trouble reconciling this determined, confident man with the quiet, unobtrusive employee she'd worked with for years. At least it had distracted her from Scott and the store, and she'd fallen asleep with her lips still tingling.

The beeping of a text alert woke her the next morning just five minutes before her alarm would have sounded. Blearily she pulled the phone off its charger and opened one eye, more than half expecting to see a message from one of her staff announcing they were unable to come in to work. It was too soon for any of them to have found a new job—the formal media announcement hadn't even gone out yet—but that didn't mean someone wouldn't call in sick.

Instead, she read a text from Drew. *Do you have a minute to talk before you go to work? I won't take long.*

She pushed to a sitting position and typed quickly back. *Of course.*

She barely had time to rub the sleep out of her eyes before her phone rang. "Is everything okay?" she said as soon as she saw Drew's face on the screen.

"Yes, it's fine." Drew grinned. "Nice hair. Sorry to call so early. I waited as long as I could. I have a thing this evening so can't call later."

Patting her hair with her free hand in what was probably a futile attempt to tame it, she said, "What's up?"

"Just a minute." Drew's face disappeared and she saw a random jumble of a crowded sidewalk, a flash of the side of a red bus, and dark, indistinguishable shapes. When he reappeared, he said, "I had the afternoon off but I'm heading back to the office now. We're hosting a reception tonight."

He wore a small-brimmed hat and a plaid scarf around his neck. Water droplets clung to both. "Is it raining?"

"Ugh. When isn't it? It's worse than Vancouver." His expression turned serious. "Dad called me yesterday."

Leeza couldn't help the scowl creasing her forehead. "I know. I told him not to."

"Yes, he said that." Drew sighed. "You have to stop doing that."

"Doing what?"

"Telling Dad what to do. Specifically, when it comes to me."

On the defensive after this unexpected complaint, she said, "I'm just looking out for you. It's what mothers do."

"I know. But he's my dad, and I'm an adult. It's up to me to figure out how to deal with him."

He had a point. She *hated* that he had a point. "Fine. I'll try. It's just that—"

"No." He waved a finger at the screen, which was jostling and jumping with the movements of the bus. "He and I have got to work this out on our own. It's not the same as when you were together. You can't run interference anymore."

"I said I'd try. That's as good as you get." Leeza resisted the urge to pout. She was almost fifty years old, for Pete's sake. Grown women shouldn't pout.

"So, about the cabin. He said you'd agree to put it up for sale if I said I didn't want it."

Leeza bolted upright at that bit of bullshit. "I did *not* say that. If you want it, of course I'd say no to selling it. But even if you don't, I didn't say I would." Her convoluted response hurt her own brain, but Drew seemed to know what she meant.

"Well, don't worry about it. I just talked to him again and told him I needed more time to think about it. And by time, I mean several weeks, if not longer. I love that cabin. I need to make sure I won't regret my decision, and I'm not in the right head space to do that now."

Relief deflated her like a pricked balloon. "You said that?" she said with heartfelt gratitude.

"He wasn't happy about it, but he seemed to accept it. For now, at least."

How had she been so lucky as to end up with such a bright, level-headed son? "If you do decide you don't want it, I won't make a fuss. It's your decision. I mean it."

"I know. Anyway, I wanted to let you know what I'd told him, and also..." His voice trailed away as he looked off screen for a second. "My stop is coming up."

"Wait! What else did you want to tell me?"

He hesitated, and then said, "I've met someone. Her name is Danica." Her view changed as he stood up. "I'll tell you more soon, but I've got to go. I'll call you later, okay? Love you." And he was gone.

CHAPTER FIFTEEN

September 15th, 1942
It's over between me and Daphne.

Charlene opened the door to her home with an exuberant swing. "Welcome!" she said with a bright smile. "Come on in!"

Gavin waited for Leeza to precede him into the apartment. After Charlene's divorce, she'd bought an apartment in a small but exclusive building. Polished concrete floors, vaulted ceilings, expansive windows, and austere white paint gave the space a modern but chilly feel. Tonight, however, the air was heated by the press of bodies, and Leeza gladly handed over her wool coat.

"Make yourselves at home," Charlene said. "I think you know most of the people here, Leeza. Be sure to introduce Gavin." She turned to him and her smile amped up another degree. "*So* glad you could make it."

Up until yesterday, Leeza hadn't been sure she'd attend Charlene's annual New Year's Eve party. But Drew's unexpected announcement about Danica had served to reinforce once again how everyone else was moving on with their lives, and she was determined to do the same. In a spirit of defiance—and for the security of his company—she'd invited Gavin along.

As Charlene snaked her way through the crowd, bearing their overcoats into a backroom, Gavin turned to Leeza. "Would you like a drink?"

"I'll come with you."

The bar was set up on the glossy—uninterrupted white, like the walls—kitchen counter. On their way there, Leeza greeted several people, introducing Gavin as a friend. By the time they'd reached the alcohol she was vaguely irritated at the number of surprised glances she'd been given—as if no one had expected her to bring a date.

"What will you have?" Gavin said, surveying the extensive selection. Charlene never skimped when entertaining, and the variety would shame a small restaurant.

Leeza opened her mouth to ask for her usual red wine, but the itch of rebellion was still tickling. "Rum and Coke, please." The drink itself wasn't very adventurous, but the fact she had chosen it over her favourite was.

She watched Gavin make up two drinks. He handed her one and they worked their way through the crowd, finding a relatively clear spot by the electric fireplace inset into one of the stark walls.

"So, do you really know everyone here?" he said, letting his gaze roam the room.

"Most of them. They're either friends of Charlene's that I've met at events like this over the years, or friends from my marriage."

As often happened at Prince George parties, the guests were an eclectic mix ranging from sleek to rustic. Leeza pointed discreetly at an older gentleman in faded jeans and a red down vest. "That's Carl Lomak."

"Him, I know," Gavin said. "A friend of mine is his accountant. Owns a trucking company."

"As well as houses in Palm Springs and Maui, and a hunting lodge in Northern Ontario." At Gavin's raised eyebrow, Leeza shrugged. "Scott is his real estate agent. What about her? The woman in the navy-blue shirt dress over your right shoulder?"

He looked subtly in the direction she'd indicated. "No."

"She runs a holistic healing service out of her basement. Does Tarot card readings and makes herbal remedies."

Gavin's mouth tightened and his eyes narrowed. Sensing disdain in his reaction, she said, "Hey, don't knock it 'til you've tried it. I had her read my cards once, as part of a girl's night out with Charlene. It was supposed to be a lark, but her comments were amazingly accurate."

He snorted. "That may be. I guess I just prefer more scientific methods. When Nancy was sick—" He broke off. "Never mind. This is a party."

It wasn't hard to guess that, in the desperate search to cure her cancer, Nancy had tried alternative medicines. To take Gavin's mind off troubling times, she said, "Did I tell you about Drew? He has a girlfriend."

She saw him shake off whatever dark memories her innocent comment had awoken. With a smile he said, "Really? That was fast."

Without mentioning the part of their discussion that involved the cabin, she recapped Drew's cliff-hanger phone call. "I got more details out of him this morning via text. When I talked to him at Christmas, he sounded so lonely. Turns out she was away visiting her parents, and some of his dejection was because of that. She works for the Department for International Trade with the British government. Graduated from the London School of Economics.

Was born and raised outside of London but lives in the city now." Sipping her drink, she added, "She's also blond, beautiful, and has the most bewitching accent. Alliteration all Drew's."

"And you hate her."

Choking on a laugh, Leeza exclaimed, "I do not! I don't even know her."

"Okay, hate might be too strong a word. But you're scared she'll keep Drew away. I can understand that."

"I'm an awful mother. I *want* him to be happy, I do. But it was hard enough letting him go halfway around the world without the added worry he might never come home."

Even as she said the words she flashed to William's journal. He'd met women in Britain, during his training and while waiting to be called into action. His mother would have worried about the same thing Leeza was worried about. But she also had the added anxiety that William might never come home for a much darker, more tragic reason.

"I know when Sarah first started dating..."

Leeza didn't hear the rest of Gavin's reply. Her attention was frozen on the newest arrival to the party.

Scott.

He walked in with the self-assured swagger she used to find sexy. He was carrying a large bag and Charlene greeted him as if he were a saviour, with a smacking kiss and a tight hug, before taking the bag from him and heading to the kitchen.

Leeza felt a stab of betrayal. Charlene hadn't hidden that she was still in touch with Scott, but Leeza hadn't imagined she would invite them both to the party. And not just invited Scott, from the looks of it. Had asked him for help with supplies.

"Does it bother you to see him?" Gavin's voice in her ear drew her out of her gloomy thoughts.

She answered hurriedly, turning her back on her ex and her friend. "No, of course not."

"I take it you didn't realize he'd be here." His expression was soft with sympathy.

Lifting her chin, she said airily, "He has every right to be here. He's Charlene's friend, too. It doesn't bother me at all. Besides, there are so many people here that it will be easy to avoid each other. Not that it would matter if we did meet. I can be civil."

"It's lucky you say that." Gavin's gaze was tracking something behind her. "Because he's on his way over."

Leeza had only a few seconds to prepare before she heard Scott's voice. "Hello, Leeza. Nice to see you."

She turned and smiled with false brightness. "Hello, Scott. How are you?"

His gazed travelled down and then slowly back up her body. She stood straight, thankful she'd taken special care with her appearance tonight. The bright red dress was new—well, new since her separation from Scott—and it hugged her figure in a fit that flattered and flaunted. The neckline was daring, and she'd drawn attention to her cleavage with a heavy metal pendant. The hem stopped just above her knees, and she wore silvery heels that added inches to her height.

"You look great," he said.

Slightly startled at the sincerity in his voice, she said, "Thanks. You look good, too."

His dark blond hair was cut in a style that Leeza thought was a touch too young for him. Yet she couldn't deny he was trim and fit, and he wore a sport coat over a V-neck shirt in a casual yet put-together look. She waited for the zing of sensual awareness she used to experience just looking at him—and felt nothing.

As if just noticing Gavin standing next to her, he smiled a wide, professional smile and stretched out a hand. "Hi. I'm Scott."

"You've met," Leeza said with irritation, "and more than once. Gavin works at Millar's."

"Oh, sorry." Scott's bland expression as the two men shook hands made Leeza wonder if he'd only pretended to forget. "Do you mind if I speak with Leeza for a bit? Alone?"

Gavin looked at Leeza and she gave a small nod. "Why don't I freshen up your drink?" he said, plucking the squat tumbler from her unresisting hand. "I'll be right back."

"I refuse to discuss the cabin," Leeza said as soon as he turned away. "Drew told me what he told you."

Scott held up his palms in a gesture of surrender. "That's fine, I get it. You both obviously feel strongly about it. That's not what I wanted to talk to you about."

She regarded him suspiciously. He'd acquiesced too easily, which made her wonder if he had another bomb to release. "What?"

"I want to apologize."

Her mouth dropped open. "Apologize?"

One corner of his mouth lifted in a shamefaced grin. "It occurred to me that I've never apologized for my behaviour when we were married. You didn't deserve what I did to you. And I deserved everything I got after it all came out."

"You decide to tell me this *now?*" Leeza waved a hand at the loud, noisy party going on around them. As her glance swept the crowd, she realized that numerous pairs of eyes were casting sidelong looks their way. Almost everyone knew their history. They were probably waiting greedily for a dramatic scene.

She tamped down her exasperation. Sedately, she said, "Thank you. I appreciate the gesture." Not that she was convinced of his candor. He wasn't above using an insincere apology to try and soften her up.

"I want us to be friends." He took her hand in both of his and pressed it to his chest. "I miss you."

She tugged out of his grip. "You don't have the right to miss me anymore, Scott. And I can't be friends with you."

He took a step closer, his face open and ingenuous. She backed away. "You're right. What we had together was too intense to let us be just friends now."

She couldn't help it. She laughed. "Did someone write that line for you? You sound like an actor on a soap opera."

A flicker of annoyance flashed across his features before he schooled them to friendliness again. "I know I screwed up, but can't we put that behind us? Build a new relationship?"

Gavin was standing by the bar, obviously waiting for a sign to return. Leeza waved him over, giggles tickling her throat. It was *delightful* to be able to laugh at Scott. He'd hurt her so badly that, for a time, she'd wondered if she'd ever laugh again. "You know what, you're right. We should put everything behind us."

Gavin reached them and handed her a glass. She raised it in a toast. "To new beginnings. What better night than tonight to start afresh?" Without waiting for either man to reply, she took a healthy swallow.

Scott regarded her with a puzzled expression. "Okay, then. Great."

With a recklessness that felt unfamiliar but empowering, Leeza said, "So where's your girlfriend? The one you left Yvonne for?" Just because they'd decided to move on didn't mean she couldn't be a little catty.

Scott's face turned wary. "She's not coming

tonight."

"That's too bad. You could have introduced us."

It was Scott's turn to back away. "Maybe another time. It's been good talking to you." He nodded goodbye and lost himself in the crowd.

Triumph flooded through her and she turned to Gavin with glee. "That scared him off, didn't it?"

"Who knew politeness could be so deadly?"

She snorted, the inelegant noise muffled as her nose was in her glass while she took a swallow. "You've obviously never read a Regency romance. Venomous civility was an art form."

"I'll keep that in mind the next time you're being especially nice to me." His shoulder brushed hers as he surveyed the room. "The two of you did draw some attention, though. Do you want to leave?"

She considered the offer briefly. "The show is over now, so no, I don't think so. Let's mingle."

CHAPTER SIXTEEN

December 18th, 1942
We're constantly training on beaches on the
Isle of Wight or near Norway. I'm guessing
that we're going to be landing on enemy
beaches. This isn't too comforting. They
checked our feet two days ago after marching
over forty-five miles and climbing cliffs and
later enemy planes tried to bomb our camp as
you can see we are a busy bunch.

By the time the countdown to midnight began,
Leeza and Gavin had spoken to almost everyone in
the room. Many of the friends she'd avoided since
her separation had been delighted to see her, which
made her wonder if she'd been partly to blame for
her own isolation. Of course, a few made sly
comments about Scott's newest fling, but she shut
them down fast. Serious thoughts were for another
day, and she laughed and joked and shed the last
scales of depression.

While she wasn't drunk, her defiance was
bolstered by alcohol, and she felt pleasantly giddy as
they watched the countdown begin on the large
television hanging above the fireplace. She gripped

Gavin's bicep and he smiled down at her. He hadn't left her side, other than to refill her glass, and had been his usual quiet self. She felt a sudden qualm. Had he been too quiet?

"Thanks for coming," she said. "I hope you had a good time."

"Ten...nine...eight..." shouted the crowd around them.

"I did," he said. "I enjoyed meeting your friends."

"...seven...six...five..."

"I might have gone home—you know, after Scott—if you hadn't been here."

"...four...three...two..."

"I don't think so. You're too strong to let him chase you away."

"...one!"

As noisemakers buzzed and streamers were tossed, Gavin pulled her in close and kissed her. His hands were hot through the thin silk of her dress, his hair cool and smooth against her fingers. Her mouth opened in welcome, and their tongues danced erotically against each other. By the time he let her come up for air, she was limp and bewildered.

"Let's get out of here," he said. His expression gave nothing away to anyone watching, but his eyes... Leeza shivered at the need blazing from their hazel depths.

She nodded and let him pull her down the darkened hall. In the bedroom where Charlene had laid out all the guests' coats, he kissed her again. She pressed against him, purring at the thrust of his erection against her belly. His hand slid from her hip to her breast. She moaned and leaned back to allow him greater access.

When he pulled away his breath was ragged, his cheekbones and the tips of his ears flushed with desire. "Your coat. Now," he commanded.

They scrabbled through the pile with indecent haste, and hurried hand in hand down the hall. Without a word to Charlene, they slipped out the door.

"Ever made out in an elevator?" Leeza said breathlessly as the doors slid closed behind them.

"No." Gavin tugged her into his arms, leaning back against the wall. They hadn't taken the time to fasten their coats, so she could feel his heat from breast to thighs.

"Me, neither." She dragged his mouth down to hers.

Through the drugging lust of his kiss, Leeza wondered how his normally placid exterior could hide such passion. He demanded her response without apology or hesitation, and she offered it willingly. Her pulse beat hard and fast, her breasts tingled and swelled.

When he broke the kiss, she made a sound embarrassingly close to a whine. He chuckled and brushed her nose with his. "This is our stop."

She hadn't even noticed the door behind her opening. Gavin's arm about her waist, they headed through the vestibule to the sidewalk. The bitter winter night took away what breath Gavin had left her with, and she shuddered. He pulled her closer. "I started the car," he said. "Let's hurry."

The concrete was slick with old ice and packed snow, but she moved as quickly as she could on her teetering heels. How had he had the presence of mind to use his car starter, when she could barely put one foot in front of the other? Maybe she'd had more to drink than she thought. It couldn't only be Gavin's kisses that had her so befuddled.

He opened the passenger door and she slipped onto the seat, huddling into her coat. The interior was only marginally warmer than the night outside, but at least she was out of the wind, and in a few seconds, she could feel the seat warmer kick in.

Gavin slammed his door shut and rubbed his hands briskly before turning the heater to high. The air warmed quickly and Leeza's shivers subsided.

"Oh, that's better," she sighed.

"You have to stop doing that," he said, his eyes riveted to her mouth.

"Doing what?"

"Making those sexy little noises."

The desire that hadn't quite faded in their rush to the car flared brightly. "Like this, you mean?" She made a soft sound of appreciation deep in her throat, like the sound she'd make after tasting a sumptuous chocolate dessert.

Or Gavin's mouth.

"Exactly." He gripped the back of her neck, his fingers chilled against her flushed skin, and drew her toward him so he could nibble along her jaw. "We'll never get home if you keep tempting me to tease more of those noises out of you."

She was leaning awkwardly across the seat between them but had no intention of complaining. The moist heat of his mouth travelled from her chin down her neck and she couldn't help making a hum of approval.

"Damn it, Leeza." She felt the words as much as she heard them. "Can I take you home? Will you let me stay the night?"

"Yes," she said.

Thank god Prince George *is a small town,* Leeza thought as Gavin drove quickly through the deserted midnight streets. Her body buzzed with need, and she didn't want to lose that delicious sensation. In less than fifteen minutes he pulled to a stop outside her door. Her home was in the middle of a block of tall, narrow houses, most of which were dark and silent even on this New Year's Eve. The outdoor light she'd left on beckoned, and she opened her door almost before Gavin had put the car in park. She waited impatiently for him to round the hood, and then strode to the front and punched the entry code with shaking fingers.

Inside, a light from the second storey hallway cast a glow down the stairwell, leaving the entryway dim and shadowy. Gavin closed the door. His silent presence heightened Leeza's nervous tension.

"It's been a while," she blurted.

"Me, too." He slipped his jacket off and hung it on the newel post.

"And only ever with Scott." She turned her back so he could help her with her overcoat.

Gavin's hands hesitated on her shoulders, and then continued their motion. Her arms hung limp at her sides as the sleeves slid off.

"We started dating in Grade Eleven. I've never slept with anyone else," she said, turning back to face him.

He tossed her coat over his, and then ran his palms down her arms and lifted her hands. Clasping them together in both of his, he kissed each knuckle. The gesture was sweet and reassuring and so romantic it made her knees wobble.

"I haven't slept with anyone but Nancy for almost thirty years. After all that time, I don't think my first two lovers count."

Haven't slept, not *didn't*. "You haven't been with anyone since—"

He shook his head, his lips whispering over the backs of her fingers.

"Oh, god. No pressure," she said unthinkingly.

He threw back his head and laughed, a rich rolling rumble that made her toes curl.

"You don't have anything to worry about." He drew her toward the stairs. "I assume the bedroom is this way?"

Was she really going to do this? Was she really going to bare her almost fifty-year-old body to someone other than Scott? Scott, who had rejected her, thoughtlessly and cruelly?

When she didn't follow, Gavin cocked his head. "Leeza?"

"I quit taking the pill after Scott left. And shouldn't we use a condom? Isn't that the usual thing? I certainly don't have any, so unless you have one tucked away in your wallet like in the movies—"

Gavin cut off her babbling with a gentle finger on her mouth. "Having second thoughts?"

"Yes. No." She leaned forward and pressed her forehead against his shoulder. His arms came around her and they stood like that for a moment. "I want you," she said, her voice subdued. "You make me feel things I haven't felt in a long, long time. But I don't know if I'm ready. And I know we both dismissed the boss/employee conflict, but it's one thing when we're just seeing each other, and another completely if we're sleeping together."

His hands made soothing circles on her back and she relaxed further into his solid support. "You've got a lot going on in that head of yours, don't you?" he said.

"I'm sorry. This is not what I thought would happen when we left Charlene's."

"Timing is important." He held her away from his body and stared intensely at her. "And so are you. If you're not ready, that's fine. I've waited this long. I can be patient."

His words set up an echo in her memory. Hadn't he said something similar once, about waiting? If he meant what she was beginning to think he meant, the implications were too complicated to deal with now.

"I'm sorry," she repeated.

"Don't be. Thank you for being honest. Thank you for feeling you *can* be honest with me." He kissed her forehead. "Happy New Year, Leeza."

"Happy New Year, Gavin." She cupped his chin in one hand. "Thank you for coming to the party with me."

"You're welcome."

After he left, Leeza trailed wearily up the stairs. She knew she'd done the right thing, sending Gavin away, but—

—why did the right thing have to suck so much?

CHAPTER SEVENTEEN

December 25th, 1942
Today was similar to last year's Christmas. We
were able to meet a few orphans and evacuated
kids from cities close by. It was fun, but boy did
the kids remind me of Maureen. I feel even
worse than I did last year. I hate holidays, they
make me so home sick. Hopefully they'll get us
to start training again, at least that way I think
less about the family.

The process for closing Millar's was
heartbreaking and exhausting. January flew by in a
haze of inventory control, stock-taking, and
personnel issues. As she'd predicted, most of her
employees moved on at the first chance of other
work, and who could blame them? Her own
severance package would give her a few weeks of
grace after the store shut, but her part-timers
wouldn't have that luxury.

As staff dwindled, Leeza worked more and more
hours. The little spare time she had was spent
quietly. She and Gavin continued to see each other
away from the store, but neither re-initiated the
passion that had flared on New Year's Eve. She

assumed Gavin was being true to his word and was waiting for her to make the next move. But a lowkey depression gripped her as she watched Millar's shelves slowly empty, and she lacked the energy and courage to do so.

William's diary should have provided a much-needed distraction, but the search seemed to have stalled. John from the Regimental Museum had got back about the mis-read initial and Rodney as a middle name. He agreed both were possibilities and promised he'd be in touch if he confirmed anything, but as Leeza had feared it didn't get them any further ahead. She had joined a number of promising groups on Facebook, with no success, and Gavin had heard nothing from any of the organizations he had contacted, either. Once Millar's was closed, she promised herself, she would concentrate on William. It would be her reward for surviving a stressful month—a chance to do something just for herself, for no reason other than because she wanted to.

By January 31, Gavin, Carrie, and Leeza were the only staff remaining. The store had closed to the public the day before, and the three of them were packing up everything unsold. The vast majority of inventory had been shipped off to the surviving Millar's locations already, but there was still enough left to have Leeza's back aching from the stooping and carrying.

Finally, the last box was taped shut and placed in the pile at the back door, waiting for the shippers to arrive. She pushed her hair off her sweaty forehead with a grimy hand and smiled weakly at Gavin and Carrie.

"Thanks so much, you two," she said. "And not just for today. For everything since you came to Millar's. I'm so sorry it's ending this way."

Gavin simply nodded, but Carrie enveloped Leeza in a strong hug. "You have nothing to be sorry for. I'm going to miss working with you." She backed away, wiping her eyes. Leeza's own welled up.

"No crying," she said sternly. "If you start, I will, too."

"I'm not crying," Carrie said, sniffing and blinking. "I guess I'd better get going. Sheila's waiting for me."

Gavin spoke up. "I was thinking we could have dinner together, the four of us. My treat. Take our mind off things. A farewell meal."

Carrie kissed him on the cheek. "That's sweet, but Sheila and I already have plans. Goodbye, Gavin." She hugged Leeza one more time. "Bye."

Her steps clattered rapidly through the echoing space, followed by the rattle of the security gate at the front of the store. Leeza looked at Gavin. "I guess it's just us."

"Yes. My offer of dinner still stands."

"I feel grubby," she said, making a face. "Dinner sounds lovely, but I really want to go home and shower."

"We could meet at Leonardo's in an hour." The pizza restaurant had become a regular hangout for them. Leeza was now greeted with almost as much fervor as Gavin.

"I could manage that."

Together they walked through the darkened store, and out the security gate one more time. Gavin dropped his key into Leeza's palm, and she added it to the bundle she needed to drop off at the administration office on her way out.

For a moment she stood, looking through the metal grate. She didn't have Carrie to blame this time when tears flooded her eyes. A few escaped down her cheeks, despite her best efforts.

A warm, solid arm came around her shoulders and Gavin pulled her in close. "It's okay to cry, Leeza."

"It's just a store," she said, her voice quavering. "It shouldn't hurt this much to leave it."

"It was a part of you, for a long time." His chin rested on top of her head for a moment. "And me, too. I wasn't in a good place when I started working here. I'd left a career I had spent two decades building without a backward glance, was still stumbling through my grief for Nancy. Millar's saved me. It brought me back into the world." He took her by her shoulders and turned her to face him. She couldn't see his face very well through the blur of tears. "*You* saved me, Leeza. You gave me a reason to get up in the morning, and something to look forward to when I went to sleep at night."

She laughed through a tear-clogged throat. "I gave you a job, Gavin. Nothing more than that."

"Trust me, it was more than a job." He hugged her tight, and she clung to his waist.

After a few minutes, her tears subsided, and she pulled away. "Okay, enough nonsense," she said, searching her purse for a tissue. "Leonardo's in an hour?"

He nodded. "You bet."

And for the last time, they walked out of the empty mall together.

Sixty-five minutes later, Leeza sat at the table in the far corner of Leonardo's—the one she was beginning to think of as *theirs*. She was surprised that Gavin hadn't yet arrived but was happy enough to wait with the glass of robust red wine she had ordered.

It hadn't hit her yet—the fact that she wouldn't be getting up in the morning and heading to Millar's. She had been given fifteen weeks of severance, which should be more than enough time for her to find another job. At least she hoped so. It wasn't the money as much as it was the fact she needed to *do* something. If only to stop her from getting cabin fever.

She let her mind drift, relaxing in the moist warmth generated by the huge wood-fired oven that dominated one wall of the restaurant.

She supposed she should be looking forward to no responsibilities. With Drew in London, Grampa-Great gone, and her parents not due back in town for a couple of months, she had almost no commitments. Oh, she imagined Charlene would drag her out of her house occasionally, and her parents were trying to get her to come visit them. She probably would, but not right away. For now, she needed time to herself, space to rewire her brain to the new reality.

The glass of the interior door flashed, reflecting the candles placed on each table, as Gavin swung it open. He waved at the young man wielding a huge wooden spatula near the oven and made his way directly to Leeza.

"Sorry I'm late," he said, hooking his overcoat on the back of the chair across from her and sliding onto the seat, "but I wanted to finish something before I came."

"No problem."

The server came to take Gavin's drink order. "I'll have wine. Whatever she's having is fine."

Leeza raised her eyebrows. "Wine? That's a change."

"It feels too momentous an occasion for a soft drink."

Momentous seemed an odd choice of words, and Leeza's attention sharpened. Instead of the rather subdued aura she might expect from a man who'd just lost his job, she realized Gavin was radiating a tense excitement.

"What?" she said. "What happened?"

His eyes gleamed behind the lenses of his glasses. "I was late because I was answering an email. From the North Nova Scotia Highlanders Regimental Museum."

Her spine straightened, a matching exhilaration fizzing. "From John? About William?"

"Not directly. Someone from his diary."

"Who? Other than his superiors and family, I don't remember him mentioning anyone other than Rodney."

"Here, I brought the transcript." He pulled a small sheaf of papers out of the inside pocket of his blazer. "Read August 15, 1941."

She took the pages and found the entry.

Nothing much going on yet. I've been meeting lots of new guys. Some are practically my neighbours, if you can believe that. I went to school with some of them. Some of them are jerks but I get along with most of them. There's this one guy called Grant Howard. He has to be the funniest guy I have ever met. He just keeps telling us these great stories from back home and old girlfriends and we can laugh at them non stop for 15 minutes. My stomach and my face hurt so much because of that.

"Grant Howard." She sank in her seat, surprise making her limp, and stared at Gavin. "I don't even remember reading that name."

"I've been going through the diary, making a list of any places or people that are mentioned. I figured one of them had to give us a lead. William only mentions the full name of two soldiers—Grant Howard and a Private Mitchell Holmes who was injured in a jeep accident while they were still in

England. I did the usual searches and came up blank again. That's partly why I didn't mention it before. I figured they were more dead ends. But as a last resort, I emailed your gentleman at the museum. It's been days, and I'd almost given up on getting a reply, but I finally heard back."

Leeza rested her crossed arms on the table and leaned in, drawn to Gavin's intensity. "What did John say?"

"He told me he knows of a Grant Howard who served in World War Two. A Grant Howard who was in the North Novies."

He paused. Her breath caught. "And?"

"He's still alive, Leeza." Gavin's face lit with a fervent glow. "Grant Howard is still alive."

CHAPTER EIGHTEEN

February 28th, 1943
It has been too long since my last entry. I can't
sit down and spend time writing anymore, I
hardly have time. We've been training
constantly and marching. It's really hard, but
I'm starting to enjoy all the marching. I've
become very strong and I feel much more
confident about myself. I'll try to write more
often.

Stunned, Leeza could only repeat Gavin's words. "He's still alive?"

"Ninety-five years old, and according to John, razor sharp. Needs a scooter to get around and very deaf, but otherwise hale and hearty. He's in a care complex near Truro."

She frowned. "Ninety-five, you say? That makes him five years younger than my grandfather. If William wrote about him in 1941, that means he was only—" She broke off at the enormity of her thought.

"Sixteen. He wouldn't have been the only one to lie about his age in order to enlist."

A thrill chased itself across Leeza's shoulder blades. They'd found someone who had spoken with

William, laughed with him, trained with him.

Who might also have known her grandfather, given the fact they were all Novies. She still hadn't constructed a reasonable scenario for how Otto had come to possess William's journal. Maybe she never would.

But maybe Grant Howard could supply the answer.

The server returned with Gavin's wine and they ordered their meals. Too churned up to continue her tradition of experimenting with a new pizza each time they dined at Leonardo's, she fell back on her first favourite, the margherita.

Grant Howard might be as close to finding William as they'd ever get. "There's no way he'll remember William and Rodney," she said, hoping Gavin would deny it.

Unfortunately, but logically, he agreed with her gloomy outlook. But she could hear the same hopefulness in his tone that she'd tried to hide in hers. "Chances are very slim. We have no idea how long he and William might have been stationed near each other during the years leading to D-Day. And even if they were close, there were hundreds of soldiers. They probably lost touch."

"We can't just ignore him, though."

Gavin shook his head vehemently. "Of course not. It gives me goosebumps just thinking about talking to someone who might have known William and Rodney," he said, unconsciously echoing Leeza's own thoughts. "Even if he doesn't lead us to their families, it's something to show for all our searching."

"You said he's deaf. Do you think we could call him?"

"I don't know. It might be difficult to communicate over the phone." His fingers smoothed the shiny metal of the knife lying on the crisp white napkin in front of him. "I think we should go to him."

Leeza's mouth opened in a surprised *O*. "Go to Nova Scotia?"

Gavin dropped his eyes and continued to fidget with his silverware. She realized with a start he was nervous. "You deserve a holiday after the last few weeks you've had. I've never been to the Maritimes. I thought..."

He trailed off.

Both charmed and flattered by his flustered appearance, Leeza said, "Both of us?"

He shot her a quick glance. "Why not?"

Why not indeed? Her stomach fluttered, and not from hunger.

Over Gavin's shoulder she saw the server approaching, large plates in each hand. Before she could lose her nerve, she said, "Okay."

Gavin's gaze sharpened. "Okay?"

"I want to meet Grant. I want to talk to him and learn what we can. And I want to do that with you."

He said nothing as Leeza's pizza was placed in front of her, leaning back as the server did the same for him. After assuring her they needed nothing more, he lifted his wine glass in toast. Leeza matched his action.

"To courageous soldiers, honourable veterans, and the search for family," he said.

"To Nova Scotia," she answered.

The ringing of crystal chimed like a promise between them.

Leeza couldn't believe the speed at which everything came together. The efficiency she appreciated in Gavin as an employee was nothing compared to his competence in arranging flights, hotel, and rental car. Early on the Thursday morning following Millar's closing, she was in a cramped airline seat, Gavin on her right, as the plane's wheels touched down at Halifax Stanfield International Airport.

She had called Drew to tell him she'd be travelling for a few days—which had necessitated explaining the whole diary quest and her friendship with Gavin. He'd been remarkably encouraging. "Go for it, Mom," he said. "It sounds like a cool adventure. Have I met Gavin?"

"Probably a couple times when you dropped into the store."

"Well, if you like him, I'm sure he's a good guy."

She didn't remind him her track record was not that great, given that the *not-that-great* guy was Drew's dad, but she appreciated the thought.

She and Gavin had left Prince George the day before, and after a short layover in Vancouver had boarded the redeye to Nova Scotia. Even then it still hadn't been a direct flight—they'd stopped in Calgary for an hour or so but hadn't deplaned.

As they taxied to the terminal, she rolled her shoulders, working out the stiffness of a night attempting to sleep upright. She noticed Gavin noticing, but he didn't say anything. When they'd been booking the tickets, he'd diffidently offered to upgrade their seats to business class. "I can use my points," he had said, referring to the loyalty program available through his credit card. "It won't cost me anything."

She'd been tempted, knowing the overnight flight would be a lot more bearable in the plushier compartment. Besides, she'd never flown anything other than Economy. But it wasn't right to use them. He wouldn't be going on this trip if it wasn't for her, so she'd regretfully refused.

It was a relief to stand, retrieve her carry on from the overhead rack and move along the jetway into the terminal.

"Did you get any sleep?" Gavin asked as they followed the crowd to the baggage area. Neither of them had checked any luggage, but according to the signs, the rental car counters were just past the revolving carousels.

"A bit. How about you?"

He shrugged. "I'm a night owl anyway, so considering it's only about three in the morning Pacific, I'm good." He slid her a sidelong glance. "Worried I'll fall asleep on the drive to Truro?"

"Of course not." She was jittery, though, and recognized it as a symptom of her own lack of sleep. "*I* can't promise not to nod off on the way."

"You'll barely have time for a nap if you do. It's only about a forty-minute drive."

They reached the rental car counter, and Leeza waited while Gavin completed the paperwork. She'd won the battle about business class but lost it on the rental. He'd insisted that would be on his tab. She figured she'd pay for the gas and a few of his meals to even things up.

Then she saw the car.

"Is that a Mercedes-Benz?" She stopped in front of the vehicle, her eyes widening, the damp, bitter February wind whipping her hair into her face. "You *rented* a Mercedes-Benz?"

He grinned and beeped the locks. "I love cars. When I travel, I splurge a little."

"I didn't know you could rent something this fancy from an airport lot." She stared at the sleek lines. The grill with its distinctive logo glistened, the narrow side windows were tinted, and the indents that swooped from front wheels to back along the metallic blue sides told her it was meant for speed.

"It's cold, Leeza. Get in the car." She climbed inside and he shut her door with a solid *chunk* before stowing their luggage in the trunk. The heater whirred into efficient action when Gavin started the engine.

Scanning the dash, which boasted a touch screen that had more apps than her smart phone, she said, "You drive a sedan. A nice sedan, don't get me wrong, but a...a *normal* one."

"I have a 'Vette in my garage."

"Really?" Once again, she was having to re-evaluate what she thought she knew of Gavin.

"I'll have to take you for a spin in the spring. The Mistress doesn't go on the roads until they're clean and clear."

She laughed. "The Mistress?"

"That's what Nancy called her." She watched for any sign of sadness, but his smile remained wide and open. "I didn't take her out at all, the summer after Nancy died, but since then I've driven the Oregon Coast and a few other long road trips in her."

Leeza had done her best to accommodate her part-time employees when they'd requested extended time off. But she'd never asked Gavin what he did during his weeks away. *Maybe I should have,* she thought as he deftly set up the rather complicated looking navigation system. She felt like she'd failed him by not inquiring.

He reversed out of the parking stall, and following the prompts, negotiated his way onto a wide, four lane freeway. Leeza glanced at the screen.

"Veterans Memorial Highway?" she said.

"That seems apropos, doesn't it? Maybe it will bring us good luck."

Acceleration pushed her back in her seat. Gavin controlled the power effortlessly, his hands stroking the steering wheel. "Oh, I love her already. She handles like a dream."

The sensuousness in his tone danced across Leeza's skin, as if he was touching *her*. Looking out the window, she watched bushy evergreens and barren shrubs flash by. For a month now she'd been pushing back memories of New Year's Eve, too caught up in dealing with Millar's. Maybe it was time to remember.

Maybe it was time to act.

The freeway swept over gently rolling land with a wide grey sky lowering above. Signs indicated several communities existed behind the wall of trees, and once in a while she caught a glimpse of homes and farms. After about twenty minutes they crossed a muddy, narrow waterway which the navigation system said was the Shubenacadie River. She became suddenly aware that her eyes were closed and opened them just in time to see an enormous, elephant-shaped creature silhouetted against the skyline to her right.

"Is that—" she said blearily.

"A mastodon, according to the sign I just saw."

At least she wasn't hallucinating in her sleep-deprived state. "But why—"

"I have no idea. We'll have to look it up later."

Her eyelids fell weightily, blocking her gaze again, and the next she knew the sides of the freeway where populated with stores and businesses with unfamiliar names. Except for Tim Horton's. She recognized that one.

"Are we there already?" she said, groggy from too short a nap.

"Just a few minutes from the hotel. It's way too early to check in, but we could try."

"It has a restaurant, right? I'd kill for a good cup of coffee. Maybe two. And something sugary for breakfast."

The navigation system directed them unerringly to their hotel. Gavin parked and Leeza stepped out, huddling into her coat as the cold damp breeze slid icy fingers down her neck. Gavin rounded the hood, and she chuckled when he gave it a tender pat on his way by, as if promising he wouldn't be away long.

In the lobby, their luck was in. A cheerful staff member assured them their rooms would be ready in less than an hour and pointed the way to the restaurant where they could wait. Leeza fortified herself with coffee and a huge cinnamon bun. Gavin joined her in the coffee but made a healthier choice of yogurt and fruit.

Following a long, hot shower in her neat and tidy but soulless room, she felt refreshed and eager to get on with their mission. She and Gavin hustled from the lobby to the car, the biting wind smelling of mud and marshy rotting things. "So, where to?" she said as she clicked her seatbelt.

Gavin tapped industriously on the navigation screen. "The care home is on Vimy Road."

The spectre of nightmare rippled down Leeza's spine. How ironic that a soldier who'd survived one of World War Two's most notorious battles now lived on a road that shared a name with the World War One conflict that was the bloody birth of Canadian patriotism.

Her fingers clenched and unclenched, the leather of her gloves squeaking. "Don't you think we should let him know we are coming?"

"When I called on Tuesday, the nurse I spoke with said she would pass on our message." Gavin swung the purring vehicle onto the road and joined the busy stream of traffic. "She also said he is a veteran who doesn't mind talking about the war, and she implied he would be more than happy to meet us. I left it at that."

They drove over a green iron bridge with a sign saying *Welcome to Bible Hill*, and through a community that was a mix of white-sided homes with small front gardens and neatly kept businesses. Further on the area became more agricultural, and Gavin signalled a left turn.

As they continued along Vimy Road, she broke

the silence. "We've come a long way for nothing if the nurse is wrong."

He took his eyes from the road briefly to give her a quick look. "Not for nothing," he said. "It's an adventure no matter what. And you wanted to go to the museum in Amherst, too. We'll be able to do that at the very least."

"How far away is it?"

"The shortest route takes about an hour and a half, according to Google Maps." He leaned forward to get a better look at a sign up ahead on the right. "Here we are."

A long driveway led up to a low building with a portico entrance and two long wings stretching back on either side. Gavin pulled into a visitor's parking stall and, as if disappointed the drive had been so short, the powerful engine sighed to a stop.

For a moment, they sat in silence. Nervous anticipation bubbled in Leeza's chest, making her feel short of breath.

"Ready?" Gavin said.

She looked him in the eye and nodded. "Ready."

CHAPTER NINETEEN

May 4th, 1943
Four days ago, they brought us to Stratford-on-Avon to visit Shakespeare's theatre, Warwick castle and I forget the other one. It was really great and interesting. Too bad David couldn't see this, he just loves all that literature stuff. I bought him a little bookmark and a Shakespeare biography at the gift shop. I couldn't find anything that mom or Maureen would enjoy. Next time I'm in London I'll get them something, I've got all the time in the world. War seems far from over.

No shrubs or flowers softened the long stretches of brick and stucco, and that bareness, along with the few inches of snow covering the strips of grass on either side of the path, gave the building a rather sterile appearance. Inside, the institutional feel was alleviated somewhat with wood-grain laminate flooring, built-in bookshelves, and sofas and armchairs scattered about in inviting conversational groupings. A man wearing a mulberry coloured polo shirt smiled at them from behind a long, U-shaped desk.

"Hello and welcome to Vimy Court. I'm Peter. How can I help you?"

"We'd like to speak with Grant Howard," Gavin said. "I called a couple of days ago. Gavin Fletcher and Leeza Boychuk."

The smile on the younger man's face wavered. "I'm sorry, but Mr. Howard isn't available this morning. He's at the hospital."

Leeza gripped the edge of the counter, her fingertips turning white. She steadied at the touch of Gavin's hand, warm in the small of her back. "I hope he's not seriously ill," she said.

Peter made a non-committal motion with one shoulder, and then his face brightened. "Well, look at that. You're in luck," he said. "I see the van pulling up now."

Through the wide glass entrance doors, Leeza saw a small bus with a colour decal of smiling, cheerful seniors plastered proudly on the side. The bifold door opened and a ramp slowly lowered. A stout woman wearing a mulberry coloured parka and khaki pants stepped off the ramp and waited as an electric scooter crept cautiously down the slight incline.

The tiny man driving was so bundled up he was barely visible. Once on the pathway leading to the front door, the scooter trundled to the entrance, the woman walking briskly beside. She pushed a button on the exterior wall and the double doors leading into the building opened slowly.

Together the man on the scooter and the woman in the mulberry coat entered the building, the doors shutting automatically behind them.

"Margot," Peter said, "these folks are here to visit Mr. Howard."

The woman escorting Grant Howard leaned toward the muffled figure and said, "Mr. Howard, you have visitors waiting for you at the front desk."

The scooter hesitated briefly, and then changed course and approached Gavin and Leeza. They stepped forward to meet it.

"Hello, Mr. Howard," Leeza said. "I'm Leeza Boychuk. I'm very happy to meet you."

A hand encased in a thick glove rose shakily and pulled off the woolen toque. Hair, too thin and fine to have a colour, was scattered across his scalp, and he wore hearing aids in both ears. "What was that?" he said, squinting at her as if that would help him hear. His blue eyes were almost lost in the wrinkles of his elfin face, but they regarded Leeza with sharp intelligence.

"I'm happy to meet you, Mr. Howard," Leeza repeated, speaking distinctly. "My name is Leeza Boychuk. This is Gavin Fletcher."

Margot said, "I mentioned these people to you yesterday, Mr. Howard. They want to talk to you about the war."

"Yes, yes, I remember, Margot. You don't have to tell me twice." He waved her off testily. "I don't have time to talk. I've spent the morning being poked and prodded, and it's almost time for my lunch."

Gavin nodded. "We're in town for a few days," he said. "We wanted to stop by and introduce ourselves, but we can come back another time if you like."

"Speak up, there, man. What did you say?"

"We can come back later if you like," Gavin repeated, louder.

"I think that would be best." The expression on Grant's face transformed from cranky to boyish. "I'm not usually in such a bad humour, but I hate doctors and I spent the morning with them. What can they do for me, at my age? I wish they'd just let me live my life the way I want to and quit trying to fix what can't be fixed." He winked. "I'll have my lunch and a nap, and I'll be ready to chat. How does two o'clock sound?"

"Just fine," Leeza replied with a smile at his feistiness. "We'll be back then. Is there anything we can bring you?"

"Now, that's a lovely offer." He glanced craftily at Margot, who was in a discussion with Peter. He leaned toward Leeza, and she bent closer. "Rum. The darker the better," he said, a hand raised to his mouth as if imparting a secret. "They don't approve of liquor here, but I sneak it into my coffee once in a while."

"I'll see what we can do," she said, patting his arm through the puffy down parka he wore. His lap was draped with a plaid wool blanket that hid his legs and feet.

"Good girl." He nodded approvingly. "I'm off then. See you later."

In contrast to his cautious entrance, he zipped down the hall and out of sight with a jaunty air.

Leeza grinned at Gavin. "He's going to be fun," she said.

Margot looked up from the desk. "Did he ask you to bring booze?"

Leeza felt her face freeze guiltily.

Peter laughed. "Don't worry. He's allowed to have it, in moderation, of course. But he likes to claim we'll confiscate it. Feel free to pretend to sneak it in. It'll make him happy."

Leeza's shoulders relaxed and Gavin chuckled. "Will do," he said. "See you later."

In the car, Gavin glanced at Leeza as he started the engine. "It won't take long to find a liquor store and buy a bottle. Any ideas on how we can kill the time until we come back?"

His tone was innocent, but heat flushed Leeza's cheeks and she turned away, hoping he couldn't read the direction her thoughts had taken. "Not really," she said. "Why don't we get Grant's rum and take it from there?"

It was simple enough to locate a Nova Scotia government liquor store using the navigation system. Just before they turned off Queen Street on their way to the shopping mall that housed it, they passed a narrow park wedged between two streets, and Leeza spotted a sign.

"Truro Welcome Centre," she said, pointing. "That might be a good place to start."

"And right across from the liquor store." Gavin parked in the large lot. "Let's get Grant's bottle first, then head over."

A few minutes later they emerged with an unmarked bag in which nestled a bottle of Ironworks Bluenose Rum and after stashing it behind her seat they made their way to the Welcome Centre.

The building made her think of an old-fashioned bandstand, with its grey-shingled, pyramid-shaped roof topped by a cupola. The walls, instead of being open to the elements, consisted of long, vertical windows framed in white. Gavin pulled on the handle of the glass door but met with resistance.

"Oh, no," Leeza said, staring at a sign taped to the window next to the door. "Closed until May!"

"I guess tourists don't exactly flood in at this time of year." Gavin leaned forward and, cupping his hands around his eyes, peered into the interior. "Wait, I think there's someone in there." He knocked loudly on the glass. "Hi! Can you help us?" he called.

The reflections on the glass made it hard for Leeza to see. "Are they coming?" she asked hopefully.

Her question was answered when the door pushed toward them, causing Gavin to step back and brush against her. She clutched his jacket to keep from stumbling, and he wound an arm over her shoulder. It was a warm, strong weight, and she resisted the urge to snuggle closer.

"I'm sorry, we're not open. Tourist services are based in the municipal building during the off season." The young man who had answered Gavin's call was long-legged and hunch-shouldered, reminding Leeza of a heron, an impression only enhanced by his long grey jacket and white and grey slouch toque.

"Can we just ask a couple of quick questions?" Gavin asked. "We've come all the way from British Columbia."

The man looked at his phone. "I guess I have a few minutes for people who've come that far." He stepped back and allowed them in.

The space they entered gave every indication of being abandoned for the season. Long white shelving was empty of all but a few scattered brochures, and a desk with two computer terminals was bare and clean. A walled off area bore symbols declaring it a unisex washroom. In the absence of any seating, the young man leaned against the reception desk and Gavin and Leeza stood before him.

"BC, hey?" he said, his expression curious. "My brother works out there. Whereabouts are you from?"

"Prince George," Leeza replied. "About a nine-hour drive north of Vancouver." The room wasn't much warmer than outside, but at least they were out of the wind. She rubbed her hands together, missing the comfort of Gavin's embrace.

The young man's eyes widened. "Go on!" he said, his soft Atlantic drawl evident even in the simple syllables. "That's where Scooter lives!"

A few minutes of rapid conversation determined that the young man—whose name was a much more mundane Dave as compared to his brother—worked for the local Parks and Recreation division, that he had only stopped by the Welcome Centre to pick up a box of brochures that had been stored there, and that no, neither Gavin nor Leeza knew his brother.

"Although I do recognize the name of the company he works for," Gavin said. "Reforestation, right?"

Dave nodded. "Scooter went out as a tree planter about fifteen years back, summers when he was on break at university. Ended up staying there after he graduated." His phone chimed and he glanced at the screen. "I have to get back to the office soon. What can I help you with?"

Leeza explained their quest as briefly as possible. "We were hoping for suggestions of other places we could visit that might help us find William."

"What a fascinating project," Dave said with sincerity. "I'm not really up on military history, although when you are raised here you can't avoid it all together. I grew up near Debert, about ten minutes away from here. During the Second World War it was a military camp. My grampa told me that thousands of soldiers trained there before being shipped over to Europe. There's a good chance your guy spent some time there."

"Would your grampa be willing to talk to us about it?"

"He passed last year." He nodded his thanks as Leeza made appropriate condolences. "I don't think he would have been able to help, anyway. He was only a kid during the war." His forehead creased in thought. "I think your best bet would be the Colchester Historeum."

"The what?" Gavin asked.

"The local museum. It has a terrific genealogical section. And it's right next to our new library, which also has local history displays and collections." His phone chimed again. "Look, I've got to go. But I'd love to catch up with you later, hear more about all this. If I give you my number, will you call me before you head back to BC?"

Gavin entered Dave's number into his phone and promised to get in touch. Then Dave ushered them out of the building, locked the door behind them and hurried off, cardboard box under one arm and his jacket flapping behind him.

CHAPTER TWENTY

June 24th, 1943
I picked up a nice new floral dress for Mom. I
hope she likes it, it was from the new summer
collection. Still didn't find anything for little
Maureen.

After they parted from Dave at the Welcome
Centre, Leeza and Gavin decided to postpone a visit
to the Historeum until after they had talked with
Grant.

"He might have new information for us," Leeza
said as they hustled across the road back to the rental
car. "And besides, we only have a little over an hour
before he's expecting us. Better to wait so we're not
rushed."

They had lunch at Murphy's, a tiny café in a
nondescript strip mall. The location was nothing to
brag about, but the fish and chips were the best
Leeza had ever had. Gavin took a different route
back to Vimy Court but Leeza was too wound up to
pay much attention to the passing scenery. They'd
come more than five thousand kilometres to talk
with Grant, and now the time was finally here the

nerves were churning in her stomach.

The breeze that had been blowing all day had kicked up a notch, and when they were once again parked at the care home, Leeza scurried from the car to the foyer, her arms wrapped around her middle in an attempt to keep the heat from leaching out from under her jacket. She wished she'd thought to bring a hat. Gavin, on the other hand, seemed oblivious, his hair ruffling in the wind, his glasses catching the hint of sun that crept weakly through the overcast sky as he held the door open for her.

Peter still sat at the reception desk. He smiled and kept his eyes averted from the paper bag Leeza carried. "Mr. Howard's waiting for you," he said. "Down that hall, fourth door on the right."

Grant Howard's room had a large window with an uninspired view of the parking lot. The bed with its side rails and adjustable mattress was neatly made with a colourful quilt, and the dresser and nightstand were obviously personal pieces. Framed photos hung on the walls at a height that would allow a man who used a scooter to see them easily. A black and white photo of a young couple with the clothing and hairstyles of the forties was placed so that anyone lying in the bed would see it first upon awakening.

Grant sat in a comfortably upholstered recliner set parallel to the window, the footrest raised to support his legs. The plaid blanket covered his lower limbs, and in his current position it was easy to see what the same blanket had hidden when he was sitting in his scooter.

Grant Howard was missing his left leg from the thigh down.

"Hello, there!" he said cheerfully, any earlier surliness no longer in evidence. "I had them bring in an extra chair. We could go to the lounge to chat, but it's often noisy in there, and my hearing's not what it used to be."

Leeza handed him the bag. "I hope this is okay. I wasn't sure what brand you liked."

Grant peered into the bag and cackled. "This will do just fine, thank you. Do you mind stashing it away for me? Bottom drawer of the dresser, under my boxers."

Hiding a smile, Leeza did as she was asked before taking a seat next to Gavin in one of the wooden-armed chairs set at the foot of Grant's recliner.

"So, Margot tells me you have questions about someone I might have known in the war." He folded his hands on his lap and tilted his head inquiringly. "What's so important you've come across the country to see me?"

Now the moment had arrived, Leeza found the words dammed in her throat. Gavin took her hand and clasped it in his, resting on the snugged-together arms of their chairs.

"Do you ever remember meeting someone name William Smith?" he asked. "William Henry Smith. He was a North Nova Scotia Highlander, one of the Originals that went over in 1941."

"William Henry Smith?" Grant frowned as Gavin confirmed he'd heard right. "I wasn't an Original. But we all trained together. Did he go by William or Bill? Or maybe Willy?"

Leeza shook her head. "We don't know. All we've got is his diary, and he doesn't write about himself that way. In fact, he doesn't mention too many people by name at all, except for his friend Rodney, and he doesn't give his surname. Gavin noticed the name Grant Howard in an entry from August 1941, and he contacted the Regimental Museum in Amherst. They directed us to you."

"Does he say where he met me?"

"The entry a few days before says he was

stationed in Aldershot. It was only a few weeks after he arrived in England," Gavin said.

Leeza shot him a respectful glance. "Do you have the whole thing memorized?"

He grinned. "Not quite. But I did re-read it on the flight last night."

"There were thirty thousand Canadians in Aldershot," Grant mused. "All training together, eating together, bickering together."

"William's entry says he met some guys he went to school with, some who were his neighbours. It was probably naive, but I had hoped you might have been one of those guys, someone who would have known him from before the war." Leeza offered a half-embarrassed smile.

"Well, now, I haven't said I can't remember him. It's just that Smith isn't exactly an uncommon name in Nova Scotia."

"Or anywhere else, for that matter," Gavin agreed.

Once again, the staggering odds against ever finding William's family took Leeza's breath away. As she contemplated the unlikely task she had initiated, Gavin said, "Do you mind if I ask you a personal question, Mr. Howard?"

The tiny old man waved a hand, gesturing at his missing leg. "Want to know how I lost this?"

Gavin looked honestly surprised. "Actually, that's not it. What I wanted to know is—we did the math. You would have been sixteen in 1941. How did you come to enlist?"

Grant stared at him, and then laughed, a crackly and broken chuckle thick with age, cigarettes, and alcohol. "Cottoned on to that, did you? To some, all old people are the same. They don't bother to count." As if Gavin had passed some kind of test, Grant leaned over, slid open the drawer of the end table beside his chair, and lifted out three small glasses. "I smuggled these in from the dining room. Let's open up that bottle you brought."

After Leeza had unearthed the rum and poured out three portions, he lifted his in toast. "To boys and war and those I left behind." With a practised gesture, he tossed back the dark liquid. Smacking his lips, he held out his glass for a refill. Leeza glanced at Gavin and Grant caught the look. "Don't be asking him for permission, missy. I'm ninety-five and any minute could be my last. Do you really want to be the person who refused to fulfill my final wish?"

She burst out laughing and poured him another healthy dose, and then capped the bottle and tucked it into the drawer, out of sight and, hopefully, away from temptation. She handed Gavin his glass, picked up her own, and then took her seat and waited.

Grant looked out the window, twisting the glass absently in his fingers, and his expression softened in remembrance.

"I left school at fourteen. My dad had passed, and Mother needed me to earn my keep, help support her and my three younger brothers and sisters. That would have been about the time the war started, so it wasn't hard to find work, what with all the men joining up. But piling lumber was pretty dull compared to the excitement of the war." He smiled, and Leeza had the sense he'd forgotten they were listening. "A boy of fourteen wants so bad to be a man, and men were becoming soldiers, fighting the Nazi terror. The pay was better, too. So, I signed up. It wasn't hard to do. I was never a big man, but I had some heft on me from slinging boards, and I'd been shaving for a while, so I looked older.

"We spent weeks in Debert, waiting to ship out. I tell you, those were some of the best days of my life. Everyone was eager to get over to Europe, and we worked hard to learn what we needed, to fit into army life. But there was time for fun, too. We used to come into Truro, go to the theatre, the dance halls. No one called me a kid when I was wearing my uniform. It was exactly what I'd hoped for."

His gaze focused back into the present, switching from Leeza to Gavin and back again. "Even England wasn't bad. Lots of marching and carrying gear and practicing sea landings, but ball games and more dances and girls. It was only a day or two before the Normandy Landing that things got serious for us. And, of course, everything was different after D-Day."

He fell silent, memories clouding his face with grief. Leeza held still, giving him the time he needed to gather his thoughts. After a moment, he shifted in his seat, pushing himself up with his arms, and said, "What else can you tell me about your William?"

"He survived D-Day," Gavin answered, "but there are very few entries after June 6. Rodney, his best friend all his life, died just days after the landing, and William seemed to blame himself for that. The last entry is July 7. William had been injured and was getting shipped out. He was going home. But we don't know if he made it. We can't find him on casualty lists or the war graves registry, but we also can't find him here. Even the North Nova Scotia Highlanders Regimental Museum has no record of him."

"The army has a genius for making a hash of things, even records. And in the chaos of Europe, it's not surprising, I suppose. How'd you lay hands on the diary, anyway?"

Leeza's heart clutched and she swallowed. They were in Nova Scotia because of William, but she hadn't forgotten his story was tied to her grandfather somehow. Would Grant know how they were linked? "I found it in with my grandfather's possessions. He passed away last fall, at the age of 99. I was cleaning up his books. We don't know how he ended up with

Brenda Margriet

the journal, but he was a North Nova, too, and sailed on the *Orion*. His name was Otto Friberg."

Grant's bushy grey eyebrows rose toward his non-existent hairline. "Now there's a name you'd remember. It stands out, between all the McNeils and McKinnons and McDonalds."

"Do you?" Leeza asked eagerly. "Do you remember my grandfather?"

Grant's gaze turned inward, and Leeza waited, barely breathing. After moments of tense silence, he said slowly, "Tall fellow, blond hair, blue eyes?"

"Yes." She leaned forward in her seat. "You met him?"

"I think I might have. I can't be certain. It was a long time ago." He sighed and sipped his drink. "It's easier to remember the ones we lost, sometimes. Their faces never fade."

Leeza searched for something that might tweak Grant's memory. "He played the harmonica," she said. "And loved solitaire more than any other card game. And darts. He was amazing at darts."

Grant nodded enthusiastically. "*That's* why the name was familiar. Every pub in England has a dart board. I won some money on your granddad, betting on him against the locals."

Tears brimmed in Leeza's eyes. "You remember him. I can't believe it." Gavin's hand rested on hers and she tilted her head to rub her cheek against his shoulder. "I hadn't thought... It's so incredible. I knew there was a possibility you might remember him, but I couldn't let myself hope. I can't believe it."

"You just made the trip worthwhile," Gavin said, and in the low rumble of his voice she could hear the same wonder and awe compressing her chest. "Even if you can't lead us to William, it's been great to meet you."

"I'm right sorry I can't help more." Grant looked crestfallen. "I'll keep thinking. Something might

159

twig. What exactly did the entry say? Maybe that will help."

"I can read it for you. Just give me a minute." Gavin pulled out his phone and started tapping. Leeza sat in silence, trying not to stare at the wizened old man who had known Grampa-Great when he was younger than Drew was now. It was both heartbreaking and wonderful.

"Here it is," Gavin said. "He wrote: *There's this one guy called Grant Howard. He has to be the funniest guy I have ever met. He just keeps telling us these great stories from back home and old girlfriends and we can laugh at them non stop for 15 minutes. My stomach and my face hurt so much because of that.*" He raised a brow at Grant, his eyes gleaming with amusement. *"Old* girlfriends, hey? Pretty precocious for a sixteen-year-old."

Grant snorted. "Had to fit in, didn't I? Couldn't let all those guys know I'd never even kissed a girl until I'd been in England for six months. I had an older cousin who used to brag about his girlfriends. I stole his stories, and no one ever knew." He chuckled, and then sighed. "We had a grand time in England. Lucky we didn't know what was waiting for us in France."

CHAPTER TWENTY-ONE

July 16th, 1943
Our softball team won. We beat the Highland
Light Infantry 2 days ago and we're the
champions. Rodney pitched a great game. He
should have made it to the Major League! He
saved our team.

By the time they said good-bye to Grant, the
emotions of the day and the redeye flight had caught
up with Leeza. She drooped in the comfort of her
heated seat, the warmth soporific.

"I can't believe he knew my grandfather," she
said sleepily as Gavin wended his way back to the
hotel. "I wouldn't have missed that for the world."

Grant had invited them back. "I'll try to
remember more about your granddad," he said.
"Maybe that will help me recall William, too." His
soft smile spoke of dignified patience. "Sometimes,
late at night when I can't sleep, the war feels more
real than the room around me. Besides, I don't have
much else to do these days but think."

Gavin had washed the incriminating glasses in
the en suite, and they'd left the old man with a

promise to return on Sunday, before their flight back to Prince George the following day.

"You look done in," Gavin said.

"I'm exhausted." She couldn't hold back a yawn. "I think I'm going to take a pass on dinner and crash, if that's okay with you."

"Of course."

She studied his profile. He looked relaxed and competent as usual, but she noticed lines of tiredness around his mouth. He'd had a long night and day, too. Reaching out, she laid her hand on his arm as it rested on the console between them. "Thank you."

He gave her a quick glance as he looked past her to check traffic while making a left turn. "For what?"

"Suggesting we come. I never would have dreamed of it. And you were right, what you told Grant. The trip is already worth it, even if we don't learn more about William."

Gavin was silent as they crossed the green iron bridge they'd driven over multiple times that day. "I might regret telling you this," he said in his calm, deliberate way, "but I'm going to, anyway."

Leeza pulled her hand off his arm. "What?" she said warily.

"I had two reasons for suggesting this trip." He kept his eyes straight ahead, both hands on the steering wheel. "The first was I hoped Grant could help us find William. The second, though..." He took a deep breath. "I wanted to spend time with you. Just you and me—no bookstore, no ex-husband, no family. Nothing but the two of us and an adventure we're sharing."

The clamp vising her heart loosened and she released a soft gasp. "Oh, you had me scared for a minute. That's not a horrible admission. I'm flattered. And if I'm honest with you, I agreed for the same reasons. I like you, Gavin. I like spending time with you, even though we haven't had much of a chance to do that lately. But I really do."

She could see their hotel in the distance, at the end of the road where it teed into another. Gavin didn't say anything, and her palms grew sweaty. Why was he so silent? She'd only agreed with him. That couldn't have come as a shock.

He parked safely in the lot. As soon as the engine stopped, she unclicked her seatbelt, primed to escape the heavy atmosphere thickening in the car. Before she could open her door, Gavin twisted in his seat and put out a hand to stop her.

"Now I can give you my full concentration," he said, the warmth of his hand seeping through her sleeve. "I like you, too, Leeza. In fact—" He broke off, shaking his head, and she felt a pang of mixed relief and disappointment. Had he been about to admit he more than liked her? What a tepid word. She more than *liked* Gavin, too. She wasn't near ready to admit that. Not out loud, at least.

"You're tired," he said. "Let's get you in the hotel."

Later, Leeza might blame it on fatigue. She felt outside herself, lightheaded, drifting. Gavin looked so serious, so caring, she wanted to give him something. Something to show him how she *liked* him.

She leaned over and kissed him.

It was no light, friendly brush of lips. It was a kiss of need and desire. She wanted to leave Gavin in no doubt of her intention, even if she couldn't say it in words. She'd pushed him aside for weeks now, and he'd let her. He'd waited for her to make the next move, and now was the time.

She stretched over the centre console, her elbows pressing on it, her hips raised off the seat. His arms wrapped around her shoulders and he dragged her closer. He took control of the kiss, his tongue demanding and exploring.

Electricity crackled in her veins, melting her bones. She forgot she was almost fifty, forgot she was in a rapidly cooling car, completely forgot they were in full sight of anyone walking by. She'd unleashed what felt like the pent-up desire of years, and she was aware only of Gavin's body, his lips, his scent, his taste.

A dull thud registered dimly in her brain, and Gavin grunted low in his throat. "I love this car, but it's not made for making out," he said, his lips whispering along her jaw. She shivered. "Can you hold that thought until we get to your room?"

She nodded, licking her lips, dazed but no longer tired. They opened their doors simultaneously and almost ran into the lobby. She headed for the elevator. Gavin grabbed her hand. "Too slow," he said and pulled her to the stairwell. "It's only three flights."

Giggling with dizzy joy, she followed him up, swinging around the corners at each landing. At their floor, before opening the door to the hall, he kissed her again. Her heart, already pounding from the swift climb, kicked into another gear, and when he finally let her go, she gulped in air.

"Where's your key?"

She wiggled the card out of the inside pocket of her purse and held it up. When they reached his door, right next to hers, he said, "Wait," and disappeared inside. She stood in the hall, impatient and eager, body throbbing. An instant later he reappeared, a glossy black box in his hand.

"You came prepared," she said.

"More like hopeful," he said. He took her key and swiped it in the lock. The light remained red. Leeza wanted to bang her head against the wall. One more delay was going to kill her. He swiped again and the light blessedly turned green. They reeled into the room, clutched in each other's arms.

Leeza ripped off her gloves and unwound her scarf so quickly she caught her earring in the woolly material. She hissed in a breath.

"Here, let me." Gavin gently untangled her, his fingers brushing the sensitive skin under her ear. She trembled but stood quietly as he tossed the scarf aside and held her face in his palms, his bare skin still carrying the outdoor chill. His lips swept across hers and she let herself lean into him.

"Too many clothes," she muttered, reaching eagerly for the zipper on his jacket. "Damn Canadian winters."

He laughed without lifting his mouth from hers. They struggled to divest each other of their outer clothing without breaking the kiss, until finally they were down to thinner layers. She pressed against him, her breasts heavy and full and a welcome heat tingled low in her belly.

Gavin backed up, bringing her with him, and fell onto the bed. She landed solidly on top of him and he *oofed*. Horrified, she tried to scramble off, but he clutched her tighter.

"No," he said. He took off his glasses and placed them haphazardly on the bedside table without taking his gaze from her. His hazel eyes were honest, intense, and she couldn't look away. "Right here. Right here is where you belong."

He certainly didn't seem to mind her weight, if the hard ridge against her stomach was anything to go by. Leeza stopped thinking—not that her thoughts had been very coherent since she'd kissed Gavin in the car—and gave herself up to the glory of being touched, being caressed, being *wanted*.

She braced her elbows on either side of his head and nibbled at his lips, teasing his with licks of her tongue, dodging away when he lifted his head trying to make the kiss deeper. He allowed her this torment only a few times, and then with a growl he flipped her over, deliciously trapping her beneath him. She wriggled, opening her thighs so he settled right where she wanted him.

It had taken her years of marriage to become bold enough to demand what she wanted in bed. She'd had to learn her own body, determine her own needs, and then be bold enough to communicate what she liked. But she'd done it. She'd taken control of her own satisfaction, knew how to get to that final cataclysmic peak.

Gavin was having none of that. He was in control, not her.

It was the most erotic experience she had ever known.

By the time they were naked, he had her whimpering and panting. He'd taken her to the edge more than once, using his hands and mouth and words, but had refused to let her fall.

"I can't," she whispered, mouth dry. "You have to let me..." Her hands gripped his skull.

He looked up from her breasts, to which he had been paying lavish attention. "You will," he said, grinning wickedly. He pressed her breasts together, aligning her nipples so he could bring both into his mouth at once.

She shattered.

Fierce sensations fired from her breasts to her core and to every particle of her being. She was a million stars falling from the night sky, a supernova expanding into fire and ice and fragments of soul, a meteor rocketing through the icy heat of space.

Slowly, awareness of her surroundings returned. She lay cradled against Gavin's chest, his hand stroking her from shoulder to hip. "What..." she said blurrily. "I've never..."

"Good." Smug satisfaction was evident in his voice. She didn't care. He deserved it.

"I didn't think of Scott once," she said in wonder.

"Even better." Gavin's voice rumbled beneath her ear, felt more than heard.

She considered asking him if he'd thought of Nancy but wasn't sure she wanted to know the answer. As vitality returned to her limbs, she set herself to making him forget anyone but her.

Gavin wasn't a cuddler, Leeza thought in amusement. Which was just fine with her. She liked her sleeping space, too.

He lay on the far side of the mattress, his back to her, curled in on himself. She scooted cautiously nearer, the bottom sheet cool against her sleep-warmed nakedness, and tucked in as close as she could without touching him. He deserved his rest.

Breathing in the scent at the back of his neck, she revelled in memories of the night. If his reactions were an honest guide, she'd made him feel just as amazing as he'd made her. She smiled in satisfaction. There was power in being a woman, and she had delighted in using every ounce of it for this man.

He sighed and she held her breath. She had no idea what time it was—it was dark outside the curtained window—and wanted to clutch these last private moments to herself a little longer. The day could wait.

Drowsily, she examined her conscience. *Clear as a bell,* she thought. Not one ounce of guilt or smidgeon of regret. Again, she marvelled that she hadn't once thought of Scott while Gavin had been caressing her. He was only the second man to touch her so intimately. Yet he hadn't felt like a stranger.

He had felt *right.*

Calm down, she cautioned herself. *Don't make*

it more than it is. Take one step at a time.

A few minutes later an indefinable change in his body signalled his awakening. Was he a morning person, she wondered, waking bright and cheerful? Or did he need time to shake off the night's languor?

His shoulders rolled toward her and she moved back just far enough so they could lay face to face. Creases marked his cheek, and his eyes blinked sleepily. Her heart squeezed with tenderness and she tucked her clasped hands under her chin, tightening her fingers into fists to keep from touching him.

"Morning," she whispered.

"Morning." He cleared his throat. He was so close she could see gold flecks in his hazel eyes. Eyes that had sparked with a joyful passion—for *her*.

Her stomach growled.

"Oh!" She dropped her hands to her belly. "I'm sorry!"

He grinned, skin crinkling at the corner of his mouth. "You're not the only one. I'm starving." He kissed her forehead. "Thank you."

She drew her brows down. "For what?"

He shrugged one shoulder. "For last night. For the last few months. For being you."

She laughed self-consciously. "I should be thanking you. For being you. For being patient. For waiting until I was ready. And, boy, was I ready."

"I hope you'll be that ready again sometime soon," he said with a roguish waggle of his eyebrows.

Her stomach growled again.

"Not too soon, I guess," he said with a laugh, flipping back the sheets and rising, naked and confident. "First, a shower. Second, breakfast. Then we'll see what happens after that."

CHAPTER TWENTY-TWO

September 9th, 1943
I won't be seeing London again for a while
because we're in Scotland now in a place right
by the ocean called Rothesay. Here, I think I've
done my most difficult training to date. First of
all, they brought us in boats 50 yards from the
shore and we had to swim back to the shore
with our complete kit and Mae West (a sort of
life vest). The problem is that the water is
freezing. I have never been in water as cold as
that. I'm thankful I can swim because lots of the
guys can't swim. You should see, those guys are
being showed how to swim in these small
swimming pools.

What happened after that was Gavin took Leeza
to watch the tidal bore.

"We can't come to the best place to see the
highest tides in the world without seeing just what
those tides can do," he said as they tucked into
breakfast. Gavin had ordered a stack of pancakes
and slathered them with butter and syrup. When
she'd commented on the change from his yogurt the
day before, he'd winked and said he needed to keep

his strength up.

She'd blushed, which embarrassed her and caused her to blush even more. Dropping her gaze to her eggs benedict—also a special treat—she focused on *not* imagining what he might need his strength for.

It turned out that Gavin, in his quiet, competent way, already knew where and when to see the tidal bore. "I did some research before we left Prince George," he said as he exited the parking lot. "There used to be a hotel near the river, but it was bought up by local governments and they're developing it for tourists. And I found a tidal chart online, too."

Born and raised in a landlocked area, Leeza had a leery fascination with the ocean and its tides. "How long will we have to wait, do you think?"

"Only about ten minutes, if I've planned this right. The tides are very predictable, so the bore should come in pretty soon after we get there."

There was a dead-end street with a view of the Salmon River which ran along the north side of Truro. They parked next to a small bus with *Truro Tourism* emblazoned on the side.

"What are the chances Dave is here?" Gavin said.

"Pretty good," Leeza said, pointing to a group of people gathered around a picnic table near the riverbank. Dave's tall form, clad once again in grey, was easy to spot. "He must be hosting a tour."

Leeza had asked Gavin to stop at a store on their way to the viewing area, and she'd quickly purchased a black toque. She put it on, pulling it as far down as it would go to protect her ears from the ever-present wind. Tucking her scarf around her neck, she zipped her coat up under her chin and followed Gavin toward the edge.

Dave noticed them pass and his face lit in recognition. He gave a short nod but didn't pause in his presentation. Leeza hovered nearby, drawn into his explanation of what was about to happen.

"A tidal bore is a wave that travels upstream, signalling an incoming tide, and only occurs in rivers with specific characteristics. The Salmon River, which empties into Minas Basin in the Bay of Fundy, is one of the best rivers in the world in which to view this phenomenon. Today's tide will be just under average, but don't worry—you'll still see something amazing."

Dave ushered his group to the top of the grassy berm that lined the river. Gavin already stood there, his feet at the edge of the soft, muddy bank. Riprap was piled along the shore, doing its best to slow the inevitable erosion. She took her place next to Gavin.

The wide, deceptively still expanse at her feet reminded her of the Fraser River as it flowed past Prince George, in that the water looked thick and silty. Instead of being hemmed in by high sandy cliffs, though, the Salmon River was surrounded by low, level agricultural plains. The current flowed from her right, snaked around the viewing area, which was on the inside of a huge curve, and disappeared around another arc far to her left.

Leeza became aware of a rushing sound, like wind through leaves. In the distance, where the river first came into sight, the water grew rough and turbulent.

"Here it comes," Gavin said. He stood just behind her, giving her the best view.

A curling wave, like the mane on the neck of a galloping horse, broke the smooth sleekness of the water. It flowed ever closer, not breaking and retreating like a wave hitting the shore. Instead it seemed to swallow the water before it, leaving frothy whitecaps behind, rolling and bumping in a confused symphony. Where the wave hit an immovable object, the spray crashed and broke with startling force. The rushing sound grew louder, and whether it was the water or just coincidence, the wind kicked up, too. Leeza shivered and Gavin stepped closer, wrapping his arms around her, and resting his chin on her crown.

The head of the bore passed the watching group and continued upstream. In just a few minutes, the entire flow of the river had reversed, and what had been a placidly meandering waterway was rough and tumbled. Even as she watched, Leeza could see the water level rising, climbing the sandy walls holding it in.

"That was breathtaking," she said softly. She felt a little like she did in a church—awed and insignificant.

"I didn't expect it to be so quiet," Gavin said. "Yet that made it almost more incredible. All that power, so silently overwhelming."

She nodded, wondering if he realized how his words could apply to himself. He didn't flaunt his strength and confidence, and for a long time she'd made the mistake of interpreting his quietness as weakness and uncertainty. Now she knew it sprang from boundless patience. Just as the tide had reversed the flow of the river, so had Gavin reversed the downward slide of her life, flooding her with a new sense of purpose and value.

He'd given her the courage to see a way forward, shown her a road they might walk together.

He'd *certainly* given her a lot to think about.

The show over, Dave's group straggled back to the van. He approached Gavin and Leeza with a long, loping stride. "Good to see you again," he said, "and excellent timing."

Leeza laughed and shot Gavin an amused glance. "That's all Gavin's doing. I didn't even know about this before he mentioned it. It was awesome."

"Yes, your timing for the tidal bore was spot on,"

Dave replied, "but that's not what I meant. I was afraid you might leave without calling me. I know you said you would, but I was worried you were only being polite. I wanted to tell you while you were still in Truro."

The hair on the back of Leeza's neck rose and she clutched Gavin's arm. "Tell us what?"

"I think I found your William Henry Smith."

As Leeza gaped in shock, Dave went on. "I don't have time to go into it now," he said, shooting a glance over his shoulder at his tourist flock. "But I only work a half day today. Can we meet at one o'clock?"

"Of course," Gavin said. "Where?"

"Do you know The Nook and Cranny? It's a brew pub on Prince Street."

"We'll find it."

"Great. See you then." He hurried off and ushered the last of his group onto the bus before climbing into the driver's seat and pulling away.

Leeza stared at Gavin. "It couldn't possibly be that easy."

"Well, if you consider months of research and a trip across the country easy, then—maybe?" He gestured toward their car, and she unglued her feet.

"You know what I mean. What if we hadn't stopped by the Welcome Centre? What if Dave hadn't been there when we did?"

"Let's find out what he's discovered first, and then start worrying about what might never have happened." He held her door open for her and she slid inside.

"Is it scary that I understood that convoluted sentence?" she said as he slid behind the wheel. "But more important—how will I be able to wait the almost three hours until it's one o'clock?"

Gavin solved that quandary by suggesting they visit the Colchester Historeum. "It looks like it's just

173

around the corner from the pub where Dave wants to meet," he said, deftly manipulating the touch screen on the car's dash.

Unfortunately, the woman in charge of the genealogical department was off sick, though expected back the next day. Though they searched as well as they could on their own in the museum's database, they didn't discover anything useful.

"We'll come back tomorrow," Gavin said. "Hopefully, the archivist will be in then and we'll have more details from Dave, too."

Any other day, Leeza would have enjoyed the modern, well laid out display featuring life in Truro and the surrounding area of Colchester County, as well as the one highlighting Nova Scotians who had influenced the province and country since Confederation in 1867. But she couldn't keep her mind on the tableaus before her and found herself reading the same paragraphs over and over without absorbing the information. It was a relief when it was almost one o'clock and she could casually suggest it was time to go. From the gleam in Gavin's eye she might not have been as nonchalant as she'd hoped but given his eagerness to agree she figured it didn't matter.

Leaving the car in the museum parking lot, they made the short walk at a brisk pace, urged on by the biting wind. The Nook and Cranny Brew Pub occupied the corner of a grey-sided building on Truro's main street. It boasted a wraparound wooden deck made for summer sunshine which looked desolate and abandoned in the February gloom. Inside, ornate tin ceiling tiles painted black, glossy midnight-hued tables, and charcoal-grey wainscoting gave the brew pub a nicely balanced vibe between honouring the past and embracing the future.

They took a table near the window and the

server brought over menus. Leeza became aware she was jiggling her knee only when Gavin's warm hand pressed on it. "Sorry," she said.

He smiled. "Nothing to be sorry for. My stomach's in knots. I get it."

She became abruptly aware of how close he was sitting. Even though they were in separate chairs, his thigh lay alongside hers from knee to hip, and his shoulder brushed hers with every breath. It crossed her mind she should move away, give him his space, but as if reading her intention in her eyes his hand gripped her knee tighter.

"We haven't really talked about it," she blurted.

He didn't pretend confusion. "Do we need to?" With his free hand he reached across and tucked a strand of her windblown hair behind her ear. "I had no inkling this is where we'd end up, the day I walked in for my interview at Millar's. I wasn't in a good place then, and the bookstore gave me a reason for getting out of the house, for not staying home and brooding. It was only as the years went by that I started looking at you differently."

She didn't have to ask what he meant. The intense heat and consuming desire he kept tamped down beneath his mild demeanor flared in his hazel eyes. Her heart thudded in her throat.

"You were with Scott, though, and I wasn't ready to move on yet." His mouth twisted in a wry, sad smile. "It takes a while to get over the love of your life."

Under the table, her hand squeezed his in wordless comfort.

"Then you two split up, and you needed to do your own grieving. I was waiting for a sign of some sort, to know when the time would be right to approach you. And then you dropped the journal at my feet." He stared into her eyes and her head spun. "Even if we never find William Henry Smith or his family, I will be forever grateful he brought you into my life."

Her mouth opened, and then closed again when she could think of nothing to say. She made small, soothing motions with her thumb on the back of his hand, and laid her head briefly against his shoulder, closing her eyes to better absorb his words.

A loud, cheerful greeting interrupted her racketing thoughts and she straightened, wiping her eyes to make sure the tears that threatened wouldn't fall. Dave stood at the doorway chatting with their server, and then headed in their direction.

"Hello, again," he said, taking one of the free seats across the table from Leeza and Gavin. "Have you ordered?"

Studying the menu and listening to Dave's suggestions gave Leeza a chance to recover her composure. Pushing Gavin's revelations to the back of her mind, she waited until the server had brought their drinks—craft beers all around, on the belief that when in a brew pub, only a brew would do—then leaned forward, elbows on the table.

"So, what did you find? What can you tell us?"

Dave sipped his beer and smacked his lips approvingly. "Your story fascinated me. It seems impossible that your young man doesn't show up somewhere. We've come to think that everything's online, and available at the click of a button or the tap of a screen." He sipped again, and Leeza had the rude urge to grab his mug and not give it back until he'd spit out his story.

"Anyway, I had some time after work yesterday, so I made a stop at the cenotaph. It's easy to forget that the names etched there were men, just like me." He twisted his glass between his fingers thoughtfully. "Many of them died much younger than I am now. I just wanted to hang out there for a bit, reflect, you know." He seemed embarrassed by the admission. "That's when I saw it."

"Saw what?" Leeza asked, bewildered.

"His name. Right there, engraved in the granite."

CHAPTER TWENTY-THREE

November 30th, 1943
Training, training. will it ever end? Why won't
they bring us on the front already? We're as
ready as we'll ever be, I just want to get this
over with!

"I can't believe it," Leeza said.

"I know," Gavin said patiently, agreeing yet again to the statement she couldn't stop repeating.

They stood before the cenotaph, staring at the stark letters. *William Henry Smith.*

They'd finished their meal, though Leeza couldn't remember what she'd eaten. Then, following Dave's simple directions, they had walked to the memorial, which stood proudly in the civic square a little further down Prince Street.

Surrounded by a circle of stone inset with grass in each quadrant, a lone soldier stood atop the massive plinth. His head was bowed sorrowfully over his hands, which were crossed on the butt of his rifle resting muzzle down at his feet. Red brick steps from all points of the compass led up to the monument to allow mourners and visitors to approach near enough to read the names.

"I knew we probably weren't going to find him alive," she said, tracing the letters with her gloved finger. "But I had hoped he'd made it home."

"We knew he was wounded. It was the last thing he wrote in his diary."

"They were sending him home. He just wanted to go home." The tears she could no longer hold back began to fall, trailing icily down her cheeks. "He wasn't even as old as Drew." She choked back a sob, and Gavin cradled her to his chest.

"I know this is silly," she said, voice muffled, her face pressed into the slippery material of his jacket. "It's not like I knew him."

"You *feel* like you knew him, though. I do, too. He comes across so vibrantly in the journal, even though there are so few entries over the span of three years."

She drew comfort from the fact that Gavin understood. She stole a few more moments in his embrace, and then pulled away and wiped her cheeks. "Now what?" she asked, somewhat dolefully.

"Now we find his family," Gavin said without hesitation. "That's what you wanted to do all along, right? Our search isn't over. Not by a long shot."

Before leaving Prince George, Leeza had set up an appointment with John at the North Nova Scotia Highlanders Regimental Museum in Amherst for Saturday morning. With the genealogical archivist at the Colchester Historeum out sick, there wasn't much they could accomplish during the remainder of this day. Leeza chafed at the delay, but Gavin was philosophical.

"It gives us time to explore," he said. "Who knows when we might next be in this area?"

The *we* in that sentence sent a shiver of

something—panic? delight?—over Leeza's skin.

They headed west out of Truro, crossing the Shubenacadie River near South Maitland, and then following the silty, rusty water north before sweeping west again. The highway wound through tiny settlements with names like Densmores Mills, Moose Brook, and Tennycape, and random vistas revealed stunning views of Minas Basin. They stopped at Burntcoat Head Park and Walton Lighthouse to stretch their legs, but the weather was not conducive to sightseeing, so only left the warm confines of the car briefly. Gavin seemed satisfied with letting the engine purr with graceful power around the twists and turns, and his effortless control lulled Leeza into sleepy contentment.

In the town of Windsor—the Birthplace of Hockey, according to the bold sign at the city limits—they had dinner in a small restaurant housed in a bow-fronted red brick building, and then returned to Truro along a much more direct, but less scenic, route. It was well after nine o'clock when they pulled into the hotel parking lot and climbed the stairs to their rooms.

Outside her door, Leeza paused, the ease and peacefulness of the day replaced with awkwardness and uncertainty. Would Gavin come in? Did he want to stay with her again? Or would he choose to be alone tonight?

Her questions were answered when he dropped a quick kiss on her mouth and without a word entered his own room. Flummoxed, she stared after him, before turning with a huff and unlocking her door.

"Fine," she muttered. "It's not like I *want* you to come in. Some time by myself would be good. I didn't get much rest last night." The reason for her lack of sleep brought a flush to her throat. She tossed off her coat, hat, and gloves and flopped onto the bed, lying spread-eagled with her booted feet dangling off the side. She'd barely started to enjoy her sulk when a soft rap had her bolting to the door.

Gavin stood on the other side, a toiletry bag in one hand and a change of clothes draped over his arm. Something in her expression had him raising his eyebrows. "What?"

"Nothing," she said, joy suffusing her being so she felt like she might float. "Come on in."

The visit to the Regimental Museum the next morning was a bust. John—while just as delightful and charming in real life as he was via email and phone—had no news for them. After explaining his researches and commiserating with them on the lack of results, he showed them proudly around the displays, and then waved them on their way back to Truro.

At the Colchester Historeum, Genevieve Johnson, the archivist, was in. Leeza waited with Gavin at the reception desk in the vague expectation of a white-haired woman with a stooped back and mismatched clothing to appear.

Instead, they were greeted by a woman of no more than thirty, with a brightly coloured headscarf framing her russet-brown face and dark eyes behind glasses molded from vibrant green plastic. She introduced herself, holding out her hand gingerly, her torso slightly hunched to the left.

"We were told you weren't well," Leeza said, eyeing her with concern. "I don't mean to be rude, but should you be in today?"

"Just a little stomach issue," she said. "Nothing contagious, and something I've managed before." With an effort she straightened her posture and smiled. "I understand you've come a long way to look at our records. My colleague, the one you spoke to yesterday, gave me a rundown on what—or rather, who—you are looking for, so I have some ideas on where to go next, but maybe you can tell me yourself, to make sure nothing was lost in the translation."

Gavin delivered the short form of their quest, which, Leeza reflected, he was getting quite adept at. He ended with, "We only learned of your archives after we arrived in Truro or we would have called ahead. Since we've struck out everywhere else, we had to give you a try."

Genevieve led them to the second floor of the museum and into a large room with rows and rows of shelves, cubicles with microfilm machines, and long tables, all but one bare and empty. Pointing to the table stacked with numerous cardboard boxes of the type used for storing documents, she indicated they should take a seat. She remained standing and with only a slight wince, pulled one box toward her.

"I can understand why you've been focused on finding William through military records," she said, lifting the lid and revealing a low stack of thin books wrapped in what looked like tissue paper. "But since that hasn't revealed anything, I thought we'd go the other way. Given that you say he clearly states he is twenty-one years old in 1941, I've pulled the school registers for Colchester and Cumberland Counties for 1925 to 1930. Men from those counties made up a good portion of the North Nova Scotia Highlanders in World War Two, and since we have those records on site it makes a logical place to start. Also, boys tended to leave school early in those days, so I thought we should focus on what would be his primary years."

Leeza stared at the tower of boxes. "How will we ever find him in all of that?" she asked in dismay.

"We won't know until we try," Genevieve said cheerfully. She handed out white cotton gloves, and then distributed the books, instructing Leeza and

Gavin on how to handle them after they were removed from their acid-free paper protection, and admonishing them to keep the books in order.

"Think of it as a treasure hunt," she said, taking a chair across from Gavin and smiling with what Leeza considered slightly sadistic glee. "A search like this is why I became an archivist."

The next two hours were filled with the quiet shushing of pages turning, murmured hopeful exclamations, and dispirited groans. Leeza's eyes ached from trying to decipher cramped copperplate handwriting and her nose itched with the dust of old paper. They'd gone through three boxes with no luck. She replaced the register she'd just finished studying back in its protective sheath and leaned back with a sigh.

"I need to give my eyes a break," she said. "I'm afraid I'm going to skim right past William if I get too tired."

Genevieve glanced at the clock hanging over the door leading to the main museum space. "We only have a couple more hours until the Historeum closes," she said. "Would you like some coffee?"

"That would be great," Gavin said, stretching his arms above his head. "Can I help?"

"No, that's fine. I'll be right back." She disappeared out the door, moving stiffly but not visibly worse than before.

"We're never going to find him," Leeza said miserably. "This is the proverbial needle in a haystack."

Gavin's finger tapped thoughtfully on the table. "It wouldn't feel quite so hopeless if we knew for certain he attended school at all. Even if we could narrow it down to a year or two..."

"He writes that his father died about five years before he left for England, right?" Leeza might not have memorized the diary as Gavin appeared to have done, but she remembered that.

"And he had younger siblings," Gavin said. "If he became the main breadwinner for the family, he would have had to quit school. He would have been sixteen or so." He sighed. "If he was even still going at that age."

Out of nowhere, a thought bolted into Leeza's brain. "His *brother* was still in school," she said, staring at Gavin. "He writes that his brother was doing well in school, and hoped he'd never see him as a soldier."

Gavin stared back, and she saw the instant he understood her meaning. "If we can't narrow down William, we can narrow down his brother." He pulled out his phone and started tapping. "Here it is. His brother David was seventeen in December 1941, and still in school."

"That box won't be here." Leeza scanned the labels anyway, just in case. "Genevieve said she'd pulled the ones from 1925 to 1930. What if she doesn't have 1941?"

"She will," Gavin said fervently. "Here she comes."

Coffee was forgotten in the excitement. Genevieve rushed to a desk phone nearby and made a quick call. "Stanley's bringing them up," she said breathlessly. "It'll just be a minute."

In more than a minute but not too much longer, Stanley appeared with three boxes loaded on a dolly. He was scrawny and missing a tooth and the waistband of his pants was hiked perilously near his armpits, yet Leeza could have kissed him. He removed the boxes they'd already scoured and left the new ones on the table, and then rolled away, whistling.

"Letters could take some time to get from Canada to the soldiers overseas," Genevieve said, "but I think we can safely assume that David must have been in school that fall." As before, she opened a box and handed out books. "September 1941," she said. "Let's go."

CHAPTER TWENTY-FOUR

January 11th, 1944
I guess I'm not the only one wondering when
we're going. There are posters everywhere now
telling us to keep our mouths shut. There's one
poster which I find particularly funny 'Loose
lips, sink ships'. Who comes up with that? I
should have gone into that business, I could
have come up with some much more original
ones than that!

Leeza began the new hunt with renewed enthusiasm. This *had* to be the break they needed. Finally, they had something solid to search for.

An hour later, her energy—and hope—was flagging once again.

Every book in the many boxes was the register for one school. They might have ten names listed. They might have hundreds. Since they had no idea where William's family had lived, they couldn't afford to ignore any of them. Some record keepers had been more meticulous than others, providing alphabetical lists with the registers. Others filled in chronologically as the children were registered and had to be scoured line by line.

And there was still no guarantee they were looking at the registers from the right counties.

Wearily she reached for another book.

Head bent over the register she was studying, Genevieve asked absently, "Did your William have siblings other than David?"

Gavin paused in his scrutiny, took off his glasses and rubbed his eyes. "He mentioned a sister. Maureen."

"She was quite a bit younger than him and his brother?"

Her tone was half statement, half question. Leeza's spine stiffened. "Yes. William writes she lost her front teeth after he left home."

Genevieve looked up, grinning widely. "I found them."

Leeza and Gavin turned as one to stare at each other, and then scrambled out of their seats and raced around opposite ends of the table to peer over Genevieve's shoulders.

"Here." She pointed with her white-gloved finger, tracing the line as she spoke. "Smith, David. Registered September 2, 1941. Date of birth, June 15, 1924. Parent or Guardian, Elizabeth Smith. And here, right below...Maureen Smith, date of birth, October 2, 1934."

Leeza's knees trembled and she clenched her hand tightly on the back of Genevieve's chair for support. "I can't read the address. Can anyone read the address?"

Genevieve leaned forward, and so did Leeza and Gavin as if connected to her with invisible twine. "It's not legible," she said, "but I don't think that matters." Placing a piece of paper at the page with Maureen and David's names, she closed the book and opened it again to the inside front cover.

There, in neat block lettering, as clear as day, was written *TATAMAGOUCHE SCHOOLHOUSE*.

Leeza rolled the unfamiliar, slightly fantastical looking word out, rhyming it with *ouch*. "Tahtah-mah-gouch?"

"Tahtah-mah-*goosh*. It's a French corruption of a Mi'kmaq word," she said, naming a First Nation often associated with Nova Scotia. "The village has a rather interesting history, actually. Acadians settled there but were burned out during the French and Indian Wars. It was revived with the arrival of Protestant settlers and became a thriving ship-building community. In the late 1880s, the railroad serving the farms and salt-mines in the area went through the village."

"William's father worked with trains," Gavin interrupted. "That's how he was killed—he was hit by one."

Leeza's heart lifted with this further confirmation—albeit circumstantial—that they'd found the right family. "What do we do now?" she asked anxiously. "How do we find out more?"

"We only have about forty minutes before the museum closes," Genevieve said with regret. She shifted in her chair and a spasm of pain creased her forehead. "Also, I think I might have done enough for today. I'm so sorry."

"You've been amazing," Leeza said contritely. "We should feel guilty for allowing you to work so long when you're obviously feeling unwell."

"I wouldn't have missed this for the world," Genevieve replied. "And there's no way you'll pry me away from it now. The museum is closed tomorrow, but I'll come in and do more digging for you. Now that we've got a location, I can check cemetery records and village minutes and a few other places for you."

"Is there anything we can do to help?" Gavin asked.

"To be honest, it will probably be faster if I do it

on my own. Leave me your number and an email address and I'll forward on what I find as soon as I can. I'm sure I'll be able to discover more for you."

After the three of them had exchanged contact information, Gavin asked for and was given permission to take a photo of the relevant page in the school register as Leeza offered effusive, heartfelt thanks. They left Genevieve and Stanley reordering the boxes before they were returned to their climate-controlled tomb in the basement and headed down the stairs. At the main desk, Gavin paid the research fee—which seemed remarkably reasonable for the breakthrough Genevieve had achieved—even though Leeza protested it should be her responsibility. When he simply shrugged and handed over his credit card to the clerk, Leeza offered her own as well and gave not-to-be-ignored instructions that any further charges were to be made to her account. Since Genevieve had promised to keep digging it only seem prudent.

They were so close!

After a celebratory meal at The Nook and Cranny, Leeza was enjoying a pleasant buzz from her third glass of wine. The last few days had taken on a dreamlike glow. After the stretched-out stress of January and closing Millar's, this complete disconnect from her regular life was both welcome and surreal. She almost dreaded their return on Monday. Scott had been remarkably quiet since New Year's Eve, but she was certain he hadn't given up his campaign to sell the cabin, and Drew's self-imposed window in which to make a decision was drawing to a close.

For now, though, she would choose to live in the moment.

In silence, she and Gavin waited for the elevator

to take them to their floor. He had his arm loosely about her waist and she gave into the temptation to lean her head against his shoulder. His hold tightened, but then the elevator opened, and they had to separate to step into the car.

Nothing was more natural than Gavin following her into her room and locking the door behind him. She turned to face him. The room stayed in motion even when she stopped, and she giggled.

"If you're not going to use your room, we should cancel it." She stepped forward and laid her hand on his chest. He'd shed his jacket but the soft sweater under her fingers was layered on top of his usual crisp button-down.

"It's fine. We're only here a couple more nights anyway."

A niggle of concern—was he keeping his room just in case he needed space?—tried to worm its way through her happy glow, but she stomped on it firmly. Tugging at the hem of his sweater, she lifted it up his chest, and he obediently raised his arms so she could strip it off.

"I can't believe we found his family," she said, returning to the discussion that had occupied them most of the evening. Concentrating on the buttons of his shirt, she continued. "David and Maureen might even be alive. We could meet them!"

Gavin remained silent, hissing in a breath when she slid her palms up his abdomen. "I like your chest hair," she said, following her statement by nuzzling his breastbone. "Not too much, not too little."

His hands gripped her upper arms but otherwise he stood stock still as she used her lips and teeth to explore him. She could feel the rapid tattoo of his heart under his skin and smiled at her ability to make this quiet, self-contained man wild and reckless. He clung to his control for now, but she was learning exactly what to do to make him lose himself.

With deliberate intent, she kept the conversation completely at odds to her actions. "I wonder how soon Genevieve will get in touch. Do you think she might find them before we have to leave?" She licked his collarbone and dropped her hands to his belt, undoing the buckle. "If she does, do you think we'll have a chance to visit them?"

Her hand slipped inside his boxers. The leash of his restraint snapped, and his hands vised her biceps as he bruised her mouth with a hard, demanding kiss that melted her knees. "No more talking," he said against her lips as he walked her backward to the bed, "unless it's to tell me where you want me to touch you. Where you want me to kiss you."

More than delighted to follow his instructions, she hugged him and let herself drop onto the mattress, pulling him with her. "Kiss me, Gavin," she whispered. "Kiss me anywhere you like."

Leeza woke to the heavenly scent of coffee brewing. She rolled to her back and stretched her arms over her head, the sheets brushing against her bare skin. Gavin stood, clad only in his boxers, beside the tiny single-serve coffeemaker, staring at it with brows lowered grumpily.

"You can have the first cup," Leeza said. "I think you need it more than me."

He looked over his shoulder and his expression lightened. "Morning. Did I look cranky? I was just thinking."

"About what?" She pushed herself into a sitting position, plumped a pillow behind her and leaned back, tucking the thin duvet under her arms. She rarely slept naked but the last few nights, with Gavin in her bed, had done so without a second thought.

Either ignoring or forgetting she'd told him to take the first cup, he brought her the heavy white mug and refilled the coffeemaker with another serving of water. As it hissed and steamed, he said, "Nothing important. Just morning thoughts."

Not confident enough to prod any further, Leeza let it go. But the memory of his expression nagged at her as they prepared for the day and had a light breakfast at the hotel's restaurant. She chattered cheerfully about inconsequential subjects and he responded easily. It seemed, though, that he wasn't quite present, that his mind was preoccupied with something he didn't want to share.

Which is his prerogative, she reminded herself. *He doesn't have to tell me anything if he doesn't want to.* It was just that she *wanted* him to share his thoughts. Their relationship was in danger of feeling lop-sided, with Gavin providing all the support and Leeza taking without giving anything of substance back.

While there was still a bite in the air, the weather had turned bright and sunny. After hours spent combing through dusty archives the day before, exploring out of doors seemed the best way to clear the cobwebs. They inquired about local walking trails at the front desk and were directed to Victoria Park. As they rambled the wooden boardwalks and dirt paths winding along Lepper Brook, Leeza tried to throw off her uneasiness. Gavin took her hand and kept it in his as they strolled along, and she started to relax.

They had just reached Waddell Falls, the destination suggested by the desk clerk, when his phone rang.

"Is it Genevieve?" she asked eagerly. It seemed too early for the archivist to have made any new discoveries—it wasn't yet lunchtime—but maybe...

"It's her." Gavin stared at Leeza as the phone rang again.

"Answer it, then!" Leeza exclaimed, waving her

hands urgently.

"Gavin here," he said, never taking his eyes from Leeza. Moments later, his expression fell, and he shook his head. Leeza's heart thumped with disappointment.

"I'm sorry to hear that," he said. "Yes, of course we understand. Thanks for letting us know. I hope she feels better soon."

Leeza frowned. If he was talking to Genevieve, who was sick?

"No, really, there's nothing to apologize for. Tell Genevieve we look forward to hearing from her when she's recovered. Thanks again."

"That wasn't Genevieve?" Leeza asked, now thoroughly confused.

"No. That was her roommate, using her phone. Genevieve had a bad turn in the night, so he convinced her to go to Emergency. Turns out she has kidney stones."

"Ouch." Leeza winced in sympathy.

Gavin nodded. "Yes. Very painful, from what I hear. She's been sent home but will be taking it easy for a while." They started walking again, continuing their roundabout route back to the car. "She asked him to call so we wouldn't spend all day waiting to hear from her. He says she'll be in touch when she has news."

"I guess that's the end of our research trip, then." Knowing she'd been unable to keep the frustration from her tone, she hurried to add, "Not that I blame her, of course. It's completely understandable."

"We'll just have to be patient a little longer." Gavin checked the time on his phone before slipping it back into his pocket. "We don't want to interrupt Grant's lunch, so I say we head back to the car and find a new place to eat before we head over to Vimy Court. Then we can spend the afternoon with Grant.

Maybe he knows something about the Smith's of Tatamagouche." He smiled at Leeza with no hint of his earlier reserve. "And if not, I bet he has other great stories. He never did tell us how he lost his leg."

But when they arrived at Vimy Court that afternoon and asked to visit Grant, they were greeted by a sombre Peter.

"I'm sorry," he said. "Mr. Howard passed away yesterday."

CHAPTER TWENTY-FIVE

February 5th, 1944
Lt. Ross is dead, a grenade exploded into his
hands. This is pathetic, how can guys be dying
on training? What is going to be written in the
telegram they send home? What a waste of life.
Guys have started dying by accident and it feels
really horrible. I can't imagine how it'll be like
when we're fighting for real.

"He had lunch as he usually did," Peter told them.
"After, I saw him settled in his chair in his room. His
door was open, as he liked it, and no one passing by
noticed anything different until it was time for
dinner. That's when we realized he'd gone."

Leeza and Gavin were seated on one of the sofas
in the front lobby area. Peter perched on an ottoman
in front of them, his hands clasped between his
knees. He'd offered them coffee or tea, but Leeza had
been too shocked to accept.

"It sounds very peaceful," Gavin said. "Perhaps
a little lonely, but he struck me as an independent
soul, so perhaps he didn't mind."

"He had been looking forward to seeing you
today," Peter said. "Your missing soldier was all he

talked about after you left."

"We were looking forward to seeing him, too," Leeza said. "We had news we wanted to share."

"About your soldier?" At her nod, he continued. "Mr. Howard told me a little about who you were looking for. He's probably in Heaven right now, talking with your missing man, telling him all about your search, letting him know he hasn't been forgotten."

The thought brought Leeza comfort, wrapping around her shoulders like a warm blanket. "I hope so."

A silence settled over them, broken only by the muted mutter of a television in a room down the hall and the whirring of the heating system. The cushion beneath her was hard and unyielding, the back of the sofa upright and uncomfortable.

"Can we go to his room?" Leeza said. "It hasn't been packed away yet, has it?"

Peter shook his head. "No, not yet. Mr. Howard's family was here yesterday, but we try not to rush these things. There will be time enough after the funeral. Do you remember the way?"

"Yes." She stood, and the two men followed suit. Peter returned to his post behind the reception desk, telling them to take all the time they needed, and she and Gavin continued down the hall.

She wasn't sure what she was expecting to see in the small room where Grant Howard had lived his last years. Despite the photos on the walls and dresser and the colourful quilt on the bed, the room already felt empty, abandoned. The plaid blanket she'd last seen draped over his lap was folded neatly on the arm of his recliner, which was still placed in such a way he could look out the window.

Gavin picked up the frame that stood in lone splendour on the nightstand near the bed. Leeza approached and studied the black and white photo with him. The young man wore a black suit, a boutonniere on his lapel. He held his bride in his arms as they danced what she imagined was their first dance as a married couple. They faced the camera, her curly dark hair brushing his chin, her white gown shiny and stiff with newness.

"They look happy," Gavin said, his fingers brushing the glass. "I wonder what their life was like."

Leeza moved to the photos on the wall. "This must be Grant's son," she said, pointing at a more modern wedding photo. "He looks just like him."

For a few minutes they perused the photos, the still images giving them a glimpse of a life that appeared happy and well-lived. When they took their leave, Peter was still at the reception desk. They thanked him and were halfway out the door when Gavin stopped and turned back.

"Do you know how Grant lost his leg?" he asked. "He mentioned it when we were here before, in a way that made it sound like it might be a good story. I was going to ask him about it today."

Peter gave a theatrical shudder. "It was one of his favourites, although I never could understand why. He lost it in the war. So many others would have been devastated at the loss of a limb. Not Mr. Howard. Said he was always thankful that he'd been injured enough to be sent home, but not enough to ruin his life."

"Was he shot?" Leeza asked.

"No," Peter said. "He stepped on a German mine the day after Normandy."

Leeza couldn't help feeling deflated as they left Vimy Court. Grant Howard's death had shaken her more than she would expect after such a casual acquaintance. That, combined with the unavoidable—but definitely excusable—delay from Genevieve, seemed to override the successes they'd had in Truro.

"You okay?" Gavin asked as he pulled out of the parking lot onto Vimy Road.

"Yes." She mustered a smile. "I don't know why it's bothering me so much. It wasn't as if it was unexpected. And he had a good life."

"He was a connection to your grandfather. I imagine that has something to do with it."

"I hadn't thought of it that way." She mulled it over as the car hummed along the pavement past homes and businesses that were beginning to have a familiar feel. "You know, I think you're right. I know so little of that era in his life. It was almost like having him back for a while."

"You were close?" Gavin slowed to a smooth stop at the intersection where they usually turned left to return to the centre of Truro. This time, he turned right. When Leeza raised an inquiring eyebrow, he shrugged. "I thought we'd go for another drive. No use just heading back to the hotel."

She leaned her head against the rest and relaxed, more than willing to let him go wherever he wanted while she worked through her thoughts. "I guess we were as close as most grandparents and children are. Those lucky enough to have each other, at least," she said. "As a child I spent quite a bit of time with him and my grandmother. My mom's parents had passed away before I was old enough to remember them, so they were the only ones I had. For a long time, though, as a teenager and through much of my marriage, we were just superficially close—birthdays, Christmas, Easter, that sort of thing. Fifteen years ago, after my grandmother died and Grandpa moved out of their big house, I started spending more time with him, bringing Drew along as often as I could. I wanted to give them the chance to know each other better."

"It's a special bond, grandparents and grandchildren. Great-grandparents perhaps even more so, for being less common."

"Are you close with Emmelyn?"

Gavin didn't answer, concentrating on a loaded logging truck making a left-hand turn in front of them. On Leeza's right, well-kept houses lined the road, and on the left a huge log yard sprawled. Once they were on their way again, he said, "I do my best. She's not much more than a baby yet. I admit, though, it's a ticklish situation. Nolan and Amrita trust me with her, but there's a hint of reservation, I think."

She studied his profile. His hair curled slightly behind his ear, and she had the sudden urge to kiss him there. Looking away to quell the impulse, she asked, "Because you're a man? And men can't be nurturing?"

"Something like that. They don't mean to be insulting, and I try not to take it that way. To be fair, I didn't have a lot to do with my children when they were—"

"Did you see that?" Leeza interrupted. "Sorry, but that sign we just passed pointed to Tatamagouche. Do you think we have time to drive there?"

Gavin pulled to the shoulder and fiddled with the navigation system. "It's less than an hour away," he said. "Want to go?"

"Do you mind?"

"Of course not."

He pulled back on the road and less than one hundred metres later made a right-hand turn. Wide expanses of fields lying fallow under the winter chill surrounded them, interspersed by solitary farmhouses.

"Only forty-eight clicks," Leeza said as they

passed a kilometre marker. "I never dreamed it was so close to Truro. Genevieve didn't mention anything. I'm so glad we came this way. Sorry I interrupted you before. You were saying you didn't spend much time with Sarah and Nolan when they were young?" She found that hard to believe. The night Leeza had had dinner with his family, he'd interacted with Emmelyn with such love and care she *knew* he'd been the same with his children.

"Nancy had trained as a nurse, but when the kids came along, she decided to stay at home. I was all for it, but that did mean we only had one income. So, I worked. A lot. I loved what I did, which made it easy to spend that extra hour or two at the office. Or a Saturday morning or Sunday afternoon." They passed through a small grouping of houses with open, unfenced yards, and then under two bridges that carried the Trans-Canada Highway, with its speeding cars and trucks, overhead. "Anyway, Nolan's main frame of reference of me as a parent is driving him to hockey on the weekends and the odd movie night I dragged him to when he was a teenager."

"I have difficulty imagining you as a disconnected dad."

"It's not that I wasn't involved. I was just less involved than Nancy." He glanced at her. "I was a workaholic, Leeza, in the old-fashioned sense of the word. Even when Nancy got sick, I didn't quit. In fact, I might have worked even more. It was something I could control, unlike her disease or the treatment for it."

"You were caring for your family the best way you knew how."

"That's a forgiving way to look at it, but not the truth. I was avoiding reality. It never crossed my mind, not until a few weeks before she died, that Nancy wouldn't recover. Sure, people died from cancer every day. But not *Nancy*. Not my wife. She was a fighter, and she wouldn't give up. It was something I knew in my bones." His knuckles were white on the steering wheel and he let out a shaky breath. "I was wrong, of course."

Leeza had no reply to that. She wondered how she'd react in the same situation. As a firm believer in the power of positive thinking, she could understand how refusing to give in might seem the best way to treat the situation. But how did you balance that with reality? How did you know when to start accepting there were things you couldn't change, no matter how hard you prayed?

They traveled in silence for a while, the atmosphere in the car strained and ill at ease. Not because she condemned him—not at all. In fact, she hurt for him, for the pain he'd suffered. No, it was Gavin who seemed tense and unhappy, as if he still had more to tell but couldn't find the right words.

When he remained quiet, she tentatively said, "You don't blame yourself, do you? For Nancy's death? What could you have done?"

The road swept around a curve and a cemetery came into view, despite no sign of a nearby church. Gavin pulled onto a long gravel road that disappeared past the widely spaced markers into a grove of trees and parked.

His hands gripping the wheel, he stared through the windshield. "I could have been there for her," he said quietly. "I could have held her hand more often, told her jokes to take her mind off the chemicals they were pouring into her bloodstream. I could have *been* there for her. Loved her better."

Pain coloured his words, but more than that, guilt and a despairing acceptance. He didn't expect to be excused for his actions, Leeza realized. He'd given up hope of that. It was his punishment for what he saw as a terrible failure. She unclicked her seatbelt and tucked her left leg under her so she could face him more fully in the confined space of the car.

"You said once that Millar's saved you," she said slowly. "That you used the job to pull yourself out of your grief for Nancy."

He twitched his head in her direction, a motion of assent so small she almost missed it.

"If you needed something to distract you, to help you move on"—she paused, gathering her thoughts, and then asked the question she'd been wondering about for weeks—"why didn't you stay at your financial firm? You said you loved your work. Why quit a career you'd built up for decades for a minimum wage job at a bookstore?"

His hands dropped to his lap and she gave into the urge to touch him, gathering his right hand in both of hers. "I suppose I was punishing myself." He reached over and his free hand joined the warm, comforting tangle of fingers. "My job had kept me from Nancy when she needed me most. I didn't deserve to have it." One corner of his mouth quirked. "Ridiculous, I know. But I wasn't thinking straight at the time."

She leaned forward and kissed him gently on the lips. A quiet spark of desire flared, and she let it seep into the caress.

Pulling back, she stared into his eyes and spoke firmly. "The past can't be changed. Cliché, I know, but true. Our choices are the path we build for ourselves. And your path led you here. To me." She kissed him again and his hands clenched on hers. "The day you walked into Millar's and applied for a job was one of the best days of my life. I just didn't know it at the time."

He leaned his forehead against hers and she closed her eyes, breathing in his scent. "Mine, too," he said quietly. "Mine, too."

CHAPTER TWENTY-SIX

March 15th, 1944
Exercises seem to be dying down. There have
been lots of important guys coming to inspect
us and give us these good speeches. I don't want
to assume but I think we're going soon...

Mid-morning on Tuesday, the plane touched down at the Prince George airport, bouncing lightly before the pilot engaged the braking system, causing everyone to lean forward in their seats. Outside the window, winter was in full force. Blowing snow and high winds yesterday had delayed their return, necessitating an unexpected night's stay in Vancouver after the flight from Halifax.

"Have you ever noticed how the air seems different when you come home, especially after a flight?" Leeza asked Gavin as they waited for the plane to taxi to the terminal. "We didn't even leave the country, but there's just something that says *home* even before I get off the plane."

"I know what you mean." The seatbelt sign dinged off, but he remained seated. All around them people began the hurry-up-and-wait ritual of deplaning—unbuckling and retrieving overhead luggage in a rush, and then standing impatiently while the attendants prepared for their exit.

"We were gone less than a week, but it feels so much longer," she said, stretching down to snag her satchel from under the seat in front of her.

"Is that a good thing?" Gavin asked.

"I think so." What *was* good was what they'd learned about William Henry Smith. But if she were honest, she was anxious about her new relationship with Gavin. She didn't want to dismiss it as a holiday fling, but real life was dealing with Scott and no job and Gavin's slightly-less-than-welcoming family. Their extra night in Vancouver had felt like a reprieve, and she'd made love with Gavin with an odd sense of finality, as if it was an ending, not a beginning. She didn't think he'd noticed anything different, but she had woken this morning wrapped in his embrace, which was unusual, given their shared preference for sleeping space.

They'd planned on taking a taxi into town, but when they entered the Arrivals area Gavin was greeted by a shrill, excited voice. "Papa! Papa!"

Releasing the handle of his carry on, he bent down and scooped up Emmelyn, swinging her in a circle. "What are you doing here?" he said. She chattered something that Leeza couldn't understand and pointed toward Nolan and Amrita, standing out of the flow of passengers.

She followed Gavin and stood on the fringe of the small family knot.

"She's been asking for you for days," Nolan was saying. "Since neither of us have classes or office hours this morning, we thought we'd come pick you up." Leeza recalled that both Scott and Amrita were working toward their doctorates at the University of Northern British Columbia while teaching undergraduate courses. She couldn't remember their areas of study—she should probably ask Gavin again before she made a fool of herself.

"What a lovely surprise." Gavin rubbed his chin against Emmelyn's silky black hair and the child giggled. "I missed you, too."

Amrita turned to Leeza. "Was your trip successful? I hope you didn't spend the whole time researching and had some fun, too."

To her horror, a wave of heat raced along Leeza's jaw and throat. Gavin gave her a cheeky grin and wrapped his free arm around her shoulders. She wriggled, hoping he'd take a subtle hint about his public display of affection, but his hold only tightened. Amrita appeared unfazed, but Nolan's eyebrows rose.

Seeking to distract them, she babbled, "It was quite successful, thanks. We think we might have found William's younger brother and sister. And we met a man who knew my grandfather. Unfortunately, he passed away shortly after we visited him, so we only talked with him once."

"We'll tell you all about it in the car," Gavin said. "We only have these"—he indicated the luggage they carried with a jerk of his chin—"so we're ready to go."

Amrita plucked Emmelyn from his arms, saying something in rapid Hindi that stopped the little girl from protesting. Nolan, however, continued to regard Leeza with a speculative look, and her spine stiffened. Heat again suffused her face and she cursed herself. There was nothing to be embarrassed about. She and Gavin were adults, unencumbered by other partners. It was none of Nolan's business what they had done while in Nova Scotia.

So why did she feel like a teenager coming home after curfew?

Nothing overt happened on the ride from the

airport, but Leeza was uneasy just the same. She sat in the back seat and more than once caught Nolan's searching gaze upon her in the rear-view mirror. Watching. Waiting.

Gavin walked her to her door despite her protests, and she dodged his goodbye kiss so it landed on her cheek. That earned her a searing glance from him, which made a change from those she'd been getting from his son.

"I'll call you later," he said, amusement tinting his voice. "If you hear anything from Genevieve, let me know, no matter what the time."

"I will." With a fair bit of relief, she closed and locked the door behind her, the sense of homecoming she'd mentioned to Gavin slightly tarnished by Nolan's reaction. And, if she was honest, by a faint whiff of loneliness. She and Gavin had spent almost every moment together since leaving Prince George, and the loss of his presence was palpable.

Needing to hear a friendly voice, she checked the time, did the conversion in her head, and decided to try Drew on Skype. Tossing her carry on at the foot of the stairs, she curled into her corner of the couch and started the call.

The sight of his face when he answered made her heart swell, his welcoming smile making everything right in her world. "Hey," she said. "Is this an okay time?"

"Of course it's okay. I want to hear all about your trip. What did you find out? How was Gavin?"

She was pretty sure he didn't want to hear about her love life, so she said, "Gavin is a great guy to travel with. You should have seen the car he rented. I'll text you a photo."

"Fancy?"

"In a low key, very expensive kind of way. But the best news is, we found out more about William."

She recounted their discoveries while Drew made appropriate noises. "Now we have to wait for Genevieve to see if she can find anything more. Hopefully, she feels better soon." As it was the polite thing to do, she asked, "How's Danica?"

Drew took the change of subject eagerly. "She's great. I know I've only known her a couple of months, but it"—he paused, his gaze unfocused, and then continued—"it feels right, you know? We just click."

Hearing her son admit, even if obliquely, to falling in love was a shock. He'd had girlfriends before, but Leeza had never had the sense that any of them were *the one*. This sounded serious, and she wasn't sure how she felt about it.

That was a lie. She knew how she felt about it. Scared and anxious, hopeful and trusting. He was a grown man, after all. She wondered if she'd ever have to stop reminding herself of that.

"I'm glad you're happy," she said truthfully, and then added, also truthfully, "although I wish you'd found someone closer to home."

Drew laughed. "The world is a small place, Mom, and getting smaller every day. Besides, it's still too early to worry about *that* yet. We should set up a time for the three of us to talk. So you can get to know her better." Leeza had 'met' Danica over Skype, but only a quick hello. "Changing the subject, have you spoken to Dad lately?"

"I have a message from him on my phone, but I haven't called him back yet." She'd seen the voice mail waiting for her when she'd turned her phone back on after landing in Prince George but had delayed listening to it. Drew's question made her palms itch with premonition. She knew instinctively he had made his decision about the cabin, which would be why Scott wanted to talk to her, to try and browbeat her again into listing the property, no matter what their son wanted.

"I gave him my agreement to sell."

Her heart punched her throat and she sucked in a gasp of air. "What?" She'd been so certain Drew would side with her, wouldn't give his permission. "Why?"

"As much as I love that place, I just don't see myself there in the future. Someone else should get to enjoy it."

She scrambled to adjust to his announcement. "Maybe you need to think about it longer."

"I have thought about it, Mom." Drew's voice was gentle, and for an instant she felt as if their roles had switched, that he was the parent giving unwelcome news and she the child being forced to accept it. "I didn't make this decision lightly. I know you're disappointed."

"Not in you," she said quickly. "Never in you."

"You still don't have to sell if you don't want to."

"I know." But she didn't really have an excuse not to, since Drew had decided to let it go. If she stood in Scott's way now, she'd just look vindictive and revengeful.

"I'm sorry."

"You don't have to apologize. It's fine. Your dad and I will work it out between us."

After disconnecting with a promise to get in touch again in a few days, Leeza sat and stared into nothingness. She should call Scott, get it over with, but she didn't have the mental resources to handle him at the moment. *He'll just have to wait until tomorrow,* she thought with defiance. *Another day won't hurt him.*

Her phone rang just as she tossed a load of laundry into the washing machine, the piano arpeggio notification echoing from the kitchen. She hurried down the hall, forgetting for a moment it wouldn't be a staff member calling in sick or some other urgent message from Millar's. She and Gavin had flown to Nova Scotia so soon after the store closing, she really hadn't absorbed how it would change her life yet. Her second thought was that it would be Scott, wondering why she hadn't called him back yet.

Instead, Charlene's name appeared on the lock screen.

Relieved to avoid Scott a while longer, she connected the call. "Hi, there. How are you?"

"More importantly, how are you?" Charlene's voice was warm with concern. "I'm sorry we haven't talked in so long. I know how busy you were with closing Millar's, and then I thought I should give you a few days to unwind. How are you holding up?"

She hitched a hip onto a barstool and propped her elbows on the counter. This was what she needed—an honest chat with a good friend. "Not bad, I guess. I just realized it really hasn't hit me yet. Gavin and I—you remember Gavin, right? From your party?"

"The slightly nerdy guy with a side order of hot? You bet."

Leeza laughed at the description but couldn't deny its accuracy. "He and I were in Nova Scotia. We just got back." She paused, waiting for Charlene to ask why they went, for a cheerful but raunchy reaction about getting back into action.

"Is that why you haven't called Scott yet? He left you a voice mail this morning." The rumble of another voice in the background came through the speaker.

Leeza frowned at the unexpected response. "Why do you care? And is someone else with you?"

Charlene's tone softened slightly, but still held reproach. "We're friends remember—me and Scott, you and me. Now that Drew has agreed to sell, you don't have a reason to put it off any longer."

The prickly sensation of premonition tickled Leeza's palms for the second time that day. "I told Scott before not to use you as an intermediary. It's not fair putting you between us."

More muffled syllables, a low bass tone that sounded vaguely familiar. "I'm not standing between you, Leeza," Charlene said. "I'm trying to help two friends work out a solution."

"So why aren't you telling Scott to quit asking me to sell? Just because Drew doesn't want the cabin doesn't mean I want to give it up."

Charlene's tone sharpened. "You said if Drew agreed to sell, you'd let it be listed."

"I did not." Not in so many words, anyway, and she'd never said them to Charlene. She and Scott must talk more often than Leeza realized. It sounded like something he would have said, believing only what he wanted to believe.

"You can't possibly want it for yourself," Charlene continued. "It's far too much upkeep, both in time and money. Now that you're out of a job..."

Irritated, and wishing she hadn't answered the phone after all, Leeza said tartly, "Now that I'm out of a job, I'll have the time, won't I?"

"But what about the money? Wouldn't it be better to let it go? With your half of the profit you wouldn't have to worry about getting another job for a long time. It would be a substantial amount."

A disquieting thought popped into Leeza's mind. "Charlene," she said slowly, "has Scott offered you some sort of reward if you convince me to sell?"

CHAPTER TWENTY-SEVEN

April 14th, 1944
We've moved to camp about 5 miles away from
Southampton.

The pause that followed told Leeza the truth, despite the denial Charlene offered. "Of course not," she said. "Why would you thi—"

Her voice cut off, and Leeza wondered if they'd lost connection. But only for a moment. The next voice she heard explained so much.

"It doesn't matter what I do with my share of the money," Scott said angrily. "You have no reason to stonewall me any further. We're going to sell that cabin, Leeza. I'll be over tomorrow with the paperwork."

It was all starting to make sense.

"You will not force me into this," she said, fury at his deceitfulness licking at her words.

"Here's the deal. I have a buyer who is willing to pay fair market value. I have another real estate agent lined up to handle the sale. I have a purpose for the money once the sale goes through. I am not waiting any longer."

"Why are you in such a rush? What do you need the money for?"

Another pause, this one just as telling as the one Charlene had made.

"You *are* giving it to Charlene," Leeza said. She wasn't sure why this seemed so treacherous, but it did. "The two of you have teamed up. Why? What's really behind all this?"

She waited, hearing Charlene's voice in the distance, but unable to understand the words.

Scott sighed. "Look, I didn't want to tell you this. But Charlene and I...well, we're together. She has a chance to expand her business but needs some capital. If we sell the cabin, I can help her out. It's just sitting there doing nothing, anyway."

It was like poking at a wound, but Leeza had to know for sure. "What do you mean, you're together?"

"What do you think I mean?"

An image flashed in Leeza's memory—Charlene and Scott at the New Year's Eve party, laughing, touching. "How long?" she asked sharply. "How long have you been together?"

"What does it matter?"

"Put Charlene back on."

"About the cabin—"

"Put Charlene back on!"

Fumbling noises and then the sense that someone was on the other end, silent and waiting. "When we met for coffee, at the beginning of December"—Leeza swallowed hard—"when you told me Scott was with someone new. That was you? He was with you?"

"You told me you didn't want him back."

"That's not the point! We were friends, Charlene. I tried to understand, when you said you kept in touch with him. But this..."

"It just happened. We didn't plan to fall in love."

"Fall in love." Leeza spit out the words. "We

were *married,* Charlene. We have a son together. And he cheated on me, not once, but multiple times. Do you honestly think it will be different with you?"

"This is why I didn't want to tell you. I knew you wouldn't understand."

"You're right. I don't understand. But you shouldn't have hidden it from me. You shouldn't have lied. I would have been hurt, been angry, but I would have been able to forgive you. But finding out this way—" She took a deep breath. "I don't want to talk to either one of you anymore."

"Scott needs to bring the papers for the cabin—"

"If anyone mentions the cabin to me again, I swear I will *never* agree to sell it."

"Leeza—"

"Goodbye, Charlene." She disconnected the call. And let the tears of rage and betrayal and humiliation fall.

A nagging headache remained after her emotional outburst. Thank goodness she'd been alone—losing control that badly wasn't something she was proud of. She felt hollow and lethargic and knew she had to eat to make sure the squeezing in her temples didn't turn into a full-blown migraine.

As she was standing in front of the open refrigerator, wondering if she could make an omelette with two wilted ribs of celery, a slightly fuzzy block of cheese, and two eggs, her phone rang again. She cringed, intending to ignore the insistent tune. But when she checked the screen—it might have been Drew, after all—and saw Gavin's name, she quickly grabbed the device and connected the call.

"Glad to be home?" he asked. Just the sound of his voice lightened the pounding in her head.

"Yes and no," she said. "Life was simpler in Nova Scotia."

"I noticed you seemed a bit upset on the ride home from the airport."

Neither love nor money would get her to mention that Nolan had made her uncomfortable. After all, the younger man hadn't done anything other than look at her. "Scott left me a voice mail while we were in flight," she said. Not a lie, but not a truthful answer to his unasked question, either.

"What did he want?"

"Drew has decided he doesn't want the cabin. So now Scott is insisting we list it immediately."

"What's his rush? Surely he can wait a few more days."

She couldn't tell him about Charlene and Scott. Not yet. Not while she still felt flayed raw by the knowledge. "Yes, he can," she said, taking strength from Gavin's support. "I was so sure Drew would want to keep the cabin, that I really haven't thought about what *I* want to do with it."

"When's the last time you were there? Maybe a visit will help you decide."

"That's a really good idea."

"I have them occasionally." The smile she could hear in his voice chased away the final flickers of her headache. "And speaking of good ideas—do you have dinner plans?"

She stared balefully at the closed refrigerator door. "I have nothing fresh in the house, so I need to hit a grocery store. Eating out is a treat on holidays, but after a while I do long for a home-cooked meal."

"I discovered a couple of steaks in the freezer, and the potatoes have survived my week away nicely. Want to come over?"

The thought of an evening alone, stewing about Scott and Charlene and the cabin, was *not* appealing. But the fact that she was missing Gavin already tipped the scales the other way—she wasn't sure she should give into the need to see him so soon. Even more—what with one thing and another, she'd never been to his home before. What did it say that he'd invited her over today of all days?

In the end, there really was no decision to make.

"I'll stop on my way to get fresh vegetables for a salad," she said, "and I have an apple betty in the freezer I can bring. See you soon."

If she'd ever wondered just how successful Gavin had been as a financial advisor, one quick glance at his house would have given her the answer.

Hoferkamp Road ran along the crest of the cutbanks lining the Nechako River, which tumbled into Prince George from the west. The area was a jumbled mixture of executive homes and single-wide trailers, all on large, private lots. As his employer, Leeza had known Gavin's address, and as their friendship had grown, she had pondered about what his home might be like. But she'd never imagined this.

She stood in front of a wall of windows rising two stories and arrowing into the peak of the vaulted ceiling above. Outside the glass a wide wooden deck jutted out over emptiness, snow piled up against the posts and bottom rails. In the near corner Gavin, wearing a downy coat, tended the barbeque, foil-wrapped potatoes glittering in the light falling from the interior. The city extended into the distance, details lost in the darkening dusk, lights pricking through the gloom. She imagined that if she stood at the deck railing, she'd be able to see the Nechako River passing by the foot of the sandy cliff on which the house perched. From where she was, she could see the wide curve of the Fraser, and the headlight of a train winding its way along the track that clung to that river's edge. Orange lights in regimented rows outlined the railyard at the eastern entrance to the city.

Gavin slid open the glass door that gave access to the deck and stepped across the threshold hurriedly, a gust of cold air following him in. Tossing his jacket onto a nearby sofa, he joined Leeza at the window.

"I could stand here all night," she said.

"I think I like the view best in the dark. But it's great in daylight, too."

"How long have you lived here?"

"Ten years this May. It was always Nancy's dream to have a house where she could see for miles. She said she didn't care what she was looking at— lake, meadow, city. She just wanted the expanse of it." He shifted his weight from one foot to the other. "More wine?"

She'd been so engrossed with the view that she hadn't realized she'd finished her drink. "I'd better not. I'd like another with dinner and two glasses will be more than enough since I'm driving home."

"Who said anything about going home?" Gavin plucked the glass from her hand and headed for the kitchen. The open concept plan meant living, dining, and kitchen areas all shared the panoramic expanse of windows.

Unaccountably nervous, she trailed her hand along the back of the leather sofa. "You didn't say anything about staying when you called, and I didn't want to assume."

"Why *wouldn't* you assume?" Gavin asked as wine glugged softly. "I thought I'd made my feelings pretty clear."

She wondered how to explain the sense of unreality that textured their time in Truro. "I thought that...maybe now we're back to real life...things might have changed."

Gavin's own wineglass, still full, sat on the dark wood dining table between her and the kitchen. He placed hers next to it and stood before her. She rested on the back of the sofa, her hands on either side of her hips.

He cupped her chin in his palms, his thumbs brushing her jaw, her lower lip. She gripped the soft leather of the sofa tighter.

"What are you worried about, Leeza? Why would things have changed?"

His gaze was warm and steady, and she searched for the right words. "I'm scared," she said finally. "Scott hurt me badly. But I think you might be able to hurt me worse."

He hissed in a breath. "I would never hurt you."

"Not on purpose. I know that. But we're not kids anymore. We *have* kids...grown ones. We know the world doesn't always work out the way we want it to." She huffed out a soft, sad laugh. "If William's diary has taught me anything, it's the fact that life can be brutal."

"You think I don't know that?" He stepped back, his hands dropping to his sides. "I watched my wife die, Leeza."

She flinched. "I'm sorry. I'm not making light of what you went through."

Gavin reached blindly for one of the wineglasses, picked up Leeza's, and drank from it. It gave her an unexpected thrill—and the thrill told her something more. It was too late to retreat. She was already in too deep to escape without pain.

"Are you sure Nolan didn't say anything to you this morning?" he asked.

She shook her head "No. He didn't *say* anything." In honesty, she added, "It was just the way he looked at me. It got me thinking."

"I love my children, Leeza. If they have a problem with the woman I—I want to be with, I'm not sure how I'd handle it. But I think you're reading something into the situation that isn't there."

"I'm sorry," she repeated. "Maybe I'm more upset about Scott and Charlene than I thought. I don't mean to take it out on you."

Gavin frowned. "What about Scott and Charlene?"

She hadn't meant to blurt that out, but she couldn't avoid telling him now. A part of her was relieved to share the news, while a much bigger part wanted to hide in a dark room. "Charlene, who I thought was my friend, is sleeping with Scott. She says he's in love with her. Part of the reason—maybe even the main reason—he wants to sell the cabin is to give her money to expand her business."

"Oh, honey." He never called her anything other than by name, and the easy endearment echoed sweetly in her bones. He sat beside her on the back of the sofa, his warmth permeating from shoulder to knee.

She gave in and leaned against him, his arm automatically encircling her waist. "I'm just so angry at her. I knew she was still in touch with Scott, but they've been together for *months* and she didn't tell me. They've been manipulating me, deceiving me. I feel so stupid."

"You trusted a friend. The world would be a very lonely place if we trusted no one."

He pressed a kiss to the top of her head, the simple gesture healing and tender. She rose and stepped between his thighs. Lights reflected off the lenses of his glasses, and she gently unhooked them from his ears, placing them behind her on the table. His hands rested on her hips, hers on his shoulders.

Staring into his eyes, she had a revelation. "I guess I'll never be lonely then. Because I trust you. Despite my insecurities, you should know that. I trust you."

"I'm glad."

She brushed a lock of hair behind his ear and trailed her fingertips along his jaw, tickled by the sensuous rasp of whiskers.

"You should also know," she said, "that while I didn't want to assume I was invited to stay, I did bring an overnight bag."

He laughed, low and rumbly, and pulled her in for a kiss.

CHAPTER TWENTY-EIGHT

May 10th, 1944
I finally found Maureen something and I didn't
have to go to London to find a little doll at a
store close by. It's exactly the type she likes. I'll
send them the presents soon since Mom's
birthday is coming up. Less than a month, June
6th to be exact.

As much as she wanted to hide away in Gavin's elegant aerie, Leeza knew she couldn't avoid the world forever. In the morning she insisted he relax while she made them breakfast omelettes, and then kissed him goodbye with gratitude and passion and returned home.

The way she saw it, there were three things she had to deal with, and she only had control over two of them. Until Genevieve got in touch, there wasn't much she could do in the search for William. That left deciding about the cabin and securing a new job.

Scott had said he intended to bring paperwork regarding the sale to her today, but that had been before she'd learned about Charlene and had told him she didn't want to speak with him. Not that she thought he'd pay attention to her dictate. However, she could leave that ball in his court for a little while longer.

Which meant getting another job was top of the list.

She'd started her unemployment insurance claim before leaving for Nova Scotia, which would only kick in after her severance money ran out—and if she hadn't found another position by then. After an exhaustive search of numerous career websites, scrolling through posting after posting looking for something that would suit both her experience and her interests, she closed the lid of her laptop and sat back with a sigh.

Damn it, she'd *loved* Millar's, despite its problems. Finding another position that would provide the same satisfaction—and compensation— might be more difficult than she'd thought.

The doorbell rang. Even before she peered through the sidelight to check who stood there, she knew it would be Scott.

"Hey," he said, smiling that half-smile that used to make her weak at the knees. Today she saw past the charm to the manipulation in his eyes. "Here. A peace offering." He thrust out a bouquet-shaped bundle encased in flowered paper and cellophane to keep it protected from the cold. The scent of carnations and roses escaped the wrapping.

Leeza took it automatically, flashing back to too many times in their marriage when he'd made the same gesture. Guilt gifts, she knew now, though at the time she'd been happy to believe he gave them just because they pleased her.

Stepping back, she said, "Come in. I'll put these in water."

She left him removing his coat and boots and headed for the kitchen. Finding a vase in the cupboard above the refrigerator, she released the flowers from their crinkly packaging and began to trim the ends of each stem.

Scott joined her, hovering on the other side of the counter as if waiting for an invite to sit. When she remained silent, he shrugged and settled on one of the barstools.

He'd never been able to tolerate quiet for long, so Leeza waited, knowing he'd be the first to speak. It was a petty win, but she'd take any she could get.

"So, are we okay?" he said finally. "Charlene was really upset yesterday."

"Well, then, Charlene should have been honest with me." Leeza snapped the handles of her kitchen shears together, sending the woody end of a rose rattling into the sink.

"She was worried about your reaction. And given how you *did* react—"

She cut him off with a glare and he held his hands up, palms outward in a gesture of surrender. "Okay, never mind."

Leeza drowned out whatever he said next with the rush of water filling the vase. When she flipped the faucet off, he began again. "I brought the papers. For selling the cabin," he clarified, as if she needed an explanation.

She concentrated on stripping leaves from the stems before placing the blooms and greenery in the vase. "I'm not signing anything today."

He slapped his hands on the counter and she jumped. "Come on, Leez! This is ridiculous. I'm doing this for you, too, you know. Selling the cabin is the best for both of us."

She shot him a scowl that he ignored effortlessly. "Right. Thanks *so* much," she said. He opened his mouth and she stopped him. "No. Just listen for a minute."

He settled back on his seat, expression peevish. Leeza went back to arranging the flowers. She and

Gavin had talked over her options last night, and she was much more confident about what to do. But that didn't mean she was going to let Scott off easily.

"I'm going to the cabin," she said, sliding a pink carnation into place. "I haven't been out for months, and I need to see for myself what kind of shape it's in. And to say goodbye."

Scott made a sharp sound but didn't speak. Maybe the instincts that had made him a top salesman for years had finally kicked in. Knowing when to talk and when to be quiet were important skills for a real estate agent.

"I'll give you my final decision on Monday, but I'm leaning toward selling. If I do agree, though, I want my own agent."

"What? Why?" Scott asked incredulously.

"I don't trust you." She turned to look him square in the face. "Do you honestly think I'm going to sign with an agent you choose and let the two of you badger me into whatever you want? No way. If you want to sell the cabin, I'll have my own agent looking out for my interests."

"Leez—"

"That's a deal breaker, Scott. If you don't agree to that, I don't agree to sell."

Looking harried and harassed, he said, "Fine. What else?"

"We split the profits five ways. Two parts each for you and me, one part for Drew."

His beleaguered expression deepened. "Drew? Why?"

"As a gift from his loving parents." She wondered if he heard her sarcasm. "He's a good son, he loved the cabin, and he deserves to benefit from its sale."

"You're killing me here."

"Take it or leave it."

Leeza gave thanks to Gavin for suggesting she

get her own agent. Something about Scott's insistence on selling—over and above the hastiness of it all—had always bothered her. Maybe the offer he had wasn't as great as he'd led her to believe. Maybe he'd planned to squeeze her out of her fair share. She hated to think their relationship had sunk to such lows, but given the look on Scott's face, she wondered sadly if those suspicions were right.

He rose and pushed back from the counter so quickly the stool rocked before righting itself with a clatter. "I expect to hear from you first thing on Monday."

"You will."

Without looking at her again, he headed to the front. The door closed behind him—not quite a slam, but not gently. With a sigh of relief, she caressed one of the yellow roses shining in the bouquet, before lifting the vase out of the sink and bringing it to the living room.

It wasn't the flowers' fault. No reason she couldn't enjoy their bright cheerfulness despite the tainted reason she'd been given them.

Giving Scott a deadline for her decision was both liberating and sorrowful. One way or the other, the dispute would end on Monday. In her heart she knew she'd agree to sell, just as she'd told Scott. Visiting the cabin one more time was necessary, for closure if nothing else.

She called Gavin, eager to tell him about the success of her conversation with Scott. Wrapping up her recounting, she said, "I was hoping you'd come to the cabin with me tomorrow. I'd like to go out first thing in the morning, but I don't plan to spend the night. What do you think?"

"I'd love to. Anything particular I should bring? Will we need to shovel our way in?"

"I pay one of the neighbours who lives out there all year long to clear the driveway when necessary, so that shouldn't be an issue. I'll pack food and drink, and I plan to take boxes along so I can bring home my personal items before it's listed. I imagine we'll sell it fully furnished. It only makes sense."

"You've made up your mind, then?"

She sighed. "I think I have. This visit may be a formality, but it's an important one." She hesitated. "Thanks for saying you'll come with me. I didn't want to go alone."

"Of course I'll come."

"I was also wondering—did you want to stay here tonight? I'd prefer to take my SUV tomorrow, and that way we can leave as soon as we're ready."

"I don't think that will work." Gavin's voice was regretful. "I'm having dinner with Sarah and Xander, and then I have a late curling game."

"Curling?" she said, distracted from her initial disappointment.

"I'm on a team in the recreation league. I've missed quite a few games with Millar's closing and being out of town, so I feel like I should go."

She wasn't sure why it amused her so much to think of Gavin tossing large granite stones across pebbly ice, but she couldn't help a grin from lightening her tone. "How did I not know you curled?"

"It's just for fun, and more of a drop-in league so I don't feel bad if I don't go every week."

"Well, enjoy yourself, and I'll see you tomorrow."

"I'm sorry I can't come over tonight." She could tell he meant it, and knowing he was disappointed, too, was gratifying.

"It's fine." And it was. It was healthy that they both had individual pursuits. Just because they were...whatever they were...didn't mean they had to spend every second together. "Until tomorrow, then."

It was only after he'd hung up that she wished she'd been brave enough to tell him the truth—that she would miss him until they were together again.

The next morning, well before Gavin was due to arrive at eight, Leeza had her SUV loaded and parked on the street so he could have access to her garage. The forecast was calling for a few centimetres of snow through the morning—nothing out of the ordinary, but it would be nicer if he didn't have to sweep it off when they returned later that day.

She fidgeted around the house, straightening knickknacks that didn't need to be straightened and fiddling with Scott's guilt flowers for no reason. She wasn't sure why she was so anxious. She wasn't worried Gavin would change his mind about going with her, and neither was she concerned about what they'd find at the cabin. The neighbour who cleared the driveway was good about keeping an eye on the property, letting her know if anything drastic needed to be done.

She just felt...off. Unsettled. At loose ends. She had always preferred life to be orderly and organized, with defined schedules and no unexpected events. The uncertainty and discord of the last few months must be catching up with her, ruffling the usual calm of her thoughts.

A few of her butterflies settled the instant Gavin pulled into her driveway. She hurried through the door connecting the hall to the garage and waved him in. A few flakes were starting to fall, and the air smelled of snow over the scents of exhaust and oil that permeated the concrete floor.

The kiss he gave her the moment he stepped out of the car went even further to making everything right in her world. Before she had a chance to reconsider, she blurted, "I missed you."

Ignoring the cold wind swirling in from the open garage door, Gavin kissed her again. She leaned into him, slipping her arms around his waist inside his unfastened coat, letting his heat surround her. Her mouth opened to greet him, her tongue tangling with his in a dance that was familiar and yet exciting, like the taste of a favoured wine.

"Morning," he said, drawing back just enough to form the words. "I missed you, too." An especially energetic swoosh of icy air raised the hairs on the back of Leeza's neck and she shivered. He enfolded her tighter in his embrace and said in a scolding tone, "What are you doing out here without a coat? Let's go inside."

Amused yet warmed by his solicitude, she said, "I'm ready to go. Everything's packed up." She handed him a set of keys, which she'd grabbed on her way to meet him. "Why don't you wait in my car? I'll be right out."

A couple minutes later, bundled in her scarf, toque, mittens, and parka, and wearing heavy, knee-high boots, she slid into the driver's seat. Pressing the button to shut the garage door, she smiled at Gavin. "All set?"

"You bet."

In no time at all they were on the highway heading west of Prince George. Light snow continued to fall, the wipers keeping up easily. Leeza was just about to ask Gavin how his curling had gone the night before when his phone let out a ding, immediately followed by Leeza's own phone signalling.

"That's my email notification," she said.

"Mine, too."

She spared him a quick glance. "Are you thinking what I'm thinking?"

"Genevieve."

Out of the corner of her eye she could see him hurriedly tapping the screen of his phone. "It's her," he said. "And it's a long message."

"Read it out loud," Leeza said. "I'll find a place to pull over once we're up this hill."

CHAPTER TWENTY-NINE

May 29th, 1944
They're telling us to bring as little of our kit as
possible. But there are so many things I know I
will need. Rodney had no problem. I sent mom
the package with all the presents, she should
get it on the day of her birthday. I can't wait to
hear how she liked it.

The highway snaked around several corners
while climbing a long, steep incline. As she listened
to Gavin, Leeza stayed in the right-hand lane letting
more impatient traffic speed past on her left.

"She starts with apologizing for the delay. She
went back to work on Wednesday and needed to
catch up on things before she had time to
concentrate on our search."

They reached the crest of the hill and the
highway flattened out. A rural road branched off to
the right and Leeza turned onto it, parking on the
shoulder a safe distance from the corner. Leaving the
vehicle running for warmth, she turned to Gavin, her
fists clenched nervously in her lap.

"I'll read the rest in her words," he said.

Starting from the fact David and Maureen were enrolled in the Tatamagouche School District in 1941, I checked the registers for the same district over the next few years. David was still registered in September of 1942. At eighteen he would have been one of the oldest students in the school and it is a bit surprising he was still allowed to attend (with his older brother at war and his father dead, I would have expected him to leave much sooner). At the time, the school only provided instruction up until Grade Eleven, so this probably would have been his last year there, no matter what. But obviously his mother supported his continued education, perhaps at the urging of his teachers, which makes me wonder if he went on to college or university. As we don't have those records on hand, I've put that aside for now, but we can take up that line of investigation if necessary.

As for Maureen, she was registered up until September of 1949, from which I assume she left school in June 1950 at the age of fifteen (her birthday being in October). This wouldn't have been unusual for the time, but because she left before Grade Eleven, I wouldn't expect to find her registered at a university (although a technical college might be a possibility). Again, I have put that aside for now.

My next step was to search the records for the local churches in Tatamagouche. There are two that were active during the period you are interested in—one Presbyterian and one United. Here I had some luck. I decided to call the United church first, and I immediately reached the secretary (which, in these smaller parishes, is harder to do than it sounds). It turns out she is also their volunteer archivist, and she was excited to help me with the search for Maureen and David.

The other stroke of luck is that this lovely lady (her name is Mrs. Langille, BTW) was born and raised in Tatamagouche. So not only is she interested in local history, she has a vast personal knowledge of the area. Unfortunately (but not unexpectedly), there are numerous Smith families in the area, and since Mrs. Langille herself was born after the war neither William, David, nor Maureen's names were familiar (that was probably too much to ask, don't you think? <g>)

Since I had birth dates from David and Maureen's school records, it only took her an hour or so to get back to me and confirm they had been baptized in the church (which meant I didn't have to call the Presbyterians at all—yay! Not that I have anything against them...). She was also able to find the baptismal record for William. I asked her to take a photo of it and send it to me (see attached). I thought you might like to see it, even though it doesn't really get us much further forward in finding any relatives still living.

At this, Gavin looked up from his phone. "You

know, since seeing William's name on the cenotaph in Truro, we've kind of given up looking for him. But we still don't know exactly how he died."

"Or where he's buried." Leeza nodded. "We can't forget that. It's probable that Maureen or David know, and if either of them is still alive the question will be answered if—*when*—we find them. But if only members of a younger generation are left, they may have no knowledge of the uncle or great-uncle that died so long before they were born. It would be nice to have the full story for them."

Gavin continued with Genevieve's email:

This morning I heard from Mrs. Langille again. She forwarded me a copy of a marriage certificate (also attached). On November 26, 1950, Maureen Elizabeth Smith married Harold Cecil Fulton. She said she could find no mention of David in the marriage registry in the years between 1942 and 1950 (which may bear out my idea he left Tatamagouche for further schooling). Sadly, she did find a record for a William Henry Fulton, parents Harold and Maureen. Baby William Henry was born May 3, 1951 and died only two days later.

A pang of sorrow at the long-ago loss twisted Leeza's heart. "She named her first baby after her big brother, the one who didn't come home. And then that baby died, too." She blinked away tears. Her own miscarriages still haunted her with the possibilities of what might have been. To lose a child after birth must have been indescribably crushing. "Do you suppose that was why Maureen didn't go back to school? If she was pregnant, I mean?"

"It's certainly possible," Gavin said, "but it's also

possible the baby was born prematurely, especially since he died. Getting married at sixteen wasn't unusual at the time."

"Another mystery to add to the list, I guess." She gestured at his phone. "Is that everything?"

"Not quite."

I don't want to get your hopes up, but Mrs. Langille thinks she might know someone who knows someone who knew Harold and Maureen Fulton. I got lost in the second cousins and brothers of best friends, so I'm not exactly sure of the connection. I'm waiting to hear back from her on that, but didn't want to wait any longer to send you what I had learned so far.

"The rest is just another apology for being sick— like she could help that!—and a promise to let us know the minute she hears more from Mrs. Langille." He shifted in his seat.

For a moment, they stared at each other. Then Leeza broke into a wide grin and Gavin let out a *whoop* of excitement.

"I'm beginning to believe we might actually find them," Leeza said. "If this lead from Mrs. Langille pans out..."

"It's a small enough village," Gavin said. "It is a definite possibility that she knows someone who knows someone."

"Who knows someone." Leeza laughed. "I guess we just have to wait. Again." She put the car in gear and drove a couple hundred metres down the road before she found a space where she could turn the SUV around. "There's no service at the cabin," she said, "so if Genevieve gets back to us today, we won't know until we're on our way to town."

"Maybe that's a good thing. It will stop us from checking our phones every thirty seconds."

Distracted by the email, Leeza hadn't noticed the falling snow had grown thicker while they'd been parked. Wind whipped it across the highway, making it difficult to see the road, especially when a larger vehicle roared by going the opposite direction. Gavin stayed silent, either recognizing she needed to concentrate or lost in thought about Genevieve's report. Less than half an hour later she took the turn onto the lake's access road. It had been plowed recently, but snow was already accumulating, and she was glad her vehicle had four-wheel drive.

"Not much further now," she said, taking one hand off the wheel at a time to shake out her fingers, stiff from white-knuckling. "I knew the forecast was calling for snow, but I didn't think it was going to be this heavy."

"We might have to shovel after all." He sounded almost eager.

"Do you *like* shovelling?"

"Kind of." His admission was sheepish, and she grinned.

Along their right, homes and cabins were barely visible through the snowfall. Some had well-cleared driveways, other gates protecting an untouched blanket of white. Leeza slowed and pulled off the road, parking parallel to two yellow posts with a heavy chain drooping between them.

"Made it." She put on the toque, mittens, and scarf she'd discarded in the warmth of the vehicle. "Let's walk in first, decide if we want to bring the car all the way in."

Together she and Gavin stepped over the low-slung chain and broke trail to the cabin, which was out of sight of the entrance, around a slight curve of the driveway. The air held a heavy hush, the snow deadening all sounds, even the whisper of their boots through the frothy whiteness.

It was plain to see that her neighbour had been doing his bit, as the edge of the lane was clearly defined with higher mounds of snow. Still, the trail they made was almost knee-deep. "It must have been snowing here all night," Leeza said, her breath making white clouds, condensing damply on the wool of her scarf.

"It's beautiful," Gavin said. "When the snow stops and the sun comes out, it will be picture postcard weather."

Leeza agreed, but not without a hint of unease. If the snow didn't stop soon, they might have trouble getting back to the highway. The access road was cleared by a local maintenance company but wasn't high on their priority list.

They rounded the bend, revealing the cabin squatting on a low ridge overlooking the lake. More than a foot of snow on the roof and tall drifts piled up against its walls made it look deserted and forlorn. The steps leading to the deck were slick with ice and they climbed them carefully as Leeza led Gavin past the back door and to the front of the cabin.

"It's not much of a view right now," she said. The far side of the lake was hidden behind a heavy veil of flakes. Snow-covered ice gave the illusion of a wide, smooth meadow, marred only by a snowmobile track cutting a silver-shadowed trail a few metres offshore.

"It has its own charm. So easy to imagine we're the only two people on earth."

She turned to him and saw him studying her with the quiet, intense look that made her toes curl. "We can't," she said automatically. "We have to move the car. If a plow comes by it will get buried."

With one gloved hand at the back of her neck, he drew her closer. His mouth touched hers, their chilled lips warming instantly. She sank into the kiss, sighing when he pulled away. The lenses of his glasses were fogged and dotted with melting snowflakes. "Let's get our chores done," he said, and then winked. "Then we'll give this cabin a proper send off."

It seemed pointless to clear the entire driveway, considering the snow was still falling and the further away they got from the road the harder it would be to get out later that day. Leeza unlocked the chain, the ends dropping to the ground and disappearing into the snow, and then she and Gavin cleared a space big enough to get her SUV off the edge of the road and be able to lock the chain again. It took them a couple of trips to bring in all the supplies she'd brought—enough food and drink for the day, plus the empty boxes and bags she'd brought to pack personal items in.

The cabin had two bedrooms with a loft above where two mattresses provided extra sleeping space. The kitchen and living areas took up the entire front half of the building, with large windows on either side of the door leading to the deck letting in daylight, diffused and softened by the fat flakes falling outside.

"It's pretty basic," Leeza said apologetically. "In the summer we have running water pumped from the lake, but I have it disconnected and drained in the fall to avoid frozen pipes." He already knew about the bathroom facilities, since he'd helped shovel a path to the outhouse tucked into the trees at the back of the cabin. "There's also a generator for electricity, but that's not set up to use during the winter, either."

"This is great." Gavin stood in the middle of the front room, hands on his hips. They were both still wearing their jackets as the temperature inside wasn't much different than out, and his nose was tipped with red. "Nancy and I talked about getting a cabin when the kids were little, but never seriously." He crouched before the woodstove and opened the door, peering into the black depths with interest.

Leeza surveyed the room, trying to see it through Gavin's eyes—and the eyes of any potential buyers. It was definitely a *cabin,* not a fancy cottage or year-round home. The scuffed linoleum floor and fake wood-panelled walls were sound but ugly, and the furniture an odd mishmash that had accumulated over the years. Sadly, she recognized that the new owners would more than likely tear down the small building. The value was in the land, not the structure. She sighed and her breath clouded the air.

"Do you want to get the fire going?" she said. "I brought hot chocolate and Bailey's if we can warm up some water."

"I can give it a shot."

While he busied himself with paper and kindling, Leeza went into the bedroom she had shared with Scott. Not that he'd been there for months, if not years, even before they separated. Almost from the moment they'd taken possession from her grandfather, Scott had pushed to make changes, to update and expand and renovate. The last thing Leeza had wanted was a second house to take care of, so she'd rejected all his plans, and he'd finally given up. The cabin was virtually untouched from the days when her grandparents had used it.

She had loved it exactly the way it was. But it was time to move on.

CHAPTER THIRTY

June 5th, 1944
They've brought us to the ports and boarded us
in these massive ships. This is it, we're leaving
tonight.

Leeza packed the few pieces of clothing and other small items that remained in the closet and dresser, and then turned to the rest of the room. One wall held a myriad of framed photos, the pictures dating from when Leeza's father was a child all the way to one of Drew diving off the dock only a couple of years ago. It reminded her suddenly of the display in Grant Howard's room—a well-lived life, frozen in time. She fetched another box and carefully placed them inside.

A cheerful exclamation alerted her to the fact Gavin had won his battle with the stove, so she carried the now-full box out and placed it by the door. She could already feel the warmth combating the chill. Filling a pot with water from the four-litre jug she'd brought, she set it on top of the stove to heat.

Over the next couple of hours, she and Gavin

sipped hot chocolate and added to the stack of boxes and bags at the door as the snow continued to fall. Finally, she was satisfied they had everything she wanted. She stood, surveying the pile, and bit her lip.

Gavin wrapped his arms around her from behind and rested his chin on her head. Since the woodstove had done its job and punched out lovely heat, they'd long since discarded their coats and sweaters. She rested her folded arms on top of his where they crossed her belly, the hair on his bare forearm tickling the inside of her wrist.

"I'm really going to miss this place," she said.

"I can understand that." He gave her a tight squeeze and kissed the side of her neck. "For what it's worth, I do believe you're doing the right thing. It's time for another family to make memories here."

She tilted her head and he accepted the invitation, drawing her earlobe into his mouth and flicking it with his tongue. Delightful shivers chased themselves up and down her spine and she pressed back against him.

"You said something about giving this place a proper send off," she whispered.

He spun her around, his hands dropping to her buttocks and lifting her slightly off her toes. She dug her fingers into his hair and let her mouth dance with his—tiny, nipping kisses and soothing licks deepening into a dark possession that had her soul begging for more.

Maybe it wasn't just Nova Scotia, she thought hazily as his fingers slipped beneath the waistband of her jeans so his hand could lay flat against the small of her back. Spending the day together doing mundane chores hadn't dispelled that sense of rightness, of passion, of companionship. In fact, it had shown her all her life could be.

A life with a man she loved.

His movements slowed and he pulled away.

When she moaned and leaned in, unwilling to let him go, he chuckled softly. "Don't worry, I'm not going far. But I brought a small bottle of champagne to toast the old place, and I left it in the SUV."

"You can get it later," she said, trailing kisses along his jaw.

"I have plans for that champagne. Plans that involve you naked in front of the fire."

"Oh." Evocative images flashed across her mind and she released him. "Hurry," she said, breathless.

Tossing on his parka and shoving into his boots, he gave her one more heart-pounding kiss and strode out into the swirling flurries. Leeza stared blankly after him for a moment, and then rushed into the bedroom and dragged off the heavy comforter and quilt, spreading them out on the floor in front of the woodstove. She was debating whether to wait for Gavin naked or let him enjoy undressing her when a loud thump and crash startled her out of her reverie. Leaning over the sink to peer out the window with a view of the side deck, she could see nothing. And nothing included Gavin.

Without bothering with her coat, she slipped on her boots and went to investigate. "Gavin?" she called as she rounded the corner. "Everything okay out—"

Her mind went blank at the sight of the figure sprawled against the snow-carpeted steps.

She flew toward him and knelt at his side. His face was screwed tight in pain, his lips moving in an unintelligible string of syllables. Her hands hovered over him and she drew in a shaky breath. "Gavin! What happened?"

"I slipped," he said grimly. "Where's the champagne?"

Blinking at this non sequitur, she said, "It's fine, it landed in a snowbank. I'm more worried about you."

"I'm fine." He bent one leg as if preparing to stand and froze with a hiss. "Well, maybe not fine. I think I put out my back."

"We've got to get you in the cabin." She could already see his jeans discolouring with damp as the snow melted on and under him. She slid an arm behind his shoulders. "Can you sit?"

In small degrees and with various vicious oaths, Gavin slowly made it to a sitting position. "Need to rest a bit," he said, sweat beading at his temples despite the cold.

Leeza bit back the urgency demanding she get him warm and dry. Without her coat, she was vividly aware of the icy chill sweeping up her back and around her neck, and the cold could be making his injury worse. With a curt nod he signalled his readiness to make a renewed effort. She crouched to face him. "If you lean on me, do you think you can stand if I support you?"

He nodded again, his lips pressed in a tight, flat line. He lifted his arms onto her shoulders, and even that movement caused his face to whiten. She gripped him around his waist and braced her foot on the lowest step for leverage. "Take a deep breath. One, two, three."

As smoothly as she could she straightened her legs, bringing Gavin with her as she did. He groaned, his head resting on her shoulder, but managed to get upright. For a moment they simply stood, panting in unison.

"Now, the cabin." In tiny, incremental steps, she and Gavin inched their way up the low stairs and along the deck. By the time they were inside, Leeza was sweating and Gavin's face so pale she feared he might faint. She dared not let him go—she could feel his muscles trembling.

Thanking god it was only a few more steps to the bedroom, she urged Gavin forward, and then helped lower him to the mattress. The groan he didn't suppress when he stretched out flat made her pulse jump with anxiety.

Keeping her voice calm and soothing, she said, "Okay, the worst is over." At least, she hoped so. "Let me get your boots off." As gently as she could, she also removed his coat by slipping his arms out of the sleeves and sliding it out from under him so he didn't have to sit up.

The bedroom was chillier than the front area, so she quickly went to the stove and added more wood, scooping up the blankets she had spread on the floor and bringing them to the bedroom. Shudders racked Gavin's frame, whether from cold or pain she wasn't sure. "I'll get you tucked up in a minute," she said, "but first we need to get you out of those pants."

"The plan was to get you out of *yours*," he said through clenched teeth.

Choking out a laugh, and immeasurably relieved he could still joke, she said, "You first. Then we'll see what happens after that."

She draped his jeans over a chair near the fire to dry them, wrapped him in the blankets, and helped him swallow some of the pain medication she always carried in her purse. Finally, she crawled onto the mattress next to him, lying on her side with her head propped in her hand. As careful as she was, the slight jarring had him blowing out a sharp breath.

"I can't believe this," he said, his fist clenching in frustration. "This is *not* how I imagined this afternoon ending."

"Don't worry about it. I just hope you're not hurt too badly."

"I've wrenched it before. It'll get better if I lie flat for a bit." He laid his hand on her knee, and his face held an odd mixture of hopefulness and pain. "You know, if we're careful and you do most of the work, we could still..."

She laughed. "Oh, I don't think so, chum. How many of those pills did you take?"

"It was worth a shot." He sighed and closed his eyes. She studied his face. Every so often his eyelids twitched and his mouth tightened, signs that, even lying still, he was still in pain. While it was better than lying in a pile of snow, the mattress was old and lumpy, providing only marginal comfort. She needed to get him home.

His eyes opened abruptly. "I meant to tell you." He shifted slightly, his brow creased at even that tiny movement. "They plowed the road, and there's a heavy windrow blocking the driveway. We'll have to clear that before we can get the car out."

"We'll worry about that later. For now, try to relax."

"Here." He slowly raised his arm. "If we're going to lie in bed together, we might as well cuddle. It wasn't what I had in mind, but better than nothing."

She tucked in next to him, resting her head carefully on his chest, one arm across his waist. Doing a quick mental inventory of the supplies she'd brought, she decided they were fine if they had to spend the night. They'd probably be a little hungry, but there was plenty of water and they hadn't yet eaten the lunch she'd brought. Besides, they weren't completely cut off from civilization. Other cabins along the road were inhabited—including that of her helpful, snow-clearing neighbour—and if she had to, she could walk over and seek help.

Gavin's muscles loosened and his breathing evened out. The silence was pervasive, broken only by the ticking of the woodstove as the metal heated. Leeza didn't think she slept, but when Gavin spoke, he startled her enough that she jerked against him, causing him to yelp.

"Sorry," she said, sliding away and rising to a sitting position, crossing her legs. "What did you say?"

"Sarah is expecting me to call her tonight. I mentioned this trip when I was at dinner with her and Xander yesterday. If we're going to be delayed, I should let her know."

"We're out of cell service here, but my neighbour, Abe, the one who looks after this place for me, has a landline. I can call from there if you like."

"I hate asking you to go out in this, but I would feel better if you did. Sarah might worry."

"No problem." It would also give her a chance to ask Abe to clear the windrow, and maybe even assist in getting Gavin to her car when he was up to it. She slid off the bed as smoothly as possible to avoid rocking the mattress. Circling around to Gavin's side of the bed, she bent down and kissed his forehead. "Don't go anywhere," she said. He snorted and she smiled. "I'll be back as soon as I can."

CHAPTER THIRTY-ONE

June 7th, 1944
As we approached the beaches yesterday, all I
could think of was one specific line in the speech
General Eisenhower wrote us before we left
England, "The free men of the world are
marching to victory!" But now, words are
jumping out at me. I still can't describe the
horror I saw yesterday as I got out of the L.C.I.
I saw my own friends a few feet away from me,
have their arms shot off or even worse die
instantly in front of me. Everything has a
different meaning once you live through it.

"Well, you're looking a lot better than yesterday,"
Leeza said, looking up from her phone as she had
coffee at Gavin's dining table the next morning.

He was still moving gingerly but was steady on
his feet and the pinched look about his mouth was
gone. In fact, with his rumpled hair and sleepy eyes,
he was looking quite delicious. Not quite ready for a
romp, she decided, tilting her head to study him as
he made his way toward her, but on the mend.

"I am better," he agreed as he lowered himself
onto one of the upright, hard-seated chairs. "Not

ready to run a marathon, but better."

In the end, they hadn't spent the night at the cabin. The snow had stopped while she was calling Sarah from Abe's phone, and with his help she had managed to clear the windrow quickly. Gavin had insisted he was able to make his own way to the SUV and he had, with only minimal support from Abe, which further relieved Leeza's worries. After all, who knew what damage he'd done to himself in the fall?

"Coffee?" She lifted the thermal carafe next to her.

"Oh, god, yes, please."

She had crept out of his bed about an hour ago. It had taken her a little time to figure out his ultra-modern brewing machine, and she had felt slightly intrusive rummaging through his cupboards looking for the necessities but hadn't wanted to wake him with questions.

It was only after setting the coffee to brew that she'd seen the email from Genevieve on her phone. She'd been waiting impatiently ever since for him to wake up so she could share the news, compulsively reading the message over and over.

"You didn't need to stay with me, you know." He had said the same thing in various ways more than once last night.

She replied with the same response she'd given then. "I know. But it didn't feel right, leaving you alone."

She'd tried to give him some distance, knowing it was frustrating—and somewhat embarrassing— for him to have her witness his weakness. When she'd suggested she sleep in the spare room, though, he'd kiboshed that idea. Which meant she hadn't slept much at all, worried she'd disturb him if she so much as rolled over.

But Genevieve's email had blown away any cobwebs remaining from her restless night.

"Have you checked your phone yet?" she asked, keeping her tone casual, staring innocently into her coffee cup.

"No. Why?"

She couldn't help the grin that split her face. "Genevieve heard from Mrs. Langille."

He straightened his spine, which caused him to grunt sharply, but his eyes never left Leeza's. "What's the news? Did she find Maureen?"

"Oh, she found Maureen, all right." Leeza's palms still tingled with the excitement that had lit inside her as she'd read the email. "The friend of a friend came through."

Gavin's eyes widened. "She has Maureen's address?"

"Well, she has an address that was current five years ago."

"Five years. That's pretty recent. When was Maureen born again?"

"1934." Leeza had already done the math, but Gavin didn't take long to catch up.

"She would have been only eighty-two then."

"Yes. Genevieve told me a bit of Maureen's story. She and her husband moved away from Tatamagouche in the sixties, which is one reason Mrs. Langille wasn't familiar with them."

"Where did they go?"

"It seems they worked their way west over the next few years, spending some time in Saskatoon and Calgary."

Gavin slumped back in his seat without a wince, evidently so preoccupied with the news he no longer felt his back. "She's in Calgary?"

Leeza shook her head. "No, not anymore." Gleefully she dropped the bomb she'd been waiting to detonate. "She's in Vancouver, Gavin. Her last known address is Vancouver."

Gavin's reaction was priceless. He stared at her,

his mouth hanging open. "She's in BC?" he said when he found his voice again. "She's *here?*"

"Not exactly *here*," Leeza replied, "but so much closer than Nova Scotia."

"I never thought...not in a million years..." He trailed off and Leeza giggled, enjoying his flabbergasted response.

"Not only do we have an address," she replied, "but we have a phone number, too."

"A phone number?" he repeated, clearly still trying to grasp the sudden turn of events. Leeza had had to read the email multiple times before she'd been able to absorb what it said, so she completely understood. "It can't possibly still be active," he said after a long pause. "Can it?"

"There's an easy way to find out." She tapped her phone with one finger, bringing the screen to life.

"I don't know if I'm ready for this." Gavin picked up his coffee cup as if seeing it for the first time and took a long swallow. "I'm not still sleeping, am I?"

"We have to be logical about this," she said, trying to control her own burgeoning hope as well as rein in Gavin's. "She's eighty-seven now. The chances of her still being in the same place are fairly slim." She didn't mention the most obvious possibility—that Maureen was no longer alive.

"Like you said, there's an easy way to find out. It's almost nine o'clock. Is that too early to call on a Saturday?"

"Probably. But I can't wait." Tapping the phone number Genevieve had provided onto the keypad, Leeza put the phone on speaker. Gavin reached out and gripped her hand as they listened to it ring.

The voice that answered was *not* that of an elderly lady. "Hello," a groggy male voice said. "Who is this?"

"I'm sorry if we woke you," Leeza said. "I have this number listed to Maureen Fulton. Is she available?" Gavin's fingers tightened on hers.

"Who?"

Leeza's heart sank. "Maureen Fulton."

"Sorry, I'm still half a sleep. Give me a second." Muffled sounds came through the speaker, including an enormous yawn. "I'm on night shift this weekend and only got to bed a couple hours ago."

"I am sorry to disturb you," Leeza apologized again.

"That's okay, I'm used to it. So, you're looking for Maureen?"

"Yes." The emotional pendulum swung back toward hope. "Maureen Fulton."

"Why?"

She wanted to screech at him to just answer the question, but said as calmly as she could, "It's a long story. We have something she might be interested in."

"We? Are you a lawyer or something?"

"No, we're not lawyers," Gavin said. "You were just speaking with Leeza Boychuk, and I'm Gavin Fletcher. We found a diary that we think might have belonged to Maureen's brother. We are hoping to return it to her."

"You found Grampa's diary? I'm sorry, I'm really confused." All trace of sleep had disappeared from the man's voice. "How did you get a hold of Grampa's diary? Who exactly are you?"

The air crystallized around Leeza. Scared the moment would shatter if she moved, she whispered, "Your grandfather?"

As if he hadn't heard her—and he probably hadn't, she'd spoken so quietly—he continued. "Look, until I know more about you, I'm not telling you anything else."

The tables had turned, and now it was Leeza who was too stunned to speak. Gavin took over the conversation. "Let us tell you what we've discovered, and then you can decide what to do."

The silence on the other end of the phone when Gavin finished with his explanation was profound.

"I don't know what to say." All belligerence was gone from the man's voice, leaving bafflement in its place. "I've never heard of William Henry. I always thought my grandfather was the oldest in the family."

"Your grandfather was David?" Leeza asked tentatively.

"Yes. He passed away about ten years ago. My dad, Henry, was his only son. Maureen is my great-aunt, Grandpa David's sister. I'm Ben, by the way. Ben Smith."

Leeza met Gavin's gaze, and only realized tears were streaming down her face when his image was blurred and indistinct. She wiped them away, sniffling.

"This phone number was given to us by a friend of your great-aunt," she said. "The last time she talked to her was five years ago." She couldn't bear to ask the question out loud. *Was Maureen still alive?*

"I moved in with her about four years ago," Ben said, "when I came to Vancouver for my residency. I'm a doctor. I rarely use the landline but haven't gotten around to cancelling it yet."

"Do you mean Maureen doesn't live there anymore?" It seemed Gavin had the same reluctance to ask the question directly.

"No, not for the last six months." Gavin's eyebrows rose. Leeza wasn't sure how to react, her heart jumping from her stomach to her throat and sinking back again. "Not since she moved into Willowmere."

A balloon of relief and excitement and thanksgiving filled Leeza's chest. She coughed to relieve the pressure. "We'd love to get in touch. Do you mind giving us her new number?"

Any doubt that Maureen was still alive vanished when Ben said, "If you don't mind, I'd like to speak with her about all this first. I don't imagine the news will upset her, but she might need some time to wrap her head around it." He laughed. "I guess *I* need some time, too. It's not every day you learn you have a great-uncle you've never heard of."

After Leeza gave him both her and Gavin's numbers they disconnected, with Ben's assurance he would talk with his great-aunt as soon as he got some sleep. "*If* I can sleep, after this," he had said cheerfully.

For a moment, she and Gavin could only stare at each other.

"I know we just got home—"

"Do you think your back feels good enough—"

Their sentences overlapped and they broke off, laughing.

"If Maureen agrees, I definitely think we should go see her in person," Gavin said.

"I can't believe we found her." Leeza had the feeling she'd be repeating that sentence numerous times over the next few days. "All this time, I've been preparing myself for disappointment. The odds were stacked against us. Now that it's happened—" She shrugged, at a loss to explain the odd mixture of relief and sadness enveloping her.

"It's almost a letdown," Gavin said, once again revealing how his emotions mirrored hers. "Like the final curtain on a play, or the last page of a favourite book. You're left with a little bit of the blues."

"Yes, exactly like that." Their chairs weren't quite close enough for her to reach him easily, so she rose and bent over, wrapping her arms around his shoulders, being careful not to squeeze too hard. "I am so thankful we did this together," she said, her lips brushing his hair as she spoke. "I like being part of a team again. Being a couple."

"Me, too." He tilted his head back and she kissed him gently. "Me, too."

CHAPTER THIRTY-TWO

June 10th, 1944
Rodney saved my life today. We were in a pit
and a potato masher grenade flew in. I was
frozen with fear but he took it and threw it back
just before it exploded. How will I ever be able
to thank him?

Leeza and Gavin decided that Ben probably
wouldn't get back to them until the next day. He'd
said he was on night shift, and they assumed that
would be at least twelve hours long. By the time he'd
gotten some rest there wouldn't be much chance for
him to get in touch with Maureen. Besides, if they
readied themselves to wait more than twenty-four
hours, it would be a pleasant surprise if he got back
to them sooner.

So Leeza did what she often did when she found
herself at loose ends—bake.

It turned out to be a good choice for killing time,
as a quick search of Gavin's cupboards had revealed
he was missing a few of the necessities. She'd passed
a couple hours with a trip to her condo to pick up
what she needed, as well as take a shower and pack

a few things for a short stay at Gavin's. Leeza had diffidently suggested she not leave him alone until his back was fully recovered—although it appeared better by the hour—and she'd been gratified by the gleam of satisfaction in his eyes when he'd agreed.

Gavin spent much of Saturday stretched out in the recliner in the living room and watched endless hours of news and sports, while Leeza made herself at home in his kitchen, doing her best to be patient while mixing batters for cookies, cakes, and muffins.

The day passed in quiet domesticity. The wonderful aromas of vanilla, chocolate and whipped sugar scented the air, and Gavin licked out the bowls with as much glee as Drew had as a child. In the evening, Leeza made a simple dinner of tuna casserole which they ate in front of the television while the Vancouver Canucks traded goals with the Calgary Flames in a high-scoring game that ended in their ultimate defeat.

Gavin clicked off the television, and a restful silence filled the room.

"Bed?" he said, his innocent tone betrayed by a teasing quirk of his mouth.

He lifted himself from his chair with barely a hint of discomfort, and though Leeza watched him carefully as he made his way to the bedroom, she could see no awkwardness in his movements. She readied herself for bed, going through her usual routine while acutely aware of Gavin waiting for her.

There was something both familiar and strange about the atmosphere tonight. They'd spent the day in such casual proximity, doing ordinary everyday things—just like a couple who'd been together for years. It had felt right, felt comfortable, but now an undercurrent of tension was making itself known in the trembling of her knees, the coiling of her stomach.

While they'd had sex numerous times over the

past ten days or so—more often than she'd had in the last months of her marriage to Scott, she realized with shock—the way they'd spent today coloured the night with a sense of fate, of destiny.

She slid into bed next to Gavin, lying on her back and staring up at the ceiling, unexplainably shy. He rolled onto his side, his face naked without his glasses, and laid his hand on her belly, a warm, stirring weight.

"I love you."

His declaration was so sudden she should have been astonished, amazed. Instead, she shuddered as a flush of heat swept over her. She turned to him with such an overwhelming sense of relief she could barely whisper the words she needed so desperately to say. "I love you, too."

"Are you sure?" His fingers traced the curve of her cheek, the sweep of her neck. "I've wanted to tell you for weeks now but was afraid to. I didn't want to ruin what we had, scare you away."

"I'm sure." How to explain to him that her love had been hiding just below the surface for a while—not as long as his for her, perhaps, but long enough to be certain.

He didn't seem to need any further assurances. Not in words, at least. He made love to her with quiet intensity and she drowned in the sensations, revelling in the freedom that her admission gave her. No more holding back, no more protecting her heart. Gavin held it firmly yet gently, and she trusted him to keep it safe.

"Take this off," he whispered, tugging at her nightgown. She wriggled out of it, flinging it aside as his mouth found her breast. Her hand stroked his back and she discovered he wore pajama bottoms. Through the haze of desire, she wondered if he hadn't been quite as confident in her response as he'd appeared to be. If she'd rejected his love, would he have left her in his bed and escaped to another room, clad with at least some dignity?

He nipped lightly on one nipple while his fingers played with her other breast. All rational thought fled. Her hips writhed, lifting off the mattress, seeking, searching, begging for fulfillment. Wanting his weight on her, his heaviness surrounding her, she reached across and tugged at his waist, urging him to cover her.

He hissed, rearing back from her breast.

"Oh, god, I'm so sorry!" she said. "Did I hurt you?"

He shook his head and dropped a reassuring kiss on her lips. "It's okay. But maybe we should do this another way." He rolled onto his back, bringing her with him.

She hovered above, braced on her hands and knees. "Are you sure? Maybe we should wait another day."

His palms cupped her cheeks, forcing her to meet his eyes, which blazed with challenge and victory and a joy that seared her heart. "You're worth a twinge or two," he said. "You're worth absolutely anything."

Without breaking their locked gaze, she slowly lowered herself onto him, careful to keep most of her weight on her knees. Her hips settled against his, his cock snugged between them, and his eyes shut. Cautiously she rocked against him. His hands clamped on her waist and she stilled.

"Don't stop," he said, exerting gentle pressure on her hips.

She slid along his length until they were both wet and gasping. His eyes still closed, he lifted his arm blindly and she leaned toward his hand. He pulled her down until their mouths touched, dominating and controlling the kiss until Leeza slumped bonelessly on top of him. His hands traced her spine, bumping along each vertebra, tender yet tickling. She squirmed weakly and he laughed, his breath huffing in her ear.

After a moment to collect her strength, she pushed to a sitting position, and manoeuvred so his tip nudged her entrance. She moaned in sensuous pleasure as she slid slowly down, anchoring herself to him.

"You are beautiful," he said as she moved against him. "Have I told you that before? You have a light that shines inside you that I can't resist."

Too overcome to reply, she laced her fingers through his and did her best to show him how much he meant to her through actions alone.

Afterward, sated and sleepy, she sighed with happiness as he curled around her. She knew it wouldn't last—they were both too restless to sleep tangled together—but she snuggled in to enjoy the connection.

"I love you," she said, already sliding into slumber, but not so far gone she didn't hear his soft, confident reply.

"And I love you."

About nine-thirty on Sunday morning, she drove Gavin to her condo so he could get his car, which had been in her garage since they'd departed for the cabin. His back was clearly close to normal, given their activities last night and again this morning. Remembering how he'd woken her had a blush rising along Leeza's cheekbones.

"When are you coming home?" he asked just before getting into his car.

The thrill that shivered across her skin was both fear and excitement. Did Gavin mean to imply his home was now hers as well? And if so, how did she feel about that?

"Around three o'clock or so," she said, the statement more of a question.

"Sounds good." He pressed a quick, demanding kiss to her mouth. "See you then."

She wandered through her house, trying to gauge her emotions. It was far too soon to talk about moving in together, but she couldn't avoid the thoughts crowding her brain. People who loved each other generally lived together. Neither one of them was young—although they weren't *old* either, she protested to her inner critic—so why waste time being separated if they both wanted to share living space? Since she'd only moved into the condo after her divorce from Scott, she felt little emotional connection with it. Moving out would not be anywhere near the wrench it had been leaving the home where Drew had grown up. And Gavin's house on the hill, though the one he had shared with Nancy, was beautiful and welcoming. Although maybe he'd prefer a fresh start in a new-to-them-both location.

Her phone notified her of an incoming Skype call, and she shrugged off her far too premature thoughts.

"Happy Valentine's Day," Drew said as soon as she connected the call.

Media made it impossible to forget the holiday for lovers, but as it had never been high on her priority list Leeza found it easy to ignore. Drew, with a new girl to impress, obviously hadn't. "Big plans with Danica?" she said, settling into her accustomed spot on the sofa. She really did like this couch. Maybe Gavin wouldn't mind if they found a place for it...

"There's an opera she wants to see," Drew was saying, "so we have tickets for tonight's show, with a late dinner after at the restaurant where we had our first date."

"Very romantic." Leeza couldn't help the teasing tone.

"I know. Me, of all people, going to an opera." He rolled his eyes, making her laugh. "It's just...I want to make her happy, you know? Sitting through three hours of unintelligible melodrama isn't asking much."

She wasn't ready to tell Drew the complete truth about Gavin, but she realized that maybe she should at least hint at the change in her life. "You remember Gavin, right?"

"Mom." Drew's exasperation was clear. "Why would I have already forgotten the guy you just spent a week travelling with?"

"Yes, right." She missed the old-fashioned phones with a curly cord connecting the handset to the base. She needed something to toy with while she talked. "I just...I thought you should know...well, we're kind of seeing each other."

"Of course you are. You've been working on that diary together."

"No, I'm mean...we're *seeing* each other."

He blinked. "Oh." Then, when the importance of her inflection registered: "Oh!"

CHAPTER THIRTY-THREE

June 12th, 1944
He's dead. Rodney is dead. He's dead. He just
lived the most painful 2 hours of his life trying
to hold his stomach from bleeding and I wasn't
even there for him. I wasn't there. Why the hell
couldn't it have been me? Why? Why did I even
volunteer to join this war, why did I force
Rodney to join with me? It's all my fault.

Leeza tried not to fret at Drew's conflicted expression. She waited patiently for him to digest the news.

"Okay, then," he said.

Her heart started beating again. "Are you sure? That it's okay?"

He paused, considering her question. "I'm not dreaming about you and Dad getting back together, if that's what you mean." He squared his shoulders and met her eyes through the screen. "I want you to be happy, Mom. And you weren't happy, not for a long time, even before the divorce."

"I wish you weren't so smart."

"I love Dad, but that doesn't mean I can't see

how badly he treated you. If you have found someone that treats you the way you deserve, then you should go for it."

Again, she had that odd sense of their roles being reversed—she the child and Drew the parent. "Thanks." She was surprised to feel lighter, freer. She hadn't realized how much Drew's acceptance meant to her until he'd given his blessing, so to speak.

"You're welcome. How is that whole diary thing going, anyway?"

Leeza updated him about finding Maureen and her great-nephew. He offered congratulations, but she could tell he didn't quite understand how important this was for her. She asked about his job, and they talked about commonplace things for a little longer, and then rang off. They still hadn't arranged a time for her and Danica to chat at length. She should probably stop avoiding that. If Drew were willing to welcome Gavin, the least she could do was make an effort with Danica.

The person she *wasn't* ready to make an effort with was Charlene. Leeza was still smarting from her deception. She could believe it from Scott, but she'd thought Charlene had some loyalty.

She'd told Scott she'd call Monday to give her decision on the cabin, but it seemed pointless to wait. Taking a deep breath, she dialled his number.

"Morning, Leeza," he answered.

With no patience for pleasantries, she dove right in. "I'm ready to sell. I'll confirm with my real estate agent tomorrow." She'd already had preliminary talks with the one she'd chosen on a recommendation from Gavin. "She'll be in touch with you and handle everything from then on. You are not to call me with anything to do with the sale."

"I don't understand why you're being so difficult about this." His tone was aggrieved, as if she'd insulted him somehow. "Selling is the best for everyone."

Everyone in Scott's world being himself and Charlene. Well, Charlene for now, at least.

"I know you don't," Leeza said resignedly. "It doesn't matter. This is the deal—my own agent, and Drew gets one-fifth the profit. If you keep pushing me on it, I'll insist he get more. To be taken out of your share."

"Fine, fine." He disconnected without another word.

For a moment Leeza sat, fingers trembling. She'd never be completely disassociated from Scott, seeing he was Drew's father. But this conversation had cut the final cord binding her old life to her new.

And Gavin was her *new*.

When Leeza let herself into Gavin's house later that afternoon, she found him on the phone.

"That's great news, Ben," he said, giving her a thumbs up. She placed her purse and overnight bag on the floor and hurried toward him.

"Yes," he said. "We'll make the arrangements as soon as we can and get back to you with details. Thanks so much. We look forward to meeting her, too. Thanks again. Goodnight." He tapped the screen and tossed the phone onto the sofa before wrapping her in an exuberant hug. "Maureen can't wait to see us," he said, lifting her off the floor and swinging her around.

"Don't hurt your back again." She laughed, sharing his excitement. How had she ever thought he was too sedate, too low key? He seemed a different person from the one she'd worked with for five years. Or maybe it was she who had changed.

"We need to look at flights." He gave her a smacking kiss and picked up his phone again. "Ben is off rotation Wednesdays and Thursdays this month," he said, staring at the screen, his thumb flicking rapidly. "He's requested we plan for one of those days, as understandably he wants to be there when we meet Maureen."

"Makes sense. Why don't I get dinner started while you look?"

"Don't worry about that," he said absently. "On Sundays the kids come over. Sarah's bringing Chinese."

Leeza stopped abruptly on the way to the kitchen, the wind punched out of her lungs. "Your family's coming over?" she said. "Do they know I'm here?"

Something in her tone must have snagged Gavin's attention as he looked up from his search, a small crease between his brows. "Yes, I told Sarah when she called to arrange the food." He peered at her. "Are you still worried about their reaction to you? To us?"

"Maybe a little. I talked with Drew today, told him about you. He seemed okay with it, but he's half a world away and knows how his father treated me. Your kids are right here, and I'll be standing next to you, where their mother should be. I wouldn't blame them if they aren't happy about that."

Gavin took her hand and led her to the sofa so they could both sit, his knees bumping hers. "We've had this discussion before, Leeza."

"I refuse to come between you and your children. If they take against me, you can't choose me over them."

"It's not going to come to that. They might need some time to get used to the idea, but it will be fine, I promise."

Sarah and Xander arrived less than an hour later, with Nolan, Amrita, and Emmelyn right behind them. While it wasn't exactly *fine*, it wasn't the disaster it had the potential to be. Leeza was careful not to appear too familiar with Gavin's home and didn't try to play hostess, instead offering to help Sarah and allowing the other woman to manage things to her liking. Gavin didn't hesitate to show his affection, touching Leeza often and casually, even kissing her in full view of everyone, which did nothing to ease her nervousness. But none of the younger adults said anything about his actions, and slowly she relaxed.

It was only when she and Sarah were clearing away the leftover food that Gavin's daughter brought up the subject. Amrita had taken Emmelyn to the bathroom to do a diaper change and put her in her sleeper, while Gavin had taken the men to *look at something in the basement*—which seemed some sort of family code for getting more beer—so they were alone in the kitchen.

"Is that your overnight case in Dad's room?"

Leeza froze, half in and half out of the refrigerator, and then closed the door before answering. "Yes."

"I wasn't snooping," Sarah said as she combined the remaining rice and chow mein into one container. "I just saw it from the hallway. I didn't think he owned anything in such a pretty paisley."

A little confounded by the lightness in Sarah's tone when she had fully expected censure, Leeza remained silent.

The younger woman snapped on the lid and turned and handed the dish to Leeza, who took it automatically, and then stood there, waiting.

"You know he loves you, right?" Sarah smiled, but her eyes remained somber. "He loved Mom, too, but with you, tonight..." She spread her arms, palms out. "He's like a teenager. He can't keep his eyes off you. Or his hands."

A blush burned Leeza's cheeks, but she took

courage from the fact Sarah seemed accepting—a little sad, perhaps, but not antagonistic. "Can I tell you something I haven't told anyone but your father? Not even my own son?"

Sarah made an encouraging gesture.

"I love Gavin." Maybe she was wrong, not telling Drew first. She sensed that Sarah was looking for reassurance, though, and this seemed the best and most honest way to give it. "I love your dad. The only other man I loved was my high school sweetheart, who, almost three decades later, I discovered had been cheating on me for much of our marriage. I'm trusting your dad not to break my heart like he did. I guess you'll have to trust me not to break his."

At first, it didn't seem as if her honesty had made a difference. Sarah wasn't making eye contact, her gaze directed over Leeza's shoulder toward the living room. Then she smiled, and with a sense of foreboding Leeza turned slowly around.

Gavin and the rest of his family were gathered on the other side of the dining table. He held Emmelyn on his hip, her head tucked under his chin, her thumb in her mouth, sucking sleepily. Amrita and Xander were smiling. Nolan, standing next to his father, had the same sober look his sister had had just a few minutes ago, but as Leeza stared at the group he gave a short, approving nod.

"Leeza." Gavin said her name and the single word held an entire world in its short syllables. He reached out his hand and she approached him, not quite feeling her feet, and took it.

"I love you, too," he said, his hazel eyes triumphant and a tad smug.

She'd make him pay for that later, but for now, she stepped into his embrace and lowered her head onto the shoulder opposite Emmelyn. Then she repeated his words back to him, but so softly only he could hear them.

Gavin and Leeza departed for Vancouver on the first flight out Thursday and took the SkyTrain from the airport into the city. A quick search on Google Maps had shown them that Willowmere, the care facility where Maureen lived, was just a short walk from the Oakridge and Forty-first Street station on the Canada Line. Their return flight was booked on the last plane that night, to give them as much time as possible with Maureen.

Just after eight-thirty, they climbed the stairs out of the subway to street level. In sharp contrast to the deep snow and freezing temperatures they'd left behind, the weather was mild and moist. No rain fell from the overcast skies, but Leeza could feel its threat in the dampness of the air.

"I think February is the only month I wish I lived in Vancouver," she said as they headed west, following the route to Willowmere. "Look—crocuses are already blooming. It will be *months* before we see grass yet."

"Hard to believe Prince George is only an hour flight away." Gavin took her hand as they continued along 41st Street. She gripped it tight and he glanced at her. "Nervous?"

"My stomach is all tied up. There's barely room for the butterflies," she said, and he laughed. "It's worse than going to meet Grant. What if I don't like her? It's silly, but I feel protective of William. If Maureen doesn't care about the diary, I won't feel right leaving him—his diary—with her." She reached into her shoulder bag and touched the protective bubble wrap envelope holding the battered little book, reassuring herself once more it was there.

"We'll know soon enough." Gavin pointed with his free hand. "We turn right, here, on Willow Street."

They waited for the lights to change, and then crossed 41st Street and headed north into a heavily residential area. Large, single family homes with tidy yards—many boasting the blooms Leeza was so jealous of—were interspersed with small apartment complexes. In a few minutes they reached Willowmere.

Standing on the sidewalk, Leeza let her head fall back to study the ten-storey building.

"This is it," Gavin said. "The end of your quest."

"*Our* quest," she said. "I might have given up without your help."

"Ready?"

"Ready."

CHAPTER THIRTY-FOUR

June 20th, 1944
I keep thinking what if I had been there with
Rodney, maybe I could have saved his life. I
could have comforted him in his darkest hour.

They entered the lobby. At the large reception desk, a man in jeans and a navy windbreaker stood chatting with a woman wearing nurse's scrubs. He glanced over his shoulder as the automatic doors swooshed shut, gave the nurse a quick smile and stepped forward.

"Gavin and Leeza? I'm Ben Smith."

Over the weeks and months of the search, Leeza had built an image of William in her mind. He'd teased his buddy, Rodney, about being short, so she had imagined William with above average height. His hair would have been close-cropped, like most soldiers, and with the Anglo-Saxon heritage *Smith* implied, neither too light nor too dark. For some reason, his eyes had become Gavin's—hazel in colour, warm and friendly in expression.

It was silly to be disconcerted because Ben in no way matched this description.

He was *well* above average height, towering over Gavin. His straight, dark hair was long enough to gather in a stubby ponytail, and his eyes, while not hostile, held a sharp intelligence in their blue depths that made her slightly wary.

He offered his hand to both Gavin and Leeza, and then motioned to the elevator. "Maureen is waiting in the lounge on her floor. She's very excited to meet you."

As they were smoothly lifted seven storeys, Ben said, "I should warn you—" He stopped, appeared to reconsider what he'd said, and started again. "Warn might be too strong a word. I should caution you that Maureen may become a little confused during your visit. While she is normally very on the ball, part of the reason she moved to Willowmere is that she has been diagnosed with mild dementia."

"I'm sorry to hear that," Leeza said.

"For the most part, she's fine. But talking about the past could trigger memories that might cause her to become disoriented."

"We'll try not to unsettle her," Gavin said as the doors dinged, and they stepped out.

The elevator opened onto another reception area, this one smaller than the one in the lobby, and more closely resembling a nurse's station. Ben greeted the two men and one woman behind the desk by name as he led Gavin and Leeza past and into a wide-open space that took up one corner of the building. On a sunny day it would be a lovely place to relax or read, and even in the current weather, the large windows and scattered groups of comfortable-looking furniture made it inviting.

A few residents were doing a puzzle at one of the tables, and a couple more were seated next to a teenage girl who was reading aloud from a paperback book. Near one of the windows, an elderly woman waited alone. Her face lit up when she saw them approach.

Even seated in the high-backed wing chair, it was easy to see she shared at least some of Ben's height. Her hair, a pristine, pewter grey, curled tightly in what Leeza assumed was a fresh perm, and she wore a dress patterned with bright flowers on a violet background. An IV cannula, discreetly taped down on her right forearm and not connected to anything, gave a hint that there might be more to her stay at Willowmere than mild dementia.

"Ben!" she said. "Are these my visitors?"

Her great-nephew bent to kiss her cheek before introducing Gavin and Leeza. A few moments were spent pulling chairs into a better configuration for private conversation, and then a light silence fell.

Maureen waited expectantly, her hands clasped in her lap and her expression bright. Ben's gaze flicked from Leeza to Gavin and back again.

Leeza took a deep breath. "Maybe I should just start at the beginning," she said. "My grandfather died last fall, and when I was packing up his books, I found a journal..."

Maureen and Ben remained silent throughout Leeza's recital. Gavin let her tell it all the way through without interruption, even though she glossed over some details of their search. She could fill in any gaps later, if necessary. For now, it was enough to provide the gist.

"...and that was how we ended up calling your number and talking with Ben."

"I wonder which of my friends from Tatamagouche it was, that the woman from the church found," Maureen said. "My husband and I kept in touch with quite a few." Her smile was soft with sadness. "So many of them are gone now."

Reaching into her bag, Leeza drew out the envelope containing William's diary and passed it to Maureen.

The elderly woman pressed her long-fingered, heavily veined hands to the padded covering. "This is it?" she asked. "This is Willy's diary?"

Leeza nodded, blinking back tears at the intimate nickname.

"How on earth did your grandfather come to have it?" Maureen said without raising her eyes from the envelope.

"We don't know. I don't imagine we ever will." Leeza hesitated, considering for a moment, and then decided to offer the solution that seemed most likely in her mind. "It's distinctly possible my grandfather and William—Willy—were together in the weeks following D-Day. Maybe, when Willy was injured, he gave it to my grandfather." Maybe the young soldier, sensing he was dying, hadn't wanted the diary to be read by his mother and had given it to Otto to keep it from being sent home with the rest of his effects. And maybe Otto had honoured those last wishes his entire life. "I'm sorry it took us so long to get it back to you."

Maureen lifted the flap and slid out the small, slim book. It fit snugly in her palm and for a moment she rested one hand on top of it, as if absorbing its words through her skin.

"I don't remember Willy very well," she said, speaking quietly. "I was only six or seven when he went to war. Mother would talk to me about him, tell of how I followed him around like a puppy when I was a toddler, how when I got older he would take me down to the pond and watch me chase dragonflies. Not that I ever caught one, of course. She says he used to laugh at that. Not in a mean way. He was never harsh with me." She smiled. "That's what I remember most when I think of Willy—the stories my mother told me. After he left, she read me his letters, of course, and we all wrote to him. Well, I wrote little notes that Mother would include in her letters. Sometimes I drew him pictures, too."

She leaned back in her chair and lifted the book to her breast. "I don't remember the war as such. It was just the way life was. Occasionally I'd hear that the brother of a friend or the son of a neighbour had been killed, but people I knew died for all sorts of reasons. My best friend in Grade Two died of a fever. I remember that distinctly—the funeral, the burial, her parents crying. So, when news came, as it did, that a young man had died an ocean away, it didn't seem out of the ordinary. I had no sense of the scope of what was going on."

Gavin took Leeza's hand and pried open her fingers to lace them with his. Only then did she realize she'd clenched her fists so tight her joints ached. She spared him a quick, grateful glance and immediately turned her attention back to Maureen.

"It's funny how memories change. You'd think they'd be fixed, but they aren't," Maureen said. She turned to Ben, sitting calm and supportive beside his great-aunt. He hadn't said a word since Leeza had started her story. "You might be too young to understand. But you'll learn. You think you remember something, but later you learn something else that changes that memory completely."

Once more addressing them all, she continued. "That's what happened to me. I was a young married woman before I connected all the dates of that summer—1944. Before I understood the agony my mother had gone through losing a child." Leeza wondered if Maureen was thinking of her own lost child, her own William Henry, but dared not ask. "At the time, all the dates were disjointed, disconnected. It was only later that I saw how they all linked.

"June 6 was my mother's birthday. We never went in for huge celebrations, which I realize now was probably partly due to rationing during the war. But that day in 1944 was extra exciting, because a parcel had arrived. A parcel from Willy.

"I was in school when it came, but I went home for lunch and it was sitting on the table. I wanted to open it right away—Mother had read the letter attached to the outside of it and she had told me it contained a present for me—but she insisted we wait for David, because there was one for him, too. He was away at university by then, but he was coming home to celebrate Mother's birthday."

Leeza shot Gavin a glance and he nodded. Genevieve had been right, David had gone on to higher learning.

"I remember fidgeting through the rest of the school day, then racing home. David had taken an early train from Halifax, so he was already there." Her eyes closed as she described the excitement of slitting open the box and lifting out each parcel. "Willy had sent mother a dress. It was wrapped in tissue paper that crackled when she unfolded it. David's gift was a book." Her mouth quirked in a grin. "I thought it wasn't a very nice gift, but David loved it. He said it was a book about the life of someone called Shakespeare. At the time, I had no idea who that was. My gift was a doll."

Opening her eyes, she sat up straight and, still holding the journal in her right hand, cradled that arm with her left, just like holding a baby. Staring at the journal, rocking slightly, she said, "She was the most beautiful doll I'd ever seen. She wore a red gingham dress with a blue apron, and when you laid her down her eyes closed. I'd seen dolls like that before but never had one of my own. I called her Willa—after Willy, you see."

For a long moment, Maureen sat there, seeming lost in her memories. Ben reached out and touched her shoulder gently. She started, as if she'd forgotten anyone else was there, and for a moment Leeza saw panicked confusion flit across her features. Then she relaxed and settled back in her chair.

"What none of us knew at the time, not even my mother," she said, "was that before we'd even woken that morning, before the parcel had arrived, Willy and thousands of other Canadian soldiers had been fighting for their lives on the beaches of Normandy. It was in all the papers soon, of course, but all I have is a vague memory of the adults talking about a great victory that cost many lives. It was only years later I connected it all. So many families, waiting for word of their boys. So many mothers, refusing to answer the door, thinking if they only ignored the knock that their son wouldn't be dead.

"I'm sure my mother must have been as terrified as all the other parents. She would have known the North Nova Scotia Highlanders, Willy's regiment, had been in the thick of things, were being touted as heroes even then. But the more days that passed, the more she would have relaxed. You can only live on a knife edge for so long. We waited to hear from Willy, but it wasn't unusual for months to go by between letters.

"When the first telegram came, I was home with Mother, weeding the garden. School was out for the summer, but I don't remember exactly what day it was. She sat down in the dirt after she read it, just plopped right down, so I knew the message was important, because Mother *never* sat on the ground. She told me Willy had been injured, that he'd stepped on a mine and his foot had been blown off, but that he was alive, and he was coming home. She was laughing and crying all at the same time, and I was frightened at first. But then she stood up and blew her nose and smiled and I felt better.

"When the second telegram came about a week later, she'd just put a pie in the oven. A cherry pie. She fainted dead away, and the man who brought the telegram carried her to bed and then sent a neighbour over to help, but we forgot about the pie and it burnt. I'll never forget that smell. Can't abide cherry pie to this day."

Leeza leaned her head on Gavin's shoulder and let the tears slip from her eyes. Throughout their search, William's mother had often been in the forefront of her thoughts. Hearing of her pain, her agony, at the loss of her son was almost unbearable.

"Mother was ill for months after. It was summer break, so David came home and looked after me. In September he had to go back to university, so he arranged for me to live with a neighbour family, and I stayed there for weeks, until Mother recovered enough for me to go home. She was never the same, though, and she died shortly after I was married. It was David who told me what happened, how Willy died. The telegram said he got an infection in his blood and died before they could put him on the ship to take him home. David tried to find out where he was buried—my mother was frantic to know, but the records had been lost or mislabelled or something. It was like he disappeared. I think that's what killed my mother—the not knowing. She stayed breathing for a few more years, but once she saw me settled, she just—stopped."

Leeza wanted to ask if she died before or after Maureen's own William Henry had lived his brief life, but the older woman looked pale and exhausted. That question would keep for another time.

Ben must have noticed his great-aunt's failing energy as well. "I think that's enough for now, don't you?" he said to her, with a sideways glance at Leeza and Gavin.

"Of course," Gavin said immediately. "Thank you so much for telling your story, Mrs. Fulton."

She nodded weakly, her eyelids drooping.

"I'll be right back to help you to your room," Ben said, rising from his seat as he patted Maureen's hand.

He walked Leeza and Gavin to the elevator.

"Do you think it would be okay if we came back this afternoon?" Leeza asked anxiously. "Mrs. Fulton might have some questions for us after she's had a chance to look at the diary."

Ben nodded. "That will probably be all right. She needs to rest now. The medication she's taking is pretty heavy duty, so it tends to wipe her out. But after lunch and a nap she'll probably want to see you again. I think you caught her on a good day."

"What do you mean?" Leeza asked as the elevator doors slid open.

"Days like these, when she's talkative and outgoing, are getting fewer and fewer. That's why I don't mind you coming back this afternoon." Soberly, he revealed the full reason Maureen had moved into the care facility. "She has inoperable stomach cancer. She's refused treatment and is only taking medication to control the pain. The prognosis is a month, maybe six weeks. You found her just in time."

CHAPTER THIRTY-FIVE

July 7th, 1944
I'm going back home. I lost my right foot on
those new German mines. We were under fire
and I was running to hide in the fields and next
thing I knew I was laying in a pool of blood in
great pain. But it's over, the nightmare is over.

Four months later, Leeza stepped out of the car,
spicy, cedar-scented air tanging on her tongue, a
light breeze tangling her hair about her face. As Ben,
Drew, and Danica alighted from the backseat, Gavin
rounded the hood and joined her, taking her hand in
his.

The five of them had come to Lockerby
Cemetery in Tatamagouche for a memorial service
celebrating William Henry Smith. Genevieve, a few
of her colleagues from the museum, and Dave from
Truro Tourism had also joined them, as had Mrs.
Langille and other members of the local United
Church, including the current pastor, who had been
invited by Ben to say a few words.

Less than a week after they had met Maureen,
Ben had called to let them know she had passed away
in her sleep. "You gave her a lot of joy in her last

days," he said. "She talked often of Willy and her mother. And I heard more stories about my Grandpa David, too. It was a great comfort for her to know none of them would be forgotten."

They had discussed what to do with the journal. Ben wanted it kept somewhere safe, somewhere it could be studied and appreciated and preserved. Leeza had no hesitation in recommending the Colchester Historeum. "It seems only fitting that it should be given to a museum near William's home, and why not the one where the biggest breakthrough was made?"

Genevieve had been more than delighted to accept the journal. Originally, Ben was going to mail it to her, but while he and Genevieve were talking, he had expressed a wish to see his great-uncle's name on the cenotaph in Truro. Genevieve immediately extended an invitation to bring the book himself, and he'd told Leeza and Gavin he was considering the idea. Gavin had diffidently suggested a remembrance service in Tatamagouche might be appropriate, and Leeza had mentioned adding a plaque to William's mother's gravestone, so that mother and son could be reunited.

"If he decides to do either of those things," she had told Gavin, "we need to go to Nova Scotia again."

When she'd been offered a job managing a local store that featured an eclectic mix of home décor, fashion, and gifts, the time off necessary to attend the ceremony had been non-negotiable from Leeza's point of view. Luckily, her new boss had accepted her ultimatum gracefully.

And that's how it came to be that on July 7, the anniversary of the last date in William's diary, the small group gathered to remember him.

They followed the minister and Mrs. Langille up the sloping hillside, the grass lush and green under their feet. Leeza glanced at the markers as they went by, noting dates from the nineteenth century up until the current year, ages from infant to octogenarian. She and Gavin had already visited Maureen's baby's grave in the Fulton section on the other side of the cemetery, the tiny plot heartrending despite the passage of time.

Near the top of the hill, the minister stopped beside a simply carved granite stone. William's parents were buried in the same grave, with their names on a single headstone. The minister waited for everyone to circle around the grassy plot, and then began his prayers.

Drew, in a short-sleeved shirt but a striped tie in honour of the occasion, and Danica, in a light summer dress that fluttered in the breeze, stood opposite Gavin and Leeza. During the last few months, Leeza had gotten to know the young woman, and appreciated her warmth and humour and intelligence. Knowing Danica was a lovely person only increased her worry about Drew ever returning home, and Gavin occasionally had to talk her down from a minor panic.

"What would you rather—he find a good woman he truly loves and live in London and be happy, or end up with someone *not* his soul-mate and be miserable here at home?"

When Drew had heard of the memorial, he'd suggested that he and Danica come as well. The four of them had met in the middle, so to speak, and once all the formalities were done, they were going to spend a few days touring Nova Scotia together. Leeza was looking forward to it.

Really. She really was.

The minister's prayer came to an end, and Ben stepped forward, taking the small bronze plaque bearing William's name and dates and a screwdriver from his pocket. Lining the plaque up with the holes pre-drilled in the granite, he fastened it securely.

Leeza wished Maureen could have lived to see her family reunited. She also wished Grant Howard had lived long enough to know they'd found William. But she believed in Heaven, and Leeza figured they were already cronies. Two young men who lost their legs to German mines were bound to bond in the hereafter, despite the fact only one of them had gone on to live a long and happy life. In Heaven, that wouldn't matter.

"Are you coming, Mom?"

Leeza blinked and looked at Drew, only then realizing the ceremony was over.

"Give me a minute," she said. A reception was planned at the local Legion hall, but Leeza wasn't quite ready to leave yet. "I'll meet you at the car."

"We won't be long," Gavin said.

She leaned into him, laying her cheek on his shoulder. The sun had warmed the light material of his shirt, and beneath it she could feel his solid strength.

"I guess it's all over now," she said.

"You should be proud," he said, his hand resting on her hip. "You brought a family closure, gave them a history they didn't know existed."

She turned to him, her hands restlessly straightening his already straight tie. "I suppose I am. I'm just a little sad that the project that brought us together is finished."

"Leeza—"

"Wait. I have something to say." She lifted her chin to face him fully. With surprise she noticed threads of grey in his hair and touched them with her fingertips. He waited patiently, his gaze firm and steady through the lenses of his glasses, his mouth curved into a small smile.

"I think we should live together," she blurted.

Gavin's eyebrows rose. "Aren't we already?"

"Mostly, I guess." They spent six out of seven

nights together, with more nights at Gavin's than Leeza's. "But I was hoping you might want to make it a little more—formal."

"What did you have in mind?"

"I think I should sell my condo and move in with you." When his eyebrows lifted even further, she hastened to add, "Only if you agree, of course. I supposed we could sell both places and move into a new space, but I love your house, Gavin. It felt like home the first time I walked into it. And you love it there. It can stay in your name, it wouldn't be my house, then if we ever separated, it would still be yo—"

"Hush your mouth." He placed his palm over her lips. "If we do this, we do it right. You sell your house, and we'll become co-owners of mine. I don't ever want you to feel like a guest in your own home."

His hand left her mouth and cupped the back of her neck. A rushing pulse in her temples made her lightheaded. "You agree then? You want to move in together?"

"I agree."

Happiness was a buzz in her veins and a balloon in her chest. "I love you," she said, pressing her mouth to his. The quick kiss she'd intended turned into a searching, passion-filled exploration of teeth and tongue, and she forgot they were standing on a hillside in a graveyard with people waiting for them.

When Gavin finally released her, she clung to him a little longer, her joy settling into a warm glow that rivalled the July sun.

"I do have one condition," Gavin said, his faint stubble catching on her hair as his chin brushed her scalp.

"What is it?" She wanted to enjoy this moment, didn't want to worry about the details yet, but whatever Gavin wanted she would give.

"While you're living with me, you have to wear

this."

He held something up in front of her face. Something that flashed in the sunlight with a million sparks of light.

If she hadn't already been clinging to him, she might have fallen. Carefully she pushed away from his chest so she could see his face. The boyish grin she loved so much lit his expression.

"Gavin," she breathed.

"Marry me, Leeza," he said. "I talked to Drew, Nolan, and Sarah before we even left Prince George, told them all that I planned to ask you during this trip. I was going to wait for the perfect time. I think this is it, don't you?"

She stared at the ring he held pinched between thumb and forefinger. It was a simple solitaire diamond floating on a smooth platinum band. But it wasn't the beauty of the jewellery that kept her silent. It was the overwhelming surge of love and gratitude and peace that swept over her.

"Yes," she said. "It is the perfect time." William Henry Smith's story might be ending here, in this cemetery, but it was a beginning for her and Gavin. A chance to rise above the challenges and tragedies of their past to build a new life. "And, yes, I'll marry you."

He slid the ring onto her finger, and a loud cheer rolled up the hill. Leeza looked over Gavin's shoulder to see the entire group—the minister and Mrs. Langille, Genevieve and her colleagues, Dave, Ben, and Danica. And Drew. Her son raised a fist in the air and his shout reached her above all the others.

Gavin smiled and took her hand.

"Ready?" he said.

She nodded, almost too full of happiness to speak. "Ready."

Together, they walked down the hill toward their future.

Acknowledgements

AFTER WORDS came to be in a roundabout way. I knew I wanted to write a story with a mature heroine and hero, and I was also toying with the idea of writing a novel with a dual timeline. The past infuses our present in so many ways, and I love stories that combine a vibrant plot in both the current day and historic times.

As I wandered around the internet, looking for ideas, I came across The Canadian Letters and Images Project. It is an online collection "devoted to the Canadian war experience, from any war, as told through the letters and images of Canadians themselves." I snooped very happily through it for hours. Then I came upon the diary of William Henry Smith.

The details of William's life mentioned in my story are based on this diary. He joined the North Nova Scotia Highlanders in time to be transported to England in July 1941, when he was about 21 years old. His father had been killed a few years before and he left behind his mother, a brother, and a sister. He spent most of the war training in England and Scotland before taking part in the Normandy Invasion, which occurred on June 6, 1944.

The diary entries at the beginning of each chapter in AFTER WORDS are the complete and (mostly) uncorrected text from William's journal. In a few cases I have deleted a sentence or two for clarity, as they related to events mentioned in entries I did not include in my story. I encourage you to read the entire diary (it is only about 4500 words long) at https://canadianletters.ca/collections/all/collection/20853. It is funny yet heart-wrenching, innocent yet brutal. Its honesty echoes through the decades, even in transcript form.

It is also true that William's fate is a mystery, and that his family is unknown to those who know of the diary. Even though he mentions leaving Canada on the *S. S. Orion*, neither William nor his best friend, Rodney, are included on the passenger list. As I write in my story, there is a William Smith listed with the middle initial B, not H, but I was unable to confirm it was a misprint like Leeza proposes. Other searches done through the Nova Scotia Highlanders Regimental Museum have revealed nothing more about this young man. There is no record of William's return to Canada or, if he died overseas, where he is buried. If you want to read more about the search for William, a blog entitled "Willy's WWII Journal" covers a lot more ground than I attempted. The link is https://michaelwwii.wordpress.com/.

Not that I didn't try. Thanks to both John Wales, Assistant to the Curator of the Nova Scotia Highlanders Regimental Museum in Amherst, and Dr. Stephen Davies, Project Director of The Canadian Letters and Images Project in the Department of History at Vancouver Island University, for their assistance. It was the first time I'd ever reached out to other professionals for help regarding one of my books, and their enthusiasm was greatly appreciated.

Since our searches ended in frustration, I was able to create my own ending for William's story. I did my best to stay true to the details that were provided by William, but I did take some liberties. In the case of William's contemporaries, if he provided a full name, I did a Google search to see if they popped up. As none of them did, I felt free to use them to solve the mystery as I saw fit.

Just a couple more notes. If you happen to check out the Nova Scotia Highlanders Regimental Museum website, you won't find Otto Friberg on the list of The Originals who travelled on the *S. S. Orion*. Also, if you are reading this book shortly after its release and are thinking I haven't done my math right in regards to the ages of some characters and the historical events I mention, I should explain that this story starts in November 2020 and continues to July 2021.

I have other people to thank in shaping this book. Ann Cameron, a fellow writer I connected with on Facebook, lives in Nova Scotia. When I decided to send my characters to Truro, she introduced me to Dave Clark, who allowed me to pick his brain for local details, and even made suggestions regarding genealogical research. It turns out that Dave and I are connected in odd and spooky ways. His son (not his brother), Scooter, lived in the same city I do, on the opposite side of the country from Truro. Also, before connecting with Dave, I had decided William would be from Tatamagouche, NS, because I loved the name. Dave was born and raised in that village, and he even wrote a romance set there. As of the publication of this book, it is currently available on Amazon.

I should also explain about Charlene Petryshyn. Charlene is a book blogger with Fun Under the Covers (you can find them on Facebook and Instagram). She is wonderfully supportive of my writing and won the right for her name to be used in this book in a contest I ran. I gave her a choice of characters, and she picked the frenemy, so don't blame me!

For many reasons, AFTER WORDS has been a

very special project. I haven't given up hope that we might find William's real family some day. Should anyone reading this have ideas or suggestions on where we might look next, I'd love to hear from you. You can email me at brendamargriet@brendamargriet.com.

Thank You!

Thanks for reading *After Words*. I hope you enjoyed it!

Reviews are a great way to help other readers learn about new authors. Just a line or two is all that's needed. I encourage you to post your honest opinion at the retailer where you purchased your copy, or on GoodReads. Thank you so much!

I'd love to connect on social media! I'm most active on Facebook and Instagram, but you can find all my links on my website, www.brendamargriet.com.

Honestly, though, the best way to stay in touch is by joining my newsletter. You will immediately receive a welcome gift of my short story, *The Life She Had Before,* and it's a great way to keep up with new releases, bonus reads, sales and more. You'll probably only hear from me once a month – unless I've got something really exciting to share. You can find the sign up form on my website.

Also by Brenda Margriet

Mountain Fire
Reserved for You
No Life But This
When Time Falls Still

The Bendixon Sisters Series
Allegro Court
Gateway Crescent
Crossroads Corner

TIMELESS Seasoned Romance
After Words

Read excerpts and find buy links at
www.brendamargriet.com

About the Author

Brenda Margriet writes savvy, slow burn, contemporary romances with ordinarily amazing characters. In her own ordinarily amazing life, she had a successful career in radio and television production before deciding to pilfer from her retirement plan to support her writing compulsion.

Readers have called her stories "poignant," "explicit and steamy," "interesting, intriguing and entertaining," and "unlike any romance you've read before" (she assumes the latter was meant in a good way).

Discover more about Brenda and her books at www.brendamargriet.com.

www.ingramcontent.com/pod-product-compliance
Lightning Source LLC
Chambersburg PA
CBHW020416260626
47156CB00007B/2408